The Better Brother

Simon Gravatt

Red Door

Published by RedDoor
www.reddoorpress.co.uk

The right of Simon Gravatt to be identified as author of this Work
has been asserted by him in accordance with sections 77 and 78 of the
Copyright, Designs and Patents Act 1988

ISBN 978-1-913062-90-3

This is a work of fiction. Names, characters, businesses, places, events
and incidents are either the products of the author's imagination or
used in a fictitious manner. Any resemblance to actual persons, living
or dead, or actual events is purely coincidental.

A CIP catalogue record for this book is available from the British
Library

Cover design: Rawshock Design

Typesetting: Jen Parker, Fuzzy Flamingo
www.fuzzyflamingo.co.uk

Printed and bound in Denmark by Nørhaven

A black eagle lays two eggs.
The first-hatched chick will peck the younger one to death
within the first few days.

Contents

PART ONE

A death in the family

CHAPTER ONE

Presumed dead

North London. June 1998

Michael was halfway through his ham and cheese sandwich when the phone rang. The ringtone indicated an external call. 'Hello, this is Michael Merriweather. How can I help you?'

'Oh, thank goodness I've found you.' The agitated voice sounded familiar, but Michael couldn't place it.

'I'm sorry, but who is this?'

'This is Monica. Monica of Merriweather's. You remember me, don't you?'

What a ridiculous question thought Michael. Of course he remembered Monica. He had known her all his life. 'Hello, Monica, why are you calling me at work?' It was unsettling; having a voice from his past, a past he was trying to forget, intrude like this.

'It's your father, Michael. I'm so sorry to tell you this, but we think he's dead.'

Think? How can you think someone's dead?

Monica continued without pause. 'He's been cremated.'

'Cremated?' The call was making no sense. 'Already?'

Monica started to say something, but Michael wasn't listening. 'Why wasn't I invited?'

There was a pause at the other end of the line. 'What do you mean?'

Michael could only focus on the cremation. 'What I mean,' he felt the anger well up inside him, 'is why wasn't I invited to the cremation? My dad's not a bloody Hindu.' Michael noticed a few heads turn in his open-plan office. He had momentarily forgotten he was at work.

'I know your dad's not Hindu,' said Monica hesitatingly, 'what's that got to do with it?'

'It means he doesn't need to be cremated within twenty-four hours,' Michael said quietly. 'You, of all people, should know that.'

'Michael, you're upset. I'm sorry I'm not explaining this very—'

Michael cut her off, 'and anyway, what do you mean you think he's dead? How can you think someone's dead? Either they're dead, or they're not. It's a binary thing.'

'Michael, I'm sorry. Please let me explain. It seems he may have cremated himself.'

CHAPTER TWO

Rest in peace

North London. June 1998

Two days later, an HR lady with a soulful expression appeared in Michael's cubicle and suggested he take a few days' compassionate leave. Speaking so quietly that he could hardly hear her, she told him to take as long as he wanted and only return when he was ready. She mistook his silence for grief whereas he was simply transfixed by her ridiculous gold-rimmed hexagonal-shaped glasses and wondered how long it would be before she left him alone. The annoying woman then put her hand on his shoulder. Now she was violating his personal space. He resisted the urge to push her away. 'I'm so sorry for your loss,' she said. Bollocks you are, thought Michael, this is the first time you've ever met me. You're only saying that because it's in your job description. It's probably from the section in *The Manual for Highly Effective HR Managers* on how to deal with bereaved employees: 'Put on a sad face and, where appropriate, provide a gentle, supportive touch on the arm. (Unless you're an older male HR manager and the bereaved is a younger female colleague, in which case, do not touch them in any circumstances.)' Michael sincerely hoped *The Manual for Highly Effective HR Managers* didn't recommend hugging.

He took his leave that afternoon, if only to get away from the weird glasses and false sympathy. Michael couldn't stand the way people always whispered in hushed tones whenever they talked about the deceased. Why do they do it? Do they think the dead are somehow listening in and need shielding from the shocking news of their demise? Or do they assume that the grieving relative has developed a sudden sensitivity to noise?

Back in his apartment, Michael didn't know what to do. He'd never taken time off work before. Had he been ill, he would have taken to his bed, but he felt fine. He'd been told to take compassionate leave, which, he assumed, meant he was expected to grieve. This was problematic. Not only did he not know how to grieve, but he felt no grief. The thought crossed his mind that maybe this meant he was sociopathic. Michael sat on the sofa in his sparsely furnished apartment, staring at the solitary poster on the facing wall. A supposedly cute kitten looked back at him. Michael hated cats. As he spent most of his time in the office, he didn't see the need for many home comforts. He didn't even own a television. The few friends who had seen his apartment teased him about his domestic minimalism, but he couldn't see the point of getting anything he didn't need. The cat poster had been the initiative of a girlfriend who had taken it upon herself to try to domesticate him. The artwork had lasted longer than the girlfriend.

Michael wondered what the proper etiquette was: were the bereft allowed to go for a walk, or should he stay out of sight and wear black? Should was one of Michael's favourite words. He couldn't understand why it got such a bad rap; as far as he was concerned, it gave clarity. Michael much preferred to be told how to behave than to have to work it out himself.

He cursed his father for dying because it meant that he was sitting there on his sofa with nothing to do. He wished his mother was alive. She would have known what to do. But she'd been dead for over twenty years.

Michael jumped as the phone rang. No one ever called him at home.

'Hello.'

'Hello. Is this Michael Merriweather?'

'It is. How can I help you?'

'Hi. I'm sorry to disturb you. This is Wilfred Owen from W. Owen Solicitors. I'm handling your father's will and need to meet with you and your brother as soon as possible.'

And so, much to his surprise, Michael found himself in Swindon the next day. He'd never been there before and hurrying from the railway station through the town centre, past rows of ugly office blocks, he was pretty sure this would be his last visit. He was late, which made him feel hot and stressed. Not late by anyone else's standards, only his own. He usually arrived everywhere at least twenty minutes before the scheduled time, and often earlier. Some of his friends, increasingly exasperated by his unacceptably early appearances, had taken to telling him their dinner party was half an hour later than they told their other guests. Otherwise, they knew he would appear before they'd finished applying the mascara and laying the table.

Michael had been early when he set out for Swindon, having added an extra twenty minutes on top of his usual twenty. But then an unexplained thirty-five-minute wait outside Didcot had blown his schedule. Although at some level he knew he was still five minutes early, every fibre of Michael's being screamed that he was at least fifteen minutes late. Thanks to British Rail, he had lost any margin of error he might need to find his destination. And as a result, he was half running, half walking through Swindon's brutal post-war architecture when he collided with an elderly couple who stopped in front of him to look at God knows what. Michael didn't consider himself to be an angry man, but people who walked too slowly annoyed the fuck out of him. He made no exception for age or infirmity. The old man waved his walking stick angrily at Michael as he helped his wife back to her feet. Michael marched on, muttering to himself that it was absurd that it was permissible to stop suddenly, without prior warning, on a narrow pavement. It wouldn't be acceptable for a car on a motorway. People, particularly the elderly and tourists, should be fitted with brake lights.

When he finally found W. Owen Solicitors, ten minutes before the appointed time, Michael did at least allow himself a smile. Tucked away in a quiet residential side street, it was as inconspicuous a location as he might have expected for anyone working with his father. The row of Victorian terraced houses, decorated with various paraphernalia of domesticity, tidy flower beds in some, bicycles, clutter and wheelie bins in others, contrasted with the busy streets through which he had just hurried. It seemed a most unlikely place for an office. There was nothing to promote the firm except a nondescript metallic nameplate in need of some polish. A thin trail of slug slime ran across the unwashed white front door and glistened in the sun. It occurred to Michael that his father would probably have found such lack of care reassuringly cheap.

Michael pressed the doorbell and heard nothing. He suspected it might not be working and wondered how his father had found such an out-of-the-way lawyer. It would have taken some sleuthing. A young man eventually answered and ushered Michael up two flights of narrow stairs into a small attic room on the top floor. A black Labrador was lying obediently in the corner of the room. The dog's tail started thumping on the carpeted floor when Michael entered and went into overdrive when he leaned over to stroke his head. 'It belongs to one of our clients,' explained the young man, who then went to make some coffee. Left alone with the dog, Michael considered why Mr Owen had been so insistent that he come all this way to discuss his father's will in person. He had wanted both Michael and his brother to attend the meeting, but Michael had told him that would be impossible, and that they would have to meet separately. Mr Owen had been unwilling to say what it was about, other than that it concerned his late father's will, or why they couldn't discuss it over the phone. He was insistent that it needed a face-to-face meeting. It irritated Michael that he had succumbed and agreed to give up a day of his time to attend a pointless meeting in a pointless place, but there had been something in Mr Owen's tone that had persuaded him to make the effort.

The young man returned with coffee, water and some shortbread biscuits. He then sat down opposite Michael and turned to the pile of papers on the table.

'Isn't Mr Owen joining us?' asked Michael.

'I am Wilfred Owen,' said the young man.

Michael was shocked. 'You're joking. You're not the guy I spoke to on the phone, are you?'

'I am. Sorry, I should have introduced myself properly, but I thought it was obvious.'

It wasn't obvious to Michael. The lawyer in front of him looked like an intern who had only recently started shaving. 'But how can you possibly be a qualified lawyer? You must be even younger than me.'

The solicitor smiled. 'Thank you, but I'm older than I look. I qualified fifteen years ago and would like to reassure you that I'm good at what I do. Your father hired me to help him with his will for a reason.'

'I have to say that with a name like Wilfred, I assumed you must be at least in your sixties.'

'Yes…regrettably, my mum had a thing about the war poets, Wilfred Owen in particular. I'm fairly sure she only

10

married my dad for his surname and the opportunity to name her son after her hero. Given how short-lived their marriage was and how incompatible they were, this would seem to be the only plausible explanation. My dad, for whom poetry only exists on the football pitch, certainly thinks so. He now believes she duped him into thinking she had fallen for his looks, only to find that it was his unremarkable surname she was after. I've had to live with it ever since.'

Michael slowly sipped his coffee as he tried to recalibrate. His late father, who had recently died in suspicious circumstances, had employed a reclusive and improbably youthful-looking lawyer named after a war poet to handle his affairs. Michael imagined these affairs would be relatively straightforward. His father had been an uncomplicated and private man who made a reasonable living from a small undertaker's business. Widowed once, divorced twice, he had lived, as far as Michael could tell, a quiet and frugal life. He had become more or less estranged from his two sons over the past few years, not least because of their lack of interest in his business. It wasn't as if Michael hadn't got on with his father; they had met once or twice a year; it was just that they had inhabited very different worlds and didn't seem to have much in common. His father showed little interest in Michael's accountancy career, other than a congratulations card when he qualified a couple of years ago. In turn, Michael was indifferent to his father's business.

In truth, it wasn't so much indifference as nausea. Michael, who had spent his childhood in a small apartment above an undertaker's shop, felt deeply uncomfortable about dead bodies. It was because he had spent his formative years in such proximity to death that he had such a problem with it. One of his earliest memories, as a three-year-old, was pushing open the unlocked door of a room, supposedly out of bounds, to find a bloated, naked corpse of a fat old man laid out on a cold metal table. As he remembered it, bodily fluids were seeping out and dripping on to the floor, although that might have been an embellishment of his memory. The cadaver was undoubtedly there, though. Michael was still haunted by it, in all its horrifying, vivid Technicolor glory, twenty-six years later. It wasn't just the thought of the putrefying flesh in the basement that so disturbed him; it was the whispered condolences, the wearing of black and the pervading air of misery around the place that he hated.

As a child, Michael had taken refuge in his schoolwork, which had enabled him to be the first in his family ever to go to university. His degree led to a job with a large firm of accountants. Michael liked accountancy. It was precise and neat. Not messy like death. Much less emotional.

'You say you're good at what you do. What exactly *do* you do?' Michael couldn't read Wilfred Owen, who looked like a fresh-faced provincial estate agent, with his shiny smile and slicked-back hair. He struggled to take him seriously. 'I'm sorry, but do you mind if I straighten that frame? It's bugging me.' Michael got up and nudged the print of Henry Scott Holland's poem 'Death is Nothing at All' so the top of its frame lined up with the dado rail.

He controlled his urge to put the chairs properly in place. Michael couldn't understand how anyone could work in such conditions. In other words, he couldn't understand how anyone could work in a room with a marginally misaligned picture frame and two chairs not fully pushed back under the table. Very few other people would notice, let alone be bothered by it. Michael had already lost a girlfriend who found his obsessiveness a little too weird. The final straw had been when he rearranged her make-up in her bathroom and hid the sanitary towels in a place she couldn't find when she needed them.

Wilfred said, 'When I was training to become a lawyer, I couldn't help observing that solicitors who specialise in wills tend only to be interested in getting it all done and out of the way as soon as possible. I couldn't find any other lawyer who properly represented their clients' interests after their death, and so I decided to stand up for the dead guy. Although I take instruction from my clients while they're still alive and work very closely with them, I only really think of them as active clients when they die. It's then that my work starts. That way my clients can rest in peace. My old English teacher used to say, "Tidy desk, tidy mind." I make sure my clients have a tidy desk when they die.'

'And the cobbler's children have no shoes.'

'Sorry?'

'Well, I wouldn't say this place is particularly tidy. Admittedly, I'm a bit obsessive, but were I to assess your business on the quality of your attention to detail, I would say "Untidy office, shoddy business."'

Wilfred smiled and put his hands up in submission. 'Fair cop. I've tried to create an atmosphere that's the opposite of a slick city lawyer. You're right, though: my old English teacher would be unimpressed.' Michael didn't respond; he was pleased to have knocked Wilfred slightly off his tracks. He didn't yet know what to make of him and had no idea where this conversation was going, which made him feel most uncomfortable.

'Let me explain why we needed to meet,' said Wilfred. 'I don't know how much you know about it, I suspect not much – but your father's affairs are quite complicated. I'm going to cut to the chase and summarise the main points of the will. Then I'm sure you'll have some questions, which we can discuss. It's a great shame that we can't have this meeting with your brother. I'm seeing him tomorrow and fully anticipate the three of us will then need to meet together.'

Michael muttered to himself that he thought this would be extremely unlikely. His internal voice said, *No way am I going to be in the same room as that bastard.* To Wilfred, he said, 'We may find it difficult to find a time we can both make.'

Wilfred said, 'I suspect that when you hear what I have to say, you'll find the time. It's going to change your life.'

CHAPTER THREE

Reduced to a cinder

South London. June 1998

'I reckon it must have been suicide.' Jack was curled up on the couch with his girlfriend, Marianne. He was absent-mindedly running his fingers through her hair, while a new Radiohead album played quietly in the background. 'It would be just like my old man to cremate himself to save on the burial costs. Dispose of his own body at the very same time as killing himself. It's certainly cost-effective.'

'Don't say that, darling, that's a horrible thought.'

'Seriously, though, it has to have been suicide. It must be impossible to cremate yourself accidentally. Particularly Dad: he was always so careful and meticulous in everything he did. It's inconceivable he could have made such a catastrophic mistake. And it's equally hard to imagine that anyone would have wanted to do him away. He's not the kind of man to have enemies. At least not the kind who would lure him into a crematorium and somehow reduce him to a cinder.'

'But why would he kill himself?'

'That I don't know.'

Thom Yorke was singing that he'd take a quiet life. Jack liked his music and had bought Marianne the Radiohead CD as part of his mission to upgrade her anodyne record collection. He believed he could read someone's character by flicking through their vinyl. It bothered him that he was going out with someone who owned a Hall and Oates LP. Either it undermined his otherwise watertight theory that musical preference reveals the truth of character, or he had got his girlfriend of six years all wrong. He couldn't even pretend it was an exception that proved the rule because, shockingly, she also had a copy of 'Agadoo' by Black Lace. They could at least agree on Leonard Cohen, who Jack had only discovered because a Marianne featured in one of his most famous songs. Whenever he made a snide comment about her musical taste, she was quick to take credit for her inadvertent introduction. 'You were just some kind of gipsy boy before you met me,' she would playfully tease him with a line from that song (their song) and Jack would be disarmed by the girl who liked 'Agadoo'.

The setting sun was reflecting off the mirror in Marianne's second-floor South London apartment and a strand of light briefly caught Jack's eye. Had he been religious, he might have read this as a sign that the spirit of his departed father was trying to commune with him. But he wasn't. His father never had any inclination to commune with him when he was alive; he was hardly going to change now that he inhabited the afterlife. Jack hadn't been particularly close to his father, but neither were they that distant from each other. Theirs was, Jack assumed, a typical relationship between a father and his twenty-three-year-old son. Or rather, had been. Now his father was dead, and Jack didn't know what, or how, to feel about it.

The world outside was changing. In short order, Britain had voted in its first left-wing government in eighteen years and then been traumatised by the tragic death of Lady Di. The internet was beginning to gain traction; dotcom companies were popping up everywhere with promises to disrupt everyone's lives. Armageddon threatened with talk of a bug that might cause a total technological collapse when the clocks struck midnight on the eve of the new millennium. Exciting, unsettling times. With his new job, Jack already felt he was surfing the waves of change. His father's death made it all the more real. Suddenly there was no grown-up in the room. Although he never had cause to turn to his dad for advice or support, he had always known he was there should he need him. Only now he wasn't there.

Jack had been at work when he had taken the call. It had been most unsettling. One of his father's colleagues had called and delivered the news in a very matter-of-fact way. Jack thought maybe it was because death was such a regular occurrence at his father's work that such a conversation was no more out of the ordinary than reporting the monthly accounts. But surely they would have been trained to deal with grieving relatives with a little more sensitivity? Maybe the colleague was in shock, too. It's not every day at work that your boss is incinerated.

Jack's employers had been understanding. Despite only being in his current job at a Soho advertising agency for ten months, they'd granted him a week's compassionate leave. Marianne had been a godsend, dropping everything (which meant missing some lectures and extending a few essay deadlines from her Master's course) to mother him for a few days. All of which led Jack to feel as if he was in some strange limbo-land. Off work, but not on holiday. Pampered, but not indulged. When he tried to explain to Marianne how he felt, all he could say was that it was unreal. He couldn't say more than that; he wasn't great at articulating his feelings at the best of times. He was a bloke, after all. It was hardly surprising then that he didn't have the vocabulary to express how he felt about becoming orphaned by an act of self-immolation.

It had, of course, made the papers. 'Undertaker Goes Up in Smoke' was one of the headlines he had seen on a local newsstand. A journalist had accosted him outside his apartment, causing him to move in with Marianne for a few days.

'My dad's lawyer called today.'

'What for?'

'He wants to meet up to talk about Dad's will. He said he would have liked to see both Mike and me at the same time, but Mike had told him that wasn't possible. There's a surprise.'

'I can't believe I've never met Mike in the six years I've known you. It's odd.' Marianne pulled herself up from Jack's lap and turned to face him. 'Don't you think it's odd?'

'I guess so, but it's all I know, so it's normal for me. He's always been like that.'

It hurt Jack that his brother had never wanted anything to do with him, but he had learned to live with the rejection. Jack was pretty sure Marianne would like him, as Michael could be perfectly pleasant when he wanted to be. He just never chose to be so with Jack, whom he had bullied when they were younger and then had just blanked his younger brother after he had left home. This, Jack had decided, suited him.

The notion of family was different for Jack than it was for Marianne. Jack's family was a dead mother, a somewhat distant and now deceased father, and a brother who hated his guts. He had no extended family that he was aware of, other than some step-relatives who had cut contact after his father's acrimonious divorce from his second wife. He couldn't explain it. His father had been a decent man. Private, but not without friends. His brother was charming to other people. And Jack himself was highly social. But as a family collective, they were utterly dysfunctional.

His father had once been summoned to Jack's primary school to discuss (explain) a picture that young Jack had drawn to represent his family. Had Mr Merriweather been an art critic, he might have detected a touch of early Edvard Munch in his son's work. Had he been a tiger mother, he might have seen the burgeoning signs of artistic genius. But he was neither. He was a provincial undertaker inspecting a graphic rendition of his family life as seen through the eyes of his five-year-old son. 'Jack said that everyone always wears black at home,' said the headmistress, by way of explaining the thick lines that dominated the picture. Mr Merriweather, who had come straight from a funeral, shifted uncomfortably in his seat, thankful that he had at least left his top hat behind in the car. The artwork was indeed devoid of colour, apart from a splash of pink on one of the stick people in a pile of stick people underneath the house. 'Jack said that there are dead bodies in the basement at your house. Is that true?' Mr Merriweather had to admit it was. 'He said the figure in the pink dress is his mum.' Had he been a psychologist, Mr Merriweather might at this point have referred himself and his sons to Social Services. The headmistress was less concerned with the thought that Jack was living above a cesspit of dead bodies, one of which was his mother, than that he had depicted himself outside the house while his father and brother were inside. 'He said that his brother had told him he didn't belong in your home.' Twenty years later, Jack wished his father had kept that picture. Not only was it early evidence of his creative gene, but also, to Jack's mind, it said it all.

Jack presumed it would have all been very different had his mother lived. Strange how a single disastrous event can have such profound consequences for years thereafter. Marianne's family, by contrast, were very close. Although he would never admit it to her, Jack at times thought cloyingly so. They were always calling each other. They were lovely people and had generously welcomed Jack as one of their own, giving him the family he didn't have, but there were occasions when Jack would have liked to have a bit more of Marianne to himself. It was also odd, he thought, that they never seemed to disagree with each other. 'That is weird,' his friend said when Jack told him about it in the pub. 'Really? They never argue with each other?'

'Never. In the six years I've gone out with Marianne, I've never heard one cross word between them. And I've seen a lot of her family over that time.'

'Wow,' said his friend. 'A happy family.'

Marianne interrupted Jack's thoughts, 'So are you going to meet this lawyer, then?'

'Yeah, Mike's seeing him today and I'm going tomorrow. He's miles away in Swindon. Not sure there's any point really, though: I can't believe there's much in Dad's will. I don't see why we have to meet, but the lawyer said there were some complications and it would be better to discuss it in person. I guess he needs to justify his fee. Death is good business for lawyers.'

'And undertakers,' Marianne added.

CHAPTER FOUR

The secrets we keep

Swindon. June 1998

Wilfred, self-proclaimed defender of the dead, said, 'Your late father thought through this will very carefully. We've been working on it together since he first contacted me two years ago. He was referred to me because I specialise in this kind of thing.'

'What do you mean "this kind of thing"?' Michael was still trying to process what on earth Wilfred had meant when he'd said this was going to change his life.

'Conditional wills. I specialise in helping people write wills that have complications. As I've just explained, I help my clients get what they want when they're no longer around to get it themselves.'

'That makes no sense to me. My father was a modest man. I can't imagine that he had much to leave in his will. It can't be complicated.'

'Just hear me out.'

Michael thought he caught a glimmer of a smile in

Wilfred's otherwise inscrutable expression and wondered if the complication related to his father's two ex-wives. That he had been married three times was strangely out of character. It suggested a bit of a philanderer, which was as far off the mark as was possible to imagine. The death of his first wife had been tragic; a catastrophic event from which Mr Merriweather never really recovered. Everyone who knew him from before said that he became much quieter and more private afterwards. His second wife had been a mistake, undoubtedly a rebound. Michael couldn't stand the second Mrs Merriweather. As far as he was concerned, she had entrapped a vulnerable widower in an unhappy marriage and proceeded to make his own life a misery for three years.

Michael didn't consider himself to be a bitter man. He didn't easily make enemies, and yet the anger he bore against his stepmother and her two daughters had been the source of countless therapy sessions. His therapist had gently asked if there might be a theme: whether he had trouble forming relationships with those closest to him. Michael had reacted with fury, 'That's nothing to do with it. They're all bastards. I'm just really unlucky.' His therapist had suggested that the loss of his mother at an early age might have led to some underlying attachment issues, but Michael still couldn't see that the problem was anything to do with him. His stepmother was a vindictive witch; her two daughters simpering sycophants who always told on him; and his brother, well that was another story.

The third Mrs Merriweather had also been a mistake,

but a different kind of mistake. She was a lovely caring woman who felt profoundly sorry for his damaged father and had tried to rescue him: but they both knew it wasn't right and annulled the marriage within a year.

Michael couldn't believe that his father would have left anything to the second Mrs Merriweather. He had once complained that the divorce settlement had been more than generous to her. He may have left something to the third Mrs Merriweather, but she had emigrated to Australia shortly after the marriage broke down over ten years ago. As far as Michael knew, she had no subsequent contact with his father. Even if he had left her something, there was no reason why it should have been so complicated as to require Michael to come all this way.

Why had Wilfred said this was going to change his life? Michael felt tense. Although the room was a little too warm, he didn't want to remove his jacket. Even though the shabby attic room felt more like a den than an office, this was a formal meeting. Michael's sense of decorum demanded appropriate attire. As it wasn't a work meeting and as it was out of town, he was wearing a blazer rather than a suit. He noticed that Wilfred was in a nondescript suit. If there was a dress code for lawyers of the dead based in Swindon, Michael imagined it would probably be the kind of cheap, innocuous grey suit that Wilfred was wearing. Michael liked rules, conventions and dress codes.

'I don't know how much you know, but from what your father said, I suspect what I'm about to tell you is going to come as a bit of a surprise. The first thing you need to know is that your father was an extremely wealthy man.' Wilfred paused to let Michael absorb this information.

Michael stared at Wilfred and sat quietly for a few seconds, before asking, 'How can that possibly be? He has – sorry had – a small undertaker's business with only three homes. My father lived modestly in a three-bedroom apartment above one of those premises. He was always worried about money and he obsessed about the cost of everything. He was comfortable, but he lived within his means.'

'I understand you haven't had too much contact with your father over the last ten years. I don't say that pejoratively, your father was a private man who was clearly proud of both you and your brother, but it might explain why there are things about him that you don't know. For a start, about eight or nine years ago he bought another substantially larger undertaker's business. You might have heard of it: Dyer's, a chain of fifteen homes in the Home Counties.'

Michael was shocked. 'I can't believe it. How did I not know that?'

'I guess you never asked. Your father didn't strike me as the kind of man who would unilaterally volunteer information.'

A load of questions came flooding into Michael's head. How? Why? How could he possibly have afforded it? Why? Why? Why? And why did he never mention it? He began to feel empty. At that moment, he realised how little he knew of the person to whom he should have been closest in the world.

Wilfred continued, 'You said your father obsessed about the cost of everything. I think he was a prudent and shrewd businessman who ran his first three homes very profitably. He successfully reinvested some of those profits and over the years built up substantial cash reserves that enabled him to expand the business. Dyer's, when he bought it, was a poorly run business and your father was able to quickly make a substantial difference by cutting out the fat and introducing the efficient practices he had perfected over the years at Merriweather's. The business soon started to deliver substantial returns. Again your father reinvested a proportion of those profits in, depending on how you look at it, some very clever or very fortunate investments and became a rich man.'

'What did he invest in?'

'I don't know the details, but he did mention he had done very well out of Dell shares.'

'Dell?' Michael was astonished. 'He knew nothing about computers. He wouldn't even know how to turn one on. The one time I suggested he should get one for his business, he dismissed the idea out of hand, saying you can't bury someone in a computer.'

'Victoria's Secrets was another.'

'Victoria's fucking Secrets? My dad? You're joking, aren't you?'

'I'm deadly serious.'

'I don't know what to say. I simply can't believe I knew nothing of this. I'm embarrassed.'

'I'm not sure we ever really know each other. In my

line of business, I continue to be surprised by the secrets that people keep from each other. Only in death do we reveal ourselves, and even then it often only raises more questions than answers.'

'So I have to ask: how much has my father left in his will?'

'Just over five million pounds.'

'How much?... Five million? Are you sure?' Michael was stunned. He sat back in his chair. 'I don't know what to say. Why did he live so frugally if he had so much money? Why didn't he tell us?' Michael knew the answer to his question. His father never talked about money. He would have seen no reason to disclose how much or how little he had.

Wilfred said, 'I'm conscious that this is a lot for you to take in, which was why I wanted to meet with you rather than discuss it over the phone. However, there is more. I need to share all the main terms of the will, and then we can return to the whys and wherefores. Your father's will leaves the bulk of his estate to you and your brother, just over two million each, but it's subject to an important condition that has substantial implications for the two of you.'

'What's the condition?' Michael tried to sound calm. But there was something in Wilfred's tone that warned him there was a catch.

A great big catch.

CHAPTER FIVE

The catch

Swindon. June 1998

As soon as he got out of W. Owen Solicitors and found a nearby phone box, Jack called Marianne. 'You won't believe this. I don't know where to start.'

Jack was five years younger than Mike. The two brothers had never got on. Jack felt that Mike never gave him a chance, was always putting him down, beating him up or excluding him. As far as Jack could remember, although he was not much more than a toddler at the time, their first stepmother was not interested and never intervened. By the time she was out of the picture, Mike was at secondary school and more or less ignored him. Their father tried his best to bring them together, but was so wrapped up in his work, not to mention dealing with the pressures of two unsatisfactory marriages, that he didn't give them much time either. His father was, anyway, no good at that kind of thing. He was great with people when they were dead, but much less competent when they were alive. His attempts

28

involved taking his two sons out to an event like a football match, something that none of them had any interest in but was the kind of activity, his dad assumed, a father should take his sons to. Other times they might go to the cinema or a dismal lunch together in a family room devoid of atmosphere at some local pub. Mostly these events were painful. His father had no small talk, Mike behaved as if his brother wasn't there, and Jack just felt miserable.

As they grew older, their father gave up taking them out and tried instead to engage them both in the business. He once said, when Jack was eleven and Mike sixteen, that he would like them to take over the family firm, but Mike quickly shut him down with a grumpy adolescent retort, 'Well, that's never going to happen.' Mike seemed to have an almost visceral reaction against the business, and flatly refused his father's entreaties to learn more about it. Jack was less opposed to it, but just wasn't that interested. He certainly didn't see himself as an undertaker. It was just too dull.

Jack's brother was a stranger to him. He had hardly seen him for ten years and had had no contact whatsoever in the six years since Mike had left home. As a young boy, Jack was desperate for Mike's approval, but over the years he had grown to feel a mix of resentment and disengagement. Fuck him, he thought, if that's what he wants, then so be it. While he couldn't say that he really knew his brother, he was aware they were different in many ways. Mike was uptight. Everything needed to be perfect. It was no surprise that he had become an accountant. Mike always wanted to be called

Michael, never Mike. Jack referred to him as Mike because it would annoy him if ever he knew, even though he never would. Jack, on the other hand, had become Jack as soon as he had any say in it. He could never get his father to call him Jack rather than Jonathan, and he didn't suppose Michael would ever call him anything other than his christened name – but everyone else knew him as Jack.

Jack was more free-spirited than his brother. Some might assume it was because he was the youngest, but he certainly hadn't been an indulged child. Instead, he had had to plough his own furrow in a cold affectionless home. He didn't doubt that his father loved him, but he never showed it.

Jack had fallen into advertising. He hadn't done well at school, where he was more concerned with impressing his friends than his teachers. After landing his latest job, he had taken to joking that he had now had had more jobs than he had GCSEs. It was a good joke at his own expense, even though he didn't like what it said about himself. Thick and unemployable. In Jack's book, a good joke trumped everything, even those self-deprecating ones. Especially the self-deprecating ones. Marianne didn't like it; she tried to stop him saying it by telling him that he wasn't stupid, in fact quite the opposite; it was just that school didn't suit him and he hadn't yet found the right job. She would have had more success had she been able to persuade him that the joke simply wasn't funny. Jack's problem in holding down a job arose primarily because his lack of qualifications meant he was unable to get a job worth keeping. None of his previous employers had taken him seriously, and so he hadn't taken them seriously. He had messed up the one job he had quite enjoyed by taking sick leave to attend a three-day music festival, where he had the misfortune to bump into his boss. His boss had commented how well he looked and then, when they were both back at work, handed Jack his P45. Jack was okay with that, though, because it made for a great story. And, as he would also say in the retelling, the headlining act at the festival were brilliant.

For once, Jack was tongue-tied. He called Marianne in great excitement, but then didn't know where to start. Marianne said, 'Darling, I really can't hear you very well. It sounds as if you're in the Arctic Circle. It's so garbled that it sounded like you said you might be a millionaire. Why don't you tell me about it when you get home. I'm dying to hear what's happened.'

Jack didn't know what he had done to deserve Marianne. Perhaps it was compensation for the lack of affection at home. They had met six years ago at the seventeenth birthday party of a mutual friend. Jack had felt an instantaneous attraction the moment he saw her. He had plucked up the courage to ask her for a dance and had never let go since. Recently though, as much as he was loath to admit this to himself, Jack sensed his grip was loosening. Although she never said as much, Jack could tell his charm and his jokes were beginning to wear thin on Marianne. Jack chose not to dwell on such thoughts.

He was bursting to fill her in once he got back to her apartment. Getting a beer from the fridge, he launched into his news. 'The meeting was extraordinary. Will Owen is the lawyer handling Dad's will. He looks about seven years old but seems to know his shit. The most amazing thing is that Dad amassed this huge fortune of around five million pounds without telling anyone.'

Marianne took a sharp intake of breath. 'Five million pounds? You're joking.'

'I'm not. I couldn't believe it. Apparently, Dad bought this second chain of undertakers a few years ago and has done rather well from it.'

'Darling, I have to say you've suddenly become a little more eligible than you were a few hours ago.'

'Yes, but there's a catch. Dad's will passes two million pounds each to Mike and me, but only if we take over the business and run it together for at least five years.'

'Whoa.'

Jack took a sip of his beer as he let Marianne absorb what he had just told her. Marianne said, 'But surely there's no way to enforce that. Who's going to know? What's to stop you or Mike taking the money and then not working in the business?'

'It's complicated, but in essence Dad has set up an elaborate structure in the form of a trust to enforce it. Will Owen specialises in this kind of thing. He calls it a "conditional" will. The payments are spread over time and are legally recoverable by the trust if certain conditions aren't met. We enter into a binding contract with the trust. Dad had been working on this for two years with Will. It seems fairly watertight.'

'And what happens if you don't accept the conditions?'

'We don't get the money.'

'What if one of you accepts it and the other doesn't?'

'Neither of us gets the money. I think Dad saw this as a way to bring us together.'

'Tear you apart, more like. And where does the money go if you don't get it?'

'Well, here's the thing. Extraordinarily, it will go to Sheila, my first stepmother, and her two daughters. I think I've told you how much Dad hated them and how acrimonious their divorce was, but he knew that we, and especially Mike, hate them just as much.'

'That's terrible. It doesn't sound like the kind of thing your father would do at all. So Machiavellian.'

'It shows how much he wants us to accept it, that he has proposed such a radical alternative. It would be hard enough to walk away from two million pounds, but to do so in the knowledge that it would all go instead to those three people doesn't bear thinking about.'

'It doesn't sound as if you have much choice, then.'

'Yes, but here's the thing. Apparently, Mike said he didn't think he could accept it.'

CHAPTER SIX

A normal life

North London. June 1998

Michael woke the next morning with a thumping headache. In turmoil after meeting with Wilfred Owen, he'd spent the evening pacing around his apartment and drinking one too many glasses of whisky. More than anything else, he was furious with his father. He resented being given an impossible decision without any opportunity to discuss it. He cursed him, thumped the table and went for a long, late walk around the park. Bastard. Why? Why would he do such a thing to me?

All his old resentments against his father, grievances he had thought were long buried, rose to the surface. He remembered the time when his father had sided with his stepsister, who had falsely accused him of breaking one of her toys. Years later his father had apologised to him for this episode, but now, in his anger, it was the incident rather than the apology he chose to remember. More than anything else, it was the fact that he had had no opportunity to talk to his father about it. But that was typical. When Michael was younger, his father was always telling him not to answer back. He was never interested in Michael's side of the story. And now he's gone and done the same thing again. Big time. Michael found himself wanting to stamp his feet and scream, '*It's not fair!*'

'And what the bloody hell am I to do with you?' The black Labrador wagged his tail cautiously.

As the meeting in Swindon had drawn to a close, Wilfred had turned towards the dog in the corner. 'And your father also bequeathed you this. No strings attached, it's yours.'

'But my father didn't own a dog.'

'He did. He got Morty eighteen months ago. He's wonderful, very well trained. I've looked after him for the past few days. It's been a real pleasure.'

'What did you say his name was? Monty?'

'Morty. His full name is Mortuary Merriweather.' The dog pricked up his ears.

Michael laughed. 'Mortuary? You're joking surely; you can't possibly be suggesting that my father had a sense of humour.'

'It would seem so. Anyway, Morty is yours now. I've arranged for various dog-walkers and dog-sitters to be on call to help you out whenever you need. Here's a list of their numbers. They're expecting to hear from you.'

Michael was flabbergasted. 'Why me? Why did Dad give *me* a dog? Why not my brother?'

'I think your father trusted you to look after Morty –

and, in fact, Morty you. He said he thought you could do with the company, and with the responsibility of having someone, or rather another creature, to look after. Morty does some good tricks. Let me show you. Morty, sit.' The dog got up from his lying position and sat bolt upright. 'Morty, dead.' The dog flopped to the floor and lay utterly still with his tongue hanging out. 'Morty, rigor mortis.' The dog rolled on to his back and stretched all four legs vertically in the air.

'Who taught him that? It can't have been my father.'

And so Michael had a companion on his journey home from Swindon. And Morty found that his new home was to be a bachelor flat in North London.

'We'll get rid of that, I promise,' Michael said to the dog when he saw him eyeing the cat poster.

The next day at work had been a bit of a blur. Not only was he nursing a small hangover, but he also hadn't slept well. He had been disorientated when the doorbell rang early in the morning, forgetting that he had booked an early start for the dog-sitter. Fortunately, the audit he was working on that day didn't require much interaction with anyone else, so he'd been able to get on with it and keep himself to himself.

'Still on for this evening, Michael?' Richard, his closest colleague at work, popped his head around the corner. 'God, you look rough. Everything okay?'

'I'm fine, yeah, thanks, Richard. Yes, I'm still on for this evening. Looking forward to it.' Michael's oldest friend Cat had thoughtfully invited him and Richard to dinner when

Michael's father had died. She anticipated that Michael might otherwise slip into his shell and internalise his grief and felt he could probably do with the company of friends. If not a shoulder to cry on, at least an opportunity for a good chat.

'Oh, Richard, one other thing, I'll be bringing a well-behaved dog with me this evening.'

'A dog?' Richard was surprised, 'okay.'

Alone in his cubicle, Michael reflected on his past few days, which had resembled a rollercoaster ride. Michael hated rollercoasters. He couldn't stand the way they slowly rumbled up a steep incline, building up tension, before a sudden descent involving a series of sharp, violent turns. Michael always imagined the car was going to get thrown off its tracks and become a headline item on the evening news. He didn't want ups and downs and sharp changes of direction. He craved certainty and predictability. He wanted a normal life.

As he was beginning to pack up at the end of the day, Jen appeared. 'Can I come in?'

'Oh, hi, Jen. Yes, of course, how can I help?'

'I wanted to check you're okay.' Michael didn't know Jen very well – they had only once briefly worked together on a significant audit – but he had always liked her. A few years senior to him, Jen was a highly respected junior partner at the firm and had recently returned from a short maternity break. Michael had enjoyed working with her because, unlike most of the other managers at Abel's, she didn't carry any airs or graces. There was something in her calm manner that encouraged him to be a little more honest in his response than the perfunctory I'm okay, thanks, that was his default response. 'I've had better weeks,' he said.

'I'm sure. I'm sorry for your loss. My parents are both still alive, so I can't imagine what it must be like for you. But when my grandfather died, I took comfort from the Chinese belief that our life continues through our descendants. I like the idea that, in some way, he lives on through my daughter and me. Maybe the same is true for you?'

'That my father lives on through me? God, I hope not. I appreciate your thought, but you've hit on a sensitive area. Right now I can't imagine anything worse than becoming my father, even if that's what he would have liked.'

'I'm sorry, it was clumsy of me to try to put myself in your shoes. I just wanted to let you know that I'm here for you. Please let me know if I can help with anything at all.'

'Don't apologise. I appreciate you taking the trouble to speak to me. I'll let you know if I need any help.' Michael was being polite. He knew he had to get through this by himself and he couldn't envisage turning to anyone, least of all a work colleague, to help navigate a way out of his current turmoil. 'I'm sorry, I'm a bit all over the place at the moment.' He didn't foresee, then, quite how portentous Jen's offer would prove.

As Michael left the office that evening, he regretted having accepted Cat's invitation. He would have preferred to be on his own, forgetting that from now on, with Morty at his side, he would rarely be alone.

'Are you out of your mind? Are you seriously going to walk away from two million pounds?' Richard was incredulous. Michael hadn't necessarily planned to share his dilemma with his friends, but it was impossible not to. Cat, who had been in the adjoining kitchen preparing the food, half in and out of the conversation, stopped her preparations and joined in this extraordinary conversation. Dinner could wait.

'*Why?*' Richard was aghast.

'Could someone please fill me in,' said Cat.

'I can,' said Richard. 'Michael, with all due respect, appears to have taken leave of his senses.'

Having been brought up to speed, Cat turned to Michael. 'Is this true? Is this how it is?'

'More or less,' said Michael.

'Can I ask why? Might it have anything to do with your brother?'

Michael leaned back and took a big breath.

CHAPTER SEVEN

Dying wish

South London. June 1998

Like Cat, Jack thought Michael's decision had something to do with him. In fact, he assumed it had everything to do with him. He wouldn't put it past his sibling to sacrifice two million pounds just so his little brother didn't get anything. He was seething. Ever since meeting Will Owen, he had found it impossible not to think about the money and start spending it in his head. Rather than a magazine of aspirational slightly-out-of-reach items, *GQ* became a shopping list. Jack found himself walking into a luxury car showroom that he had previously only admired from the outside. He went from not even contemplating owning a car to evaluating whether he would look better in an old classic such as a Mercedes-Benz 190 or a brand new Ferrari: zero to full throttle in less than twenty-four hours. His compassionate leave became not so much a time to mourn the passing of his dear departed father as an indulgence in future possibilities.

But just as Jack began to let his mind get carried away with all these exciting opportunities, his fantasies would disintegrate when he reminded himself that his brother sought to deprive him of all his dreams. It was hugely frustrating to him that he couldn't even talk to Mike. He tried calling him, breaking a six-year vow of silence between them, but the call had gone through to answerphone. He wanted to confront his brother at his home or work, but realised he didn't know where either place even was. Marianne counselled against this. Wisely, she pointed out that Jack was unlikely to persuade his brother to change his mind at the best of times, so to try to do so in the heat of the moment would inevitably only make things much worse. Jack became like a caged tiger. He tried to walk off his tension, which only led to him wandering back into the car showroom and the infinite loop of tantalising dreams, followed by crushing reality. Later that evening he would turn to alcohol, but before that he went back to Marianne's flat where he remembered to share something Will Owen had given him.

'Here, have a read of this.' He passed Marianne a letter from his father.

1 June 1998

Dear Jonathan,

I am writing identical letters to both yourself and Michael. You will by now have met Mr Owen. First of all, I would like to say that I love you. Although I realise I didn't always show it, I've always been immensely proud of you both. I appreciate I haven't been the best of fathers to you. Your mother's death was an enormous shock to me. It hit me hard and, if I'm honest, I never really got over it. I didn't know how to look after myself, let alone two young children. I'm sorry. I would like to say I did my best, but that's probably not true. I could have done so much more for you.

It upsets me more than you will know that the two of you don't get along. I never really understood why. I would have thought that what with all you have been through, you two would have been as thick as thieves: united against this cruel world. It would have devastated your mother to know that her two boys weren't the best of friends. It's my hope that you put your differences aside and overcome whatever it is that separates you. It is with this in mind that I have written this will.

I suspect your initial reaction will be to disagree with my proposal, but I hope, once you have reflected on it, you will agree to give it a go. I'm optimistic that once you start working together, you will come to realise what a great team you can be and how you have more in common than you currently think. I honestly believe you have complementary talents that could make for a formidable partnership.

I know neither of you is interested in the business. That, too, has been disappointing to me. But again, I believe this is partly a consequence of your age (I'll be the first to admit that, at first glance, undertaking looks a lot less sexy than the worlds of finance and advertising) and of circumstance. I understand that your resentment, in part, comes from the time I spent in the business at the price of attending to your needs. But it is the family business. Your grandfather started it and you will now know that I have had the good fortune to build it into a more substantial concern. It is a golden goose. I honestly believe that, with your talents, it could become something extraordinary. I don't know what you will do with it, but I would love to see it. I've taken it so far, but I can't take it any further. I just don't have the ability. You do. More importantly, though, it's the vehicle that can bring you together.

Please give it a go. I'm only asking for five years. If, after that period, you want to go your own ways and do your own things, then so be it. At least you'll have given it a fair crack of the whip.

It's literally my dying wish. And I know your mother would have wanted the same.

I love you both,
Dad

'Wow.' Marianne put the letter down and sat silently for a few moments. Jack watched her. He wanted to know what she thought should happen next. He was feeling such a swirl of emotion that he didn't know what to think. His father had killed himself; that much at least was clear now. That alone was something he needed to process and accept. On top of that, the will, with its extraordinary revelations, challenged everything he thought he knew about his father. And then his old animosity with his brother was bubbling up. All the hurt and anger he had managed to bury in recent years was roaring to the surface. He was a wreck. His father's letter was the most honest expression of emotion he had ever received from him. Why couldn't he have said this to them when he was alive? It was as if his father, who had always been more comfortable with death than life, had only found his voice once he no longer had one.

Marianne wiped a small tear from her eye and said, 'It's so sad. Poor you.' She moved to hug him. He reciprocated by wrapping her in his arms and never wanted to let go. Jack felt a deep need for Marianne. She gave him the love he had never had in the past, the love he had been deprived of when his mother died giving birth to him. He felt less alone with Marianne.

Marianne said, 'It's a lovely letter, if not a bit formal.'

'Well, that's him to a tee isn't it. He probably put on a suit to write it.'

'It's such a shame he couldn't have said this when he was alive.'

'Exactly what I was thinking. It's as if he's more himself now that he's dead. Death is bringing him out of himself, which is pretty weird, if you think about it, for an undertaker. But maybe it's not so weird. Maybe he was a great undertaker precisely because the afterlife is his natural habitat.' Jack was using humour to quell his emotions, something he always did. 'Look on the bright side of life' was something of a mantra for him, as was the sense that everything was fair game for a witty comment or a joke. 'Maybe we'll now be able to get on famously. Perhaps now that he's dead, he'll be able to live happily ever after.'

'So, what happens next?'

'I was hoping you were going to tell me what to do. Quite possibly nothing happens next; other than I lead the rest of my life tortured by the thought that I could have inherited two million pounds were it not for my bloody brother. Not that I would be bitter, of course. I would be perfectly sanguine about it all. I could feel "holier than thou" because I would know that money isn't everything and that I could be happy living a relatively impoverished life, untarnished by grubby materialism. I could smile at my odious millionaire stepsisters living a life of luxury and pity them for the superficiality of it all. Fuck that. It would drive me insane.'

'Did the lawyer explain why he thought Mike wasn't going to accept the inheritance?'

'No, he didn't. He just said Mike's initial reaction wasn't particularly favourable. I tried to press him, but he was fairly inscrutable about it and said it needed more time. He also seemed to think that it would be a good idea for the three us to meet to talk it through together. I'm not sure he appreciates that Mike doesn't want anything to do with me.'

'What do you think? Why do you think Mike might not accept the will?'

'That's obvious. He hates me.'

'There must be more to it than that. Just suppose that wasn't the issue – why else might he not want to accept it?'

It wasn't easy for Jack to put himself in the shoes of his brother. He said, 'Well, I suppose he's always been adamant that he wants nothing to do with the business. Mike always opposed, sometimes violently, my father's entreaties to involve us in any way. He once shouted at my father that it was disgusting, those dead bodies down there. He's always had a bit of a reaction against it, and so I suppose the thought of it being his livelihood might be abhorrent.'

'I would have thought that would be a pretty good reason. Didn't you say a while ago that you had heard Mike was enjoying his work as an accountant?'

'Yeah, something Dad said a couple of years ago when Mike qualified. Dad said he had always been good with numbers and that he had found himself a good career. Dad being Dad, though, went on to say that he thought he was getting useful skills for a future in the family firm. Despite all Mike's opposition to the business, Dad still saw his experience as an accountant as preparation towards taking over Merriweather's.'

'Okay, so that's a second good reason. Mike loves his job. Why would he want to give up a job he loves for a business he hates? What else?'

'Well, I guess Mike has never been that materialistic. I think it's more that he wants to be seen to do well. Although he would never admit it, I think Dad's approval meant a lot to him. He's always wanted to prove himself and do things his way. He's never wanted any help. I'm not sure Mike's particularly interested in money itself. It's probably important to him as a signifier of success, but he's not interested in money for money's sake.'

'You seem to have a pretty good steer on your brother

given that you've hardly seen him for six years.' Marianne smiled.

'Yeah, well, he looms pretty large in my life, even when he's not around. And I do pick things about him from people who know us both. Cat, for example.'

'So I think you've given me two big reasons there. He's not materialistic, and he wants to forge his own path. Anything else?'

'Well, that he hates me.'

'We're not counting that. So let me summarise. One, Mike loves his job. Two, he hates the undertaking business. Three, he wants to prove himself. And four, he's not that materialistic.'

'Yeah, I know, what have the Romans ever done for us, and all that.'

'And I would add a fifth reason, which is maybe an amalgamation of some of the others. It sounds as if Mike would hate the idea of a handout. You see? Maybe it's not all about you after all.'

'I guess so. Maybe there is a bit more to it.'

'I think I need to meet the mysterious Mike.'

CHAPTER EIGHT

Graveyard therapy

Hertfordshire. June 1998

Michael flipped the coin, but failed to catch it. It rolled a few yards down the path, where a dishevelled man trapped it under his foot. 'Heads I keep it, tails you get it back,' said the man.

'Okay,' said Michael.

'Heads it is,' said the man, and quickly pocketed the coin.

'Hey, hold on a minute, I didn't see it.'

'Okay, then do another one.'

'All right then, give me the coin back.'

'No, I won that – do another one.' Michael thought he caught a whiff of alcohol on the man's breath, but decided to play along. He flipped a second coin, which landed on the cobbled path. His opponent moved surprisingly quickly and repeated the same pattern. 'Heads. I win again.' Michael didn't bother to contradict him, although he was pretty sure it wasn't.

'Why are you flipping coins, anyway?' The man sat down beside Michael on the bench. Michael could now smell more than just alcohol.

'I can't decide what to do.'

'Between what? I'm good at making decisions.' Michael looked at the layers of shabby, threadbare clothes and wondered what might constitute a decent decision for his new friend. As if reading his thoughts, the man added, 'I made the right move coming to talk to you, didn't I? Made 20p out of it already.'

What the hell, thought Michael, who felt an urge to unburden himself. 'I can't decide whether to give everything up.'

'I did that,' said the old man, 'or rather it did it to me. Either way, I gave everything up. Hey, have you got a ciggie?'

'Sorry, I don't smoke.'

'So what are you thinking of giving up?'

'My career. My life as I know it.'

'I had a job once. Hated it.'

'I love my job.'

The old man looked in surprise at Michael. 'So why do you want to give it up?'

'I don't.'

'See, I told you I was good at decisions,' the old man said triumphantly, 'I've helped you decide to keep your job.'

'You might be right mate; you may well be right.'

'What are you doing here, anyway? I haven't seen you before and I'm here most days.'

'I've come to see my mum's grave. I thought she might know what I should do.'

'Which one is she? I know most of them here.'

'That one over there. Mrs Merriweather.'

'I know that one. I thought the dog looked familiar. Your father used to come every day with his dog. I talked to him sometimes. Nice man. Tragic, what happened to him. The gardener told me.'

'Yeah… And he wanted me to take over the family business.'

'Aah. Now I understand. That's your decision.'

'The thing is, I hate dead bodies.'

'I can see how that might be a problem for an undertaker.'

'I don't want to do what he wanted me to do. I want to do what I want to do.'

'He was a good man, your father. Very generous. You don't happen to have a spare fiver, do you?' Michael found himself giving his new confidant a five-pound note while wondering whether it was true. Generosity was not an attribute he had ever associated with his father, and the old man had already shown himself to be not entirely honest when it came to money. Still, somehow Michael believed it was possible that his father might have been charitable towards him. 'It's good to respect the dead. Maybe your father knew what was best for you.'

'Like fuck he did.' Michael surprised the old man with his sudden unexpected demonstration of anger. 'Sorry, excuse my language. He might have been a nice man, but he never had any idea what was best for me.'

'Well, as I said before, it sounds as if you should stick with your current job. It doesn't seem like undertaking is for you.'

'Yes, but here's the thing, and this is why my father was maybe not so nice. If I don't take over the family business with my brother, who incidentally I can't stand, then I'm written out of his will. All the money goes to his second wife, who happens to be a horrible bitch.'

The old man sat back and breathed out loudly. 'I thought I had problems. You're angry with your father, you don't like your brother, you don't like your stepmother, and you don't like the dead. You should take up smoking. Here, do you need a sip of this?' He proffered a dirty bottle containing what Michael supposed was neat meths. Michael shook his head. 'Does it matter if your stepmother gets the money? It seems a high price for you to pay. Money isn't everything you know.' The man reflected, apparently with some surprise, on what he had just said. 'But it does help. Any chance you could stand me a bit more?'

Michael pulled two twenty-pound notes from his wallet. 'This is what I would pay for a therapist to ask the kind of questions you're asking.' The old man took the money without a word. He seemed to agree that it was indeed a fair price for the consultation. 'After all, if I'm going to walk away from two million pounds, I might as well give you forty.'

Like the good therapist he had suddenly become, the old man said nothing. He was dumbstruck. Michael patted him on the shoulder to thank him, got up and walked out of the cemetery, all the more confident that he should stick to his convictions. As the old man said, money isn't everything.

Meanwhile, the old man was unscrewing the top of his bottle of meths and thinking precisely the opposite.

A few days later, Michael received a summons to meet with his ultimate boss, the partner in charge of his section. Michael could count on one hand the number of times he had met him in the six years he had worked at Abel's and hence felt a degree of trepidation. He suspected the meeting might have something to do with his father's death, although that seemed too personal for a work meeting. Abel's was a place of work. Senior partners tended not to indulge in small chat with the minions. Michael didn't suppose a death in the family would be sufficient reason to break this convention of complete uninterest in the personal lives of their employees. Waiting outside his office, facing a stern-faced PA, he couldn't help feeling like a naughty schoolboy outside the headmaster's office, which was precisely how he was supposed to feel. Abel's was a traditional accountancy practice. Its hierarchy had empowered and enriched five generations of partners. They weren't going to let go of their power structures in a hurry. It was one of the things Michael liked about the firm. He knew where he stood. And he looked forward to the day when he would graduate through the ranks and have his very own PA guarding his time and his self-importance.

'You can go in now.'

Michael entered an expansive office, big enough to house at least ten of his cubicles.

'Hello, Michael, please take a seat. I understand you may inherit your father's business.' Michael was taken aback. How could he possibly know that? It might have been an educated guess, or Richard might conceivably have said something, but it all seemed very Big Brother. At least the senior partner was true to form. No faux sympathy. He clearly felt it was appropriate to discuss Michael's life outside work as it concerned a potential business interest, but didn't feel any need to pretend that he was sorry for the personal loss his employee had suffered. To the senior partner, Michael's dead father was an appreciating asset rather than an expired life.

'It's complicated. I might, but there's a chance I won't.'

'Yes, I heard that. Although I think you probably will. I think you probably should.' Michael didn't feel it was his place to ask him why. 'Assuming you do take it on, I wanted to let you know that you have our support. You are well regarded here, and we would be sorry to lose you, but I would hope that would simply mean a slight change of relationship, from employee to client. If you appoint us as your auditors, you will also be able to draw on our consultancy support, and we may be able to lend you some people to help you get through the first year. That was all I wanted to say. Do consider it.' The senior partner got up and started to walk back towards his desk. He didn't expect a reply from Michael.

'Oh, yes, there was one other thing... I think you should take some time off work.' Michael thought for a split-second that the senior partner was about to reveal a hitherto well-hidden compassionate side before he said, 'It's not good for the firm having all those journalists sniffing around reception.'

The last thing Michael wanted was to be stuck at home with nothing to do. In the event, he booked himself a week's walking holiday with Morty in the Lake District to get away from it all. Including his father's memorial service.

CHAPTER NINE

Waste disposal

Hertfordshire. June 1998

'I've lost count of the number of times someone has come up to me and said, "I'm so sorry for your loss. Where is your brother?" Richard, surely Abel's must know where he is?' Jack was sheltering under a large oak tree with Marianne, Richard and Cat at the end of his father's memorial service. As Mr Merriweather had already disposed of his own body, his ashes lost to dust, there was nothing left to bury and no need for a funeral. His employees felt it was wrong not to mark the passing of a man who had given his whole life to arranging dignified departures for others, and so had organised a memorial service in the cemetery where he had spent so much of his life. They had arranged for a new gravestone so that he could be immortalised through inscription alongside the first Mrs Merriweather.

Jack, imagining it would be a small service, was shocked to find hundreds of people in attendance. It would have been a bad day to die in Hertfordshire as all eighteen of the Merriweather and Dyer's funeral homes in a thirty-mile radius had shut up shop for the day. But it wasn't just employees; customers had also turned out in force to pay their respects to the man who had buried someone close to them. As had assorted members of the local community, where Mr Merriweather, although a private man, was well known and well liked. And then there were the simply curious whose interest had been piqued by the media coverage, not to mention a smattering of journalists hoping for new angles to perpetuate the story of the undertaker who had gone up in smoke.

The weather was appalling. It had been raining all morning. The persistent rumble of a thunderstorm provided a grim, atmospheric backdrop to the occasion; although it didn't appear to have deterred anyone from attending. Jack felt like an interloper. He hadn't been involved in the preparations and yet everyone treated the occasion as if he was its lead actor. He was exhausted by it all. And not a little pissed off that his brother had chosen against sharing the burden of representing the family. At times it felt to Jack and Marianne as if they were royalty at a state funeral, accepting the commiserations and condolences from a stream of strangers. It was a surreal experience for Jack, who had always assumed his father had few friends and employed little more than a handful of staff. The sea of people filling every available spot in the cemetery provided a graphic demonstration of the scale of the business. Yet again, it showed Jack how little he had known about his father.

Two of his father's former colleagues, Royston McGinty and Monica Moody, both made time to talk with him and Marianne. Royston and Monica had assumed temporary charge of the business. They had, in fact, already been running it for many years alongside Mr Merriweather. The triumvirate had been responsible for its success, and neither Royston McGinty nor Monica Moody had any intention of letting the minor inconvenience of the untimely death of the owner change anything. They, more than most, knew that death happens and life goes on. Wilfred Owen had conveyed his client's wishes that they assume responsibility for the business until his sons joined. 'What if the fookers don't join?' asked Royston. There was no disrespect in his question; everyone was a *fooker* to Royston.

'There's a contingency plan,' said the lawyer, 'but I'm not at liberty to disclose it.' Royston McGinty was an uneducated, heavily tattooed expert embalmer who had first encountered Merriweather's in its early days when they helped bury his beloved mother. Unemployed at the time, having just left the army to care for his cancer-stricken mum, and beside himself with grief, there was nonetheless something about Royston that led Mr Merriweather to encourage him to join the firm with a promise to train him in the art of embalming. Royston took to it like a natural and over time Mr Merriweather gave more and more responsibility to this no-nonsense, brute of a man. They formed an unlikely partnership.

'The fookin' police interrogated me for fookin' hours.' Royston was aggrieved to have been the prime suspect for the first couple of days after Mr Merriweather's expiry. 'Why me? Why not fookin' Monica here?'

Jack could entirely understand why the police might have suspected Royston of having a hand in his father's death. Not only did he have the means, in that he was one of the few people with access to the crematorium and knowledge of how it all worked, but Royston McGinty also had the bearing of a hardened criminal. It wouldn't have surprised Jack one bit if Royston had been a compassionate accomplice to his father's death. His father used to say that he trusted Royston with his life. Jack wondered if perhaps he had misunderstood what his dad had meant. Despite that, he warmed to Royston. He was a character with a sense of humour. Jack also liked that his brother was terrified of Royston, which, it only then occurred to him, might be another reason for Mike's reluctance to get involved in the business.

Monica had also worked with his father for years. Initially joining as his secretary, she had grown with the business to become involved in all aspects of it. After helping to keep the books in the early days, she had then become the de facto HR manager, primarily because there was no one else to do it. This role became crucial after the takeover of Dyer's, when the two businesses needed to be integrated. Monica proved herself to be remarkably good at telling people they no longer had a job. His father once told Jack that people often make the mistake of assuming that Royston is the tough one when, in fact, it's Monica they should fear. 'Hard as nails,' he had said, 'and a volcanic temper that only erupts every 10,000 years or so, but when it does, you'll sure know about it.' Jack had never seen that side of Monica. He had often turned to her as a young boy, on those occasions he was home alone in the apartment upstairs while she was manning the funeral home below, for the emotional support he couldn't find anywhere else. He felt she had a soft spot for him. And both she and Royston had been solicitous of him and Marianne today. If they had any concerns about the future of the business and the brothers' possible involvement, they made no mention of it.

Jack was relieved that the service was over. The crowd of well-wishers was beginning to thin out. He turned down an invitation from Royston and Monica to go back to the funeral home for coffee and a light buffet. He wondered if he should go, but felt he had already done more than his duty. He was grateful for the company of Mike's friends. He had known Cat for years – their two mothers had been best friends – but this was the first time he had met Richard.

Richard shook his head in response to Jack's question. 'I'm afraid not. All I know is that Michael's been signed off work for a week or two. Last time I saw him was when he came to dinner at ours a few days ago.'

Jack turned to Cat. 'Where do you think he is, Cat? You probably know my brother better than any of us. He must have been in touch with you.'

'No, he hasn't. Mind you, I'm not surprised he's not here today. Funerals are not his kind of thing, and he seems pretty angry with your dad about the will.'

Jack was surprised. 'He told you about that, did he? I didn't think anyone else knew.'

'How do you feel about it?' asked Richard.

'What do you think? I'm incredibly fucking annoyed. But as always, there seems to be nothing I can do about it. It's like this inheritance has been dangled in front of me, but then my brother has said, "No, you can't have it." What I want doesn't seem to come into it. And I can't even talk to him about it.'

'Would you take it, if it were your decision?'

'Of course. Who wouldn't?' Jack paused, 'Other than my brother.'

Cat, who had spent much of the morning in quiet reflection, said, 'I've been thinking about the business. Being here today and listening to your father's colleagues talking about how much the company meant to him and how much it means to them, it struck me that his will isn't really about the money, it's about the business and your relationship with Michael. Do you know what happens to Merriweather's if you and Michael don't accept the will?'

'I think it goes into some kind of trust. I don't know.'

'Perhaps you could take over the firm anyway, irrespective of whether you get the money.'

'What and give up my job in advertising to become an undertaker, *without* the inheritance? You've got to be joking. Why on earth would I want to do that?' At that moment, a clap of thunder sounded in the background. Richard laughed. 'Well, it sounds like your father has something to say about that from up there.

'Exactly,' said Cat, her expression darkening like the skies. 'I'm sorry if I'm speaking out of turn here, Jack, but I think you've become completely distracted by the money. I haven't heard you once say that you want to take over the business and build on your father's legacy. And neither have I heard you talk about the opportunity this presents to build bridges with your brother. Quite the opposite. You seem completely detached from the business and just angry with your brother for getting in the way of the money.'

Marianne put her hand on Jack's shoulder, 'Cat's right, you know. You haven't said anything about wanting to take over the business.'

Jack was a little riled by this, not least because it was true. 'So what the fuck should I do? Pretend the money doesn't matter and that I'm interested in the business?'

'I'm not saying it's easy,' said Cat. 'I would hate to be in your position, but when you just said to Richard that you would accept the conditions of the will if it were up to you, I couldn't help but think about your father's business. We've seen today how much it means to so many people. That's quite a responsibility to take on. I wonder if you've thought about that at all.'

'To be honest, no, I haven't. Because it's not going to happen.'

'You're disempowering yourself. If you wanted this, I suspect there might be a chance of making it happen.'

'Why? What do you know? Have you spoken to Mike about it?'

'I'm saying this hypothetically. I did speak with Michael.

Right now I think he wants nothing to do with it, but it's not yet decided, so in theory everything's still possible. At some point in your life, Jack, you need to stand up for what you want and not run away when you can't get it.'

'Whoa, where did that come from?' Jack was surprised at Cat's admonishment. She was usually so calm and level-headed.

'Look, I'm sorry if I'm speaking out of turn. But being here today, remembering your father, who was such a kind, well-meaning man, and seeing all these people here for whom his business means so much, it just feels a bit distasteful for it all to be reduced to a sibling spat over money.'

'What siblings don't fight over money?' Richard injected.

'Speak for yourself,' said Marianne.

'You don't count,' said Jack, 'your family is too perfect. It's not normal.'

'And you and Mike are?'

'Probably more normal than you think, if not at the extreme end.'

'My point,' said Cat, 'is I think you should try to forget about the money and consider whether you want to take on the business. Could you do it and would you want to do it?'

'I dunno. I haven't thought about it.'

'Because if you did decide you wanted it, then you could start to think about how you might persuade Michael. You might not succeed there, but at least you would have tried and stopped playing the helpless victim.'

'I agree with you, Cat,' said Marianne. 'Jack, do you think you could run this?' Marianne opened her arms to gesture towards the expansive cemetery.

'One day lad, all this will be yours.' Jack mimicked a broad Yorkshire accent, followed by a high-pitched retort 'What? All the graves?' The Monty Python reference was lost on his friends, but his mimicry lightened the mood.

'Seriously, Jack.' Marianne pressed him to answer her question. 'Do you think you could run the business? You've got no experience.'

'I don't see why not. How difficult could it be? It's just a waste-disposal business with a few extras thrown in.' No one was sure whether Jack meant it. No one was ever sure whether Jack meant it. Not even Jack. Marianne caught Cat's eye and gave her a despairing look.

They were interrupted by a dishevelled man who approached the group. 'Which one of you is the young Mr Merriweather?'

Jack raised his hand slightly and said, 'That'll be me.'

'I'm sorry for your loss, son. Your father was a good man. Very generous.'

'Thank you…but generous? Are you sure?'

'Yes, he came every day and always gave me something for a cup of tea.'

'Well, I'm sorry that I can't carry on the family tradition. I haven't got any cash on me.'

'Perhaps your friends might have something. You could always pay them back once you've made up with your brother and become a millionaire.'

'How the hell do you know that? Is there anyone who doesn't know about my father's secret will?'

'I heard it through the graveyard.' The old man's smile suggested that any donations might be better spent on dental treatment than a cup of tea.

'That's funny. Marianne, have you got a fiver?'

'Thank you, sir. Your brother gave me £45.40.'

'What?'

'Nice fella, too. A bit troubled, though. Maybe you could make up with him—' the old man paused, 'then you would have a bit more to help me out.'

'If only I could.'

'What's stopping you?'

'Him. He doesn't want anything to do with me.' It was quite surreal, having an increasingly personal conversation with an old tramp in front of his friends at his father's memorial service. Jack mentally logged it as a good story for the future.

'Doesn't it take two to tango?' said the wise man.

'Exactly,' said Cat, 'that's just what I was saying to Jack. He needs to stop being the victim here.' Cat turned to the tramp and gave him a tenner from her purse. 'By the way, have you ever thought of a career as a relationship counsellor?'

'You're the second person who's said that to me. I think I might take it up. It certainly seems to pay well.'

CHAPTER TEN

A fateful meeting

North London. July 1998

Michael wasn't sure why he agreed to meet Marianne. He was vaguely aware of her as Jack's long-time girlfriend and would usually have avoided having anything to do with anyone connected to his brother. But it was a strange time. His father had just died, and all those extraordinary revelations were coming out. His friends – and Cat in particular – had encouraged him not to retreat into himself. She'd suggested he open himself up to the possibility that some good could come out of what threatened to overwhelm him. She'd encouraged him to avoid shutting out his brother entirely. 'It's hardly his fault that your mother died giving birth to him.'

'Well, who's fault was it then?' Michael had retorted. 'There was no one else in the room at the time, other than the midwife.'

'I don't really understand what you've got against him,' said Cat, 'he's a nice guy.'

'You don't know the half of it. He was a nightmare when we were growing up. Always seeking attention and asking stupid questions. He broke my toys.'

'But surely that's just kids' stuff, the rough and tumble of being brothers.'

'Maybe, but I just find him really annoying and prefer not to have anything to do with him.'

At some level Michael took Cat's comments on board and, while he had no desire whatsoever to resume contact with Jack, it did mean that his guard was down when Marianne called.

The moment that Marianne first saw Michael at the coffee shop on the Caledonian Road, she knew she was in trouble. She recognised him immediately. He was strikingly similar to Jack, but older, more mature and more composed. The suit made a difference; she had never seen Jack in a suit. Michael was five years older, which felt significant. Early twenties is closer to student; late twenties is adult. Michael looked very grown-up. She had been attracted to Jack when they first met, but had never quite felt it as strongly as he did for her. As soon as she saw Michael, though, she knew a different, more profound emotion was in play. She very nearly turned away and walked straight out of that coffee shop. But she couldn't. Instead, she just sat there, on the opposite side of the shop, and watched him. She had a sense of foreboding but could do nothing about it. She knew at that moment that once she introduced herself to Michael nothing would be the same again. For her. For Michael. And for Jack. She hated what it would do to Jack. It will destroy him, she thought, but there's nothing I can do to stop it. All of this she knew before she had even said hello to Michael.

When she finally walked over to his table, she could see it in his eyes. This is meant to be, she thought. Whatever happens, it is what it is.

Before she could introduce herself, her phone rang. It was Jack. 'Have you met him yet? How did it go?'

'No, I've only just spotted him. Give me a chance to at least say hello.' Marianne put her hand over the receiver and mouthed 'Sorry' to Michael.

When she put her phone down, Michael couldn't resist the opportunity of a dig at Jack. 'My brother, I presume? Impatient and needy, that's not like him.'

Michael, true to form, had also been in the coffee shop for about ten minutes and was beginning to regret his hasty decision to agree to meet with Marianne. While intrigued to see what his brother's girlfriend was like, he feared a haranguing. He suspected she wanted to change his mind about the will, and, although he had begun to have some doubts about his instinctive reaction to run a mile from it all, he didn't want to be told yet again that he was crazy. Least of all by his brother's girlfriend.

Michael had never liked the hackneyed expression 'take your breath away', but that was what happened when he saw Marianne making her way across the coffee shop towards him. He knew it was her, not because she had given him a timid wave, but because he just knew. She wound her way towards him, politely excusing herself as she squeezed between the other customers in the cosy, crowded room. Time stood still. She was shorter than he had expected. She looked French with her short dark hair and hooped blue and white top. Michael took a sip of coffee so as not to appear as if he was staring at her. Which he was.

He immediately regretted his snide comment about his brother. It had been a nervous release. Marianne was also tense. 'Hello, Mike, I'm Marianne.' Seeing him flinch, she remembered and quickly corrected herself. 'Sorry, I mean Michael. Well, this is going well.' They both laughed.

Michael couldn't remember what they talked about that day. He could visualise it all, frozen as it was in his mind's eye, but he had no idea what they had said to each other. Everyone else in the café blurred into the background as Marianne and the coffee table shifted into crystal-sharp focus. He could recall, for weeks afterwards, details such as the pattern of the grain of the pinkish-brown beech tabletop, with its faint circular coffee stain that could have been a deliberate part of the design. He had been in that coffee shop on numerous occasions and never noticed the quality of its furniture until then. Nor had he paid any attention to the mellow background music that assumed a trance-like, almost hypnotic quality in his memory. If asked, before meeting Marianne, he would have said he didn't think they played music in that café. Thereafter, he couldn't miss it. The chilled soundtrack became a defining characteristic of the place. He often returned there on his own to remind himself of the day he met Marianne. Bizarrely, he also remembered the sound of a passing siren as the emergency services went about their everyday duties on what had become anything but a normal day for him. At least, he thought there had been a siren, but maybe he had just imagined it.

A few days afterwards, he spotted the same top that Marianne had been wearing in a French Connection shop window – marked down in a sale. It was all he could do to stop himself going into the shop and buying it as a memento of the day that changed his life. But that would be weird. Most of all, he remembered her deep brown eyes and how unnerving, and exhilarating, the way she had looked at him had been. He wondered if she felt anything like the turmoil he did. Her poise and composure, with one hand calmly resting on the table and the other holding her coffee cup, didn't betray any anxiety. He was pleased to notice she was only wearing a couple of simple rings. He didn't know why that pleased him, but it did. He felt that there had been a connection between them, but for all he knew she had the same easy manner with everyone she met. He sensed a connection between them, but he didn't know for sure. All he knew was that he had never felt this way before.

That evening he called Cat. 'You know how you encouraged me to cut Jack some slack.'

'Yes.'

'Well, I met with Marianne today. You know Marianne?'

'I do, she's lovely. Michael, that's great. Well done.'

'The problem, Cat, is that I like her.'

'That's not a problem, Michael, that's good. I'm so pleased you've met her.'

'I mean, I really like her. I really, *really* like her. And I think she likes me.' Cat didn't respond. 'Cat, are you there?'

'Yes, I'm here, Michael. Do you mean what I think you mean? You're attracted to her?'

'Yes, seriously attracted, and I'm pretty sure it's mutual.'

'Oh, God. What have I done? When I suggested that you should reconnect with your brother, I didn't mean you should go and fuck his girlfriend.'

'Cat, it's nothing like that, I promise you. We just had coffee.'

'Well, it sounds like it to me. Michael, you can't go there, you really can't.'

'I'm not sure I can do anything about it. I've never felt this way before.'

'It would destroy Jack.'

'Don't tempt me.'

'Michael!' Cat shouted in admonishment down the phone.

CHAPTER ELEVEN

Under control

South London. July 1998

'Where are you? It feels like I haven't seen you for ages.'

'Don't exaggerate, Jack, it's only been a few days. I'm sorry, but I do need to catch up on my work. I'm going to go back to my parents' for a couple of weeks. I want to break the back of my dissertation.'

'Don't you need to be in London? To meet with your tutor and be close to the university library?'

'I've done the research I need to do for now and spoken with my tutor, who agrees that I now just need to get on with writing my first draft.'

It hadn't been hard for Marianne to reduce contact with Jack. He had thrown himself into his work as a distraction from his frustration over his father's will and had become involved on a pitch that had required him to work most evenings. Initially, he had been desperate to know how her meeting with Michael had gone, but his curiosity had been largely satisfied by Marianne being non-committal about it. She told him that Michael was indeed charming, as Jack had warned, and that he hadn't wanted to talk to her about the will other than to say that he needed a few more weeks to get his head in the right place. Strangely, Marianne thought, Jack had readily accepted this as permission to park his angst about potentially losing out on his inheritance. It occurred to Marianne that Jack, for all his bluster, didn't really like confrontation. She also marvelled at his ability to compartmentalise and wished she could do the same. Marianne was, at that moment, a complete mess. She did, as she had told Jack, need to catch up on her work, but she couldn't stop thinking about Michael and what to do about Jack. She had been economical with the truth when she told Jack that they hadn't discussed the will. While it was true that they hadn't touched on it in that first meeting, they had talked about it during their second. An encounter that Marianne had decided not to mention to Jack.

Marianne also neglected to tell Jack that she had met with Cat, who had called after she first saw Michael and insisted they both meet the following evening. Marianne had always been a little in awe of Cat. Not only was she six years older, and therefore inhabited a different life-stage planet, but she was the only friend of Michael who also stayed in touch with Jack. As such, Cat was Marianne's single point of contact with Jack's distant and mysterious family. Jack always said Cat was the sensible one who never took sides because she always saw everyone's side of the story. She was a natural peacemaker and someone to whom Jack would turn for advice. He often referred to her as the big sister he never had.

They had met in a bar in Waterloo, close to where Cat worked. She was already there when Marianne arrived. Before they even had time to order a drink, Cat jumped in and demanded to know what was going on. Marianne had never seen her quite so agitated. She wondered afterwards if she had inadvertently strayed on to Cat's territory by stealing Michael's affection. Or whether it was just that Cat cared deeply about both brothers and feared this would rip them apart irreconcilably.

'Marianne, what's going on? I had Michael on the phone last night in quite a state after meeting with you.'

'Cat, nothing's going on, I promise. I saw Michael for a coffee because, in my six years of going out with Jack, I've never met him and also because the impasse over the will is tearing Jack up. I wanted to understand for myself what Michael's issue is. Jack's convinced that Michael is going to reject the will out of spite for him. I couldn't believe that was the only reason. I also wanted to see if I could help; whether there might be an opportunity to mediate a solution that works for everyone.'

'But it seems that Michael has taken a fancy to you, to put it mildly.' Marianne couldn't help but feel her heart miss a beat upon hearing someone else validate what she knew to be true, and what she felt.

'I'm not going to lie to you. I felt it too, but nothing's going to happen. It can't. I know it can't.' Even as she was saying this, Marianne knew she was trying to convince herself.

Cat picked up on it. 'You sound as if your head is trying to tell you something that your heart hasn't accepted.'

'Cat, I've been with Jack for six years. He's the only proper boyfriend I've ever had. If I'm honest, I think our relationship may have run its course, but I know nothing can happen between Michael and me. You don't need to tell me what that would do to Jack. I know.'

'So what are you going to do about it?'

'I don't know. I really don't.'

Marianne had thought this through incessantly, but never came up with a satisfactory answer. She felt she probably had no option but to carry on as normal and suppress her feelings. It had crossed her mind, more than once, that she might need to walk away from both of them. She sipped on her wine, conscious that Cat was waiting for a fuller answer. *Why does everything have to be some complicated?* Marianne glanced around the bar to avoid Cat's patient gaze. How carefree everyone else looks, she couldn't help thinking. Eventually, she said, 'Surely there must be a way for them to put their differences aside. Perhaps the biggest thing I could give Jack would be to help reconcile with his brother.'

'Reconciliation implies there was a relationship in the first place. They've never got on.'

'But why not? Jack seems to think that Michael blames him for killing his mother.'

'He does.'

'But that's ridiculous. Michael must know it's not Jack's fault.'

'Rationally, yes, but it's not a rational thing. It's a deeply emotional reaction to losing his mother and needing to blame someone. I don't think it was helped by the awful period subsequently, with their stepmother, which just served to intensify Michael's sense of loss and anger. I'm no child psychologist, but the trouble is Michael got this notion that Jack was to blame in his head at a very early age. He views everything that Jack does through this prism: the opposite of rose-tinted spectacles. He finds fault in everything about Jack. It's hardwired in him. I honestly don't know how you change that. I'm not sure that you can. Their father never really understood it, and although he was desperately sad that his two sons didn't get on, he was helpless to do anything about it. Everything he tried just made things worse. The will is just the latest example.'

'So what do you think should happen?'

'Well, until the memorial service, I thought it was probably best that they just lived their own separate lives. It's not unusual. Plenty of families don't talk to each other.'

'I know, even though I can't relate to that. I couldn't imagine not seeing my brothers again.'

'But at the memorial service it struck me just what Mr Merriweather had built and how important it is to so many people. I had a brief fantasy that there must be some way for Michael and Jack to continue his work. I suppose I had a glimpse of Mr Merriweather's vision. But coming back down to earth, it's almost impossible to see how it could happen. It's not just that they don't get on, it's also that Michael really does have a problem with the business itself. He can't stand the thought of dead bodies.'

'Do you think there's any way he could change his mind?'

Cat sat back and thought for a while. The bar was filling up as more and more commuters sought to punctuate the end of their working day with a quick drink before catching the train home. Cat and Marianne were tucked into a corner table, seated in a thicket of standing drinkers, which created a small private oasis of calm. 'I don't know. An easier question to answer might be "What would persuade him to change his mind?" because if you ask, "Could he?" I'd have to answer no.'

'Okay, what would change his mind?'

'Well, not it seems two million pounds.' Cat gave a wry smile. 'Though I have to say, it does seem to have given him pause for thought. The thing about Michael is that he's principled. He's keen to do the right thing. He might conceivably be persuaded by an appeal to his sense of responsibility: to do the right thing by the employees and by continuing the family legacy. Although he was always angry with his father, deep down he wanted to impress him. It meant the world to him that his father wrote to congratulate him on qualifying as a chartered accountant, even although he tried to dismiss the gesture. It's a great shame he wasn't at the memorial service because it would have given him an entirely different view of the business. He thinks of it as a poky, distasteful thing, whereas what I observed last week was something almost noble. If Michael could somehow get a sense of that, he might be more amenable to the idea.'

'So different to Jack,' Marianne said, almost absent-mindedly.

'Tell me about it. Jack, bless him, doesn't give two hoots about principles. He thinks rules are there to be broken. How they're related, God only knows.'

Marianne said, 'Michael and I arranged to meet again.'

'Oh God, Marianne, I thought you said you're not going there.'

'It's not like that. I wanted to meet with Michael to understand him better and see if there might be an opportunity to engineer a reconciliation with Jack. I didn't get the opportunity to ask him about his opposition to the will. We ran out of time. I don't even know what we talked about, but it flashed by and he had to go back to work. I asked him if we could meet again to complete the conversation.'

'Oh, Marianne, that's playing with fire. That doesn't sound like completion to me, that sounds like it could ignite a whole heap of trouble.'

'You might be right, but I'm determined to keep it under control.'

'Good luck with that. Do you know your whole demeanour changed when you started to talk about Michael? You looked lighter. There are some things we can't control. Have you told Jack that you're meeting him again?'

'God, no.'

'Are you going to tell him?'

'No. I can't. Maybe I will afterwards.'

'I think maybe I should join you. It sounds as if you need a chaperone.'

CHAPTER TWELVE

Out of control

_____

North London. July 1998

Marianne occupied Michael's thoughts approximately every thirty seconds. He dreamed about her; he woke up thinking about her; she was in his head as he ate. He found it difficult to concentrate on his work, as thoughts about her kept intruding. He felt he was going mad. All his other concerns – the will, his dead father, the strange Mr Owen, the unsettling talk with his boss – were pushed to one side. He felt both deliriously happy and deeply depressed at the same time. He tried talking about it with a neutral friend who didn't know his family, but the friend quickly tired of his monologue and made his excuses, although not before leaving Michael with the sage advice: 'Just fuck her. For the love of God, just fuck her.'

This was new ground for Michael, who had always maintained high defences. Previous girlfriends had accused him of being emotionally stunted. He had never really understood what they meant, but it now felt as if the floodgates had opened over a girl with whom he had spent little more than thirty minutes in a coffee shop off the Caledonian Road. For someone who kept such a tight rein on his emotions, feeling so out of control was scary.

He was not just counting down the hours until he saw Marianne again, but mentally chalking off the minutes and seconds. He had been surprised, and disappointed, to receive her text saying that Cat would be joining them. He wondered why. Cat had been so disapproving over the phone when he told her about meeting with Marianne that her presence couldn't be a good thing. Furthermore, Cat was his closest female friend. He had at times even speculated whether he and Cat might get together in the future. He knew she cared for him, and he often wondered how she might respond if he were ever to make a pass at her. But ultimately he felt that she was too good a friend for them to become a couple. As soon as he got Marianne's text, he called Cat. It went straight to answerphone. He hadn't thought what he was going to say and so he hung up. He took out a piece of paper and jotted down a message to leave on her phone. He didn't want to get it wrong. He decided to keep it light and non-confrontational. He was going to say, *Cat, so pleased to hear you're coming this evening, but I'm a little surprised given your reaction when we last spoke. Any chance of a quick chat before we all meet?* But he didn't say any of this because the next time he phoned, Cat picked up.

'Hello, Michael.'

'Oh. Cat. I wasn't expecting you.'

'Who on earth did you expect? You called me.'

'Yeah, I know, but I thought it would go to answerphone.'

'Well, you got me for real. Lucky you.'

'Great, I'm sorry, but I have to ask: why are you coming tonight? Is it to stop me pouncing on my brother's girlfriend?'

'To be honest, yes.'

'C'mon Cat; I'm not going to do that.'

'Good, then you won't mind me coming along.'

'Oh. Okay. Of course not. See you later then.' Michael had been thoroughly disarmed.

The week he had spent in the Lake District to clear his head had helped. He had walked nearly twenty miles each day and barely spoken to another soul. Other than Morty, to whom he told everything. He had run everything through in his head thousands of times and returned determined not to be blown off course by his father's will. He had decided that he was happy with the path he was on. He was determined to make partner at Abel's and to know that he had done so on his own merit. It would be galling in the extreme if his odious stepmother and her daughters became beneficiaries of his father's will, but so be it. A month ago, he had no idea that he stood to inherit so much and had been perfectly content. Knowledge of the inheritance had only brought discord and unhappiness. He just needed to ignore it all, to put it to one side as if it had never happened and get on with his life.

Then he'd met Marianne.

For their second rendezvous, they had arranged to meet in a wine bar near Euston station. Michael had thought long and hard about where to suggest. Euston was close to his office and easy for Marianne to get to, but he had chosen it more for its casual sophistication. He also liked that it offered the flexibility of eating if they decided, as he hoped, to stay for more than just a drink. He thought Marianne wouldn't have been there before. There was no way his feckless, good-for-nothing brother would have taken her. He had no idea what kind of places Jonathan visited, nor did he much care. Although his brother had hardly featured in their conversation, Michael noticed that Marianne called him Jack rather than Jonathan. She had also called him Mike, before quickly correcting herself. It was as if he and his brother inhabited different universes with different identities. The up-market wine bar was an attempt to lure Marianne into his.

As he strolled through the streets around Fitzrovia, commuters pushing past him in their rush to catch their train home, Michael tried to picture himself serenely floating through the anxious, harried crowds. He was ridiculously early. Again. He had already killed time by walking around the shops and stopping for a milky coffee in a teashop, and now, fifteen minutes before the time they had agreed to meet, he decided to make his way towards the wine bar. He may have succeeded in looking calm on the outside, but inside he was in turmoil. What would they discuss? What should he say? Should he prepare some questions? What if he makes a fool of himself? Why were they meeting again? Marianne said she wanted to understand his animosity towards his brother. I don't want to talk about that. I want to talk about her. I want to get to know her.

Michael had nearly finished his glass of champagne when Marianne and Cat arrived together.

'Champagne. Very nice. What are we celebrating?' Cat immediately regretted her impulsive remark as she remembered her role was to dampen everything down. Some hope. She saw the way Michael and Marianne smiled at each other when they arrived, and knew her mission was doomed. Even before either of them had said anything, she felt like the gooseberry.

For the first twenty minutes, they skirted around the issue they had agreed to discuss, as well as sidestepping the elephant in the room. Cat couldn't help but notice the chemistry between the pair. They were making small chat as easily and comfortably as if they had known each other for years. Cat had never seen Michael look so relaxed and happy. Her thoughts turned to Jack, and she felt an urgent need to intervene. 'So, Michael, I think Marianne wanted to meet you originally to try to understand why you and your brother don't get along.' Cat saw a momentary flash of frustration on Michael's face. He didn't like discussing his brother, and he certainly didn't want to do so in front of Marianne.

'I dunno. We've just never got on. We're very different. I'm older. It was a difficult time at home.' Michael was speaking in short staccato sentences. 'I guess we didn't get off to the best of starts, with Mum's death.'

'I find it hard to understand, particularly now having met you.' Marianne was careful in her choice of words.

She was well aware that they had strayed into a sensitive territory and didn't want to step on any landmines. 'You're both so nice and decent.'

'Did you think I was going to be Cain to my brother's Abel?' Michael smiled as he lifted his glass and slowly took a sip.

'Oh my God,' said Cat, 'I never thought of that. Cain and Abel. How weird is that, that you work at Abel's. Had you made that connection?'

'No, I hadn't,' Michael chuckled. 'You're right, though, it is a little weird.'

'Remind me,' said Marianne. 'What happened with Cain and Abel?'

'They were the two sons of Adam and Eve. Cain was the eldest,' Cat said.

'Just like me,' added Michael.

Cat continued, 'Cain ended up murdering Abel because he was jealous of him. God thought that Cain's gift wasn't as good as Abel's.'

'Fucking religion,' said Michael, 'it's hardly surprising that everything is so messed up, given that our moral compass is based on stories of bloodshed and vengeance.'

'What was Cain's gift to God?' asked Marianne.

Michael said, 'Cain gave God some fruit of the soil whereas Abel sacrificed a young lamb. Clearly, God wasn't a vegetarian.' Michael was pleased to see how easily Marianne laughed at his joke.

'What happened to Cain? I'm sorry, I'm not up on my biblical stories.'

'Me neither. I just happen to know this one because the parallels have been pointed out to me. Not, I hasten to add, that I have any intention of killing my brother. Nor of giving God any vegetables.'

'And Cain, what happened to him?' Marianne repeated her question.

'Banished. God made him wander the earth. He eventually settled in the land of Nod and fathered a child called Enoch.'

'Enoch? Doesn't sound very religious; wasn't he a Tory politician?'

'Yes, made a racist speech about rivers of blood. Probably a direct descendant of Cain.'

'I still can't get over that you're working at Abel's.' Cat sat back in her chair and looked at Michael. 'It must have occurred to you before.'

'It honestly hadn't.'

'Maybe, subconsciously, you're paying your dues.'

'Hold on a minute, Cat; I'm not Cain. Just because I'm the older brother, it doesn't make me a murderous, vengeful, vegetarian outcast.'

'I'm not saying that, but you're the one who has cast Jack out of your life.'

'It's not just me.'

'Yes, but you're calling the shots here. Jack has always looked up to you.'

'Bollocks he has. He always tried to get me in trouble.'

Marianne joined in. 'It's true what Cat says. Jack looks up to you. Although he has now put up his defences and

85

pretends he's okay that you don't get along, I know deep down that he's desperately sad about it.'

Michael would usually dismiss such a comment with a disparaging remark about his brother, but his desire to curry favour with Marianne overwhelmed this instinct. 'Maybe. But it is what it is. I don't see how it matters. We're both leading our separate lives now.'

'It's sad. I can't imagine losing contact with my brothers. Family is so important. It's a different kind of—'

'Yes, but our mother died and so we never had much of a family. I'm sorry I interrupted you.'

'I was going to say it's a different kind of relationship. My brothers get me in a way that no one else does. We've known each other our entire lives. I appreciate that your mother died, but as your father said in his letter, that could have brought you and Jack closer together.'

'You saw his letter, did you?'

'I did. It made me cry.'

For a brief moment, no one said anything. Cat didn't know what letter they were talking about but decided to hold her peace. Marianne continued, 'How about you, Michael? How did it make you feel?'

'If I'm honest, it made me angry. My father showed little interest in me during his life. Now he's telling me what to do from beyond the grave.'

'He loved you both. He just didn't know how to show it.' Marianne reached across the table and put her hand on Michael's. She surprised herself with this action, which was probably an instinct born of familiarity with his brother. Michael felt as if he had received an electric charge and froze. Cat thought she had witnessed the crossing of a line. Marianne removed her hand, but only after leaving it there for a few seconds longer than could be passed off as a neutral gesture. Michael felt an almost imperceptible light squeeze as she let go. It spoke more than any words, and at that moment Michael wanted Marianne more than anything else in the world.

Marianne continued to press him, though. 'Is it because of Jack that you might not accept the terms of the will?'

A professional negotiator would have advised Michael to stop this conversation because he had lost control. 'It's complicated. I don't think it's because of Jack, although I can't imagine how we could ever work together. It would be a disaster. I've thought about this a lot, and it boils down to two things. I love my career and have ambitions to make partner at Abel's in the next five years. Second, I don't like the funeral business. The money would be nice, but I would prefer to make it on my own rather than rely on a handout.'

'It sounds as if you've made up your mind.'

'I have, I'm afraid.'

'Can I say something here, Michael?' Cat broke her silence.

'Of course.'

'I've known you and your family for many years. Not your mother obviously, but my mum did. She often told me what a wonderful woman she was. She also said how proud your mother was that your dad had taken on the business that her father had started, and then made it his own.' Cat turned to Marianne and said, 'Michael's grandfather set up the first funeral home. When Michael's dad married, he took on the business and ran it jointly with his father-in-law until he retired.'

'He didn't retire actually. He was crushed by a coffin.'

Marianne exclaimed, 'Oh my God, what is it with your family and workplace accidents? Sorry, that's in poor taste.'

Cat turned back to Michael. 'Anyway, the point I want to make is the family business is a much greater part of you than you might realise. At the risk of applying some cod psychology, I think your opposition to the business could be a symptom of your repressed anger against your family. Your reaction is to run away from it all, but I fear that you may regret this in years to come. Marianne's right: family is important. I don't think you've ever given yours a fair chance, and in years to come, possibly when you start your own, you might realise just what you've lost. Except then it could be too late. You could always have this big hole in your life.' Cat paused to let Michael take in what she had said.

'Wow,' said Michael, 'I need a drink. Would both of you like another glass of champagne?' He caught the attention of a wine waiter and asked for three more glasses. Cat, renowned among her friends for being fearless in telling it as she saw it, continued, 'It's a shame you weren't at your father's memorial service. It was a beautiful occasion, but what struck me more than anything else was how much your father meant to so many people. Look here's a picture.' She pulled a photograph of the packed graveyard from her bag. Michael was visibly taken aback. 'Your father has left a fabulous legacy. He took a gift from his father-in-law and turned it into something genuinely meaningful for so many people. I honestly don't think you should run away from this.'

The waiter appeared with the drinks and, noticing that the three of them were sitting in silence, said, 'I'm sorry, is this a bad moment?'

'No, no, perfect timing, I need a drink after that,' said Michael. 'Cat, why don't you say what you really think?' He smiled at her. 'How about you, Marianne, what do you think of my fucked-up family?'

'Well, obviously I don't know you or your family as well as Cat, but I have to say I agree with her. The service last week was moving. It didn't feel right that you weren't there. Or that you want to write yourself out of the family. Like it or not, it's the family you've got. Whatever happens.'

'Not much of a family. Just me and Jonathan and I'm sorry, I know you're his girlfriend, God alone knows why, but we just don't get along. Never have and never will.'

'It doesn't sound as if you've given it a chance. You made your mind up to punish him from the day he was born. Can you, hand on heart, point to one positive thing or gesture you've done in your life towards your little brother?' Marianne felt her voice waver a bit. She had been stung by Michael's slight against her boyfriend. 'I know it's up to the two of you, but I think you have a responsibility as the eldest. I know Jack, although he likes to appear diffident about it, would be receptive.'

Michael was surprised by Marianne's admonishment. He thought his jibe about not understanding how she could be Jack's girlfriend had been mild. He could have said a lot worse. It was beyond his comprehension that such a beautiful, intelligent woman had willingly chosen to be with his brother. But he didn't want to get in a fight with her about it. 'You might be right. It probably is my fault, but too much water has passed under the bridge. Maybe, over time, we will change, but I think the best chance of that is if we follow our separate paths and don't try to force it.'

'But you have a unique opportunity now to reframe your relationship. If you don't do it now, I can't see that you ever will. Yes, of course, plenty of families are estranged, mostly over what appear from the outside to be petty and ridiculous disputes. And it always involves negative emotions of anger and pain. No one, it seems, ever happily doesn't get on with their siblings. As far as I can see, it's always a sore point. I don't know you, Michael, but I do know Jack. This separation between the two of you mystifies me. You're both decent, reasonable people. There's no reason why you shouldn't be able to get on, or at the very least have a cordial relationship with each other. If there's one thing I would ask of you, it would be that you at least meet with Jack. You haven't seen him for six years. All your previous interactions were at the height of your adolescent sibling rivalry. If there's one thing I'd do for the two of you, it would be to get you to meet as adults and properly talk things through. Please do this one small thing, if not for yourself or Jack, please do it for me.'

Michael was so in the thrall to Marianne that he found he couldn't refuse her. He feared, if he said no, not that he might not ever see his brother again, but that he might never see Marianne again. He supposed that perhaps he could meet his brother briefly and then they could go their separate ways... After all, what could possibly go wrong?

CHAPTER THIRTEEN

Delegating the bodies

North London. July 1998

Michael hovered conspicuously outside Jen's office. She was on the phone, but when she saw him through the glass, she indicated that she would be with him shortly.

Jen was a couple of rungs further up the hierarchy than Michael and so got her own private space, if an office with glass walls could ever be described as private. Seen but not heard. Commonly known as the 'goldfish bowls', the junior partner offices were, nonetheless, prized. Located in the middle of the floor, they were highly visible. Many of the recently appointed junior partners loved them because they offered a very public display of their elevated rank within the organisation. Some would make great show of their status by holding as many meetings as possible in their office, often using the flip chart to demonstrate their importance to the minions working on the benches in the open-plan area outside.

Abel's, like all the large accountancy firms, was a

bottom-heavy pyramid. They sucked up large quantities of graduates with the enticing promise of professional qualifications and a socially respectable career to come. These graduates number-crunched by day and revised for their accountancy exams by night. Unlike serfs of the olden days, they did at least have the prospect of escape; although a high proportion fell by the wayside, either because they couldn't hack it anymore or because they failed their exams. Natural selection at work in the accountancy world. Those who survived and made it to the top, the one in twenty who became senior partners and lived off the fat of the firm, were cloistered away on the upper floors of the building.

The firm's hot-desk policy meant the minions didn't get their own space other than a small metallic locker for their possessions. Most of the time, many of them were away at their clients' offices. However, there were always enough of them in the building at any one time to fill the rows of long bench desks and make the place look like a modern-day Dickensian workhouse.

Those that qualified, after three or four years' hard labour, were rewarded with their very own cubicle. The cheap plastic nameplate acknowledged that the employee was now more than just a number.

Michael had a six-foot-by-six-foot cubicle with its own floor space and enough room for an additional chair. This signified that the employee had reached sufficient status to have conversations at an equal level with colleagues rather than always be talked down at. Michael, who loved the structure of Abel's because he knew everyone's place in the hierarchy, looked forward to his next move when he would possess one of the larger cubicles with a small circular table. Then he could conduct his own private meetings. People would then begin to come to him, rather than him always having to find public spaces for meetings with colleagues or meet more senior colleagues on their territory.

The goldfish bowls were the next and most significant sign that you had made it at Abel's. Junior partners were central to the day-to-day operation of the firm, wielding not insubstantial power over their underlings. They were the right-hand man or woman to full-fledged partners, and often the primary contact for the client. They got to choose their teams as well as appraise the performance of everyone who reported to them. The situation of their highly visible offices, in the centre of the floor, fuelled gossip and intrigue. Everyone could witness dressing-downs. Although it was not possible to hear the content of these exchanges, the gist was always pretty obvious. It was equally apparent when certain people were spending more time together than their work merited. One or two office romances had been foreseen way before the participants had made the first move or even been aware themselves of the slippery slope they were on. And so there were some interested observers of Michael as he waited outside Jen's office that afternoon. Upon finishing her call, she beckoned him in. As he entered, he said, 'I hope you don't mind me disturbing you, but you kindly said to me the other week that I should let you know if you could help me.'

'Of course, Michael, please come in. How can I help?'

'It's a personal matter, although it's related to work. I could do with talking to someone sensible about it.'

Jen smiled. 'I'm honoured that you think I'm sensible.'

'Would you mind if this is confidential between the two of us?'

'Of course. I hope you know you can trust me.'

Michael started cautiously by telling Jen about his father's will and the dilemma it presented. He downplayed the rift with his brother and emphasised his commitment to Abel's and his career. All this was true. While he trusted Jen, Michael was also conscious of her loyalties to her employer. Jen listened carefully and asked a few well-chosen questions that gave Michael the confidence to open up a little more. He found it therapeutic to talk with someone who didn't know him but understood what his job entailed and how much it meant to him. He lost all track of time and was amazed when Jen looked at her watch and said hurriedly, 'Gosh, I hadn't noticed the time. I'm terribly sorry, but I have to get back to my childminder. Look, I would like to continue this conversation. Might it be possible to meet again first thing tomorrow morning? I've got some time then.'

Michael knew that the junior partners at Abel's hardly ever had any spare time, as non-chargeable hours were lost revenue to the firm. He supposed that Jen would probably have to make up this time somehow, but he did want her perspective. He had done all the talking. He needed to know what she thought, and so they agreed to meet for breakfast at 7.30 the next morning.

Jen was already waiting for him when he arrived at 7.15.

He saw her through the window, thoughtfully sipping her coffee. He felt guilty about offloading his problems on to her. She had more than enough on her plate already. He was reminded of the saying: 'If you want something done, ask a busy person.' Jen always exuded calmness despite the pressure of being a single mother with a demanding work schedule. Yesterday evening she had behaved as if she had all the time in the world for him, which her abrupt ending of the meeting had made clear she really didn't. And yet here she was again, not only giving up her precious time to listen to him prattle on about his concerns, but also arriving early to do so. All of this flashed through his mind as he walked towards the small nondescript café tucked away behind their offices. Jen had suggested meeting here, saying that no one from Abel's knew about it, despite its proximity to the office. It was new to Michael, who, like all his colleagues, tended to file directly from the tube station into the office each morning.

As he entered the room, a pungent smell of fried breakfast assaulted him. The plastic red and white checked tablecloths and pine furniture gave the room a utilitarian feel. Michael was struck by the contrast between the two worlds, less than five hundred yards apart. His usual breakfast was a milky coffee and piece of toast, for which he queued in the office canteen alongside similar young professionals in a hurry. Here, it seemed from the various black cabs parked outside, taxi drivers enjoyed a full English and a chat. 'I feel a little overdressed,' he said, as he drew up a chair opposite Jen. He noticed how she had pulled off the trick that certain professional women manage: looking smart while simultaneously blending into a less formal environment. Michael, who was always overly conscious about wanting to do the right thing, was immediately aware that he was the only one here in a suit. Not that anyone noticed or cared.

Michael was desperate to hear Jen's perspective on his predicament. Once he was settled and had dispensed with the niceties of thanking her again for her time, he said, 'So what do you think I should do?'

'How honest do you want me to be?'

'Totally.' Michael hesitated. 'I think.'

'Okay, well, please know that I'm saying this with the greatest respect for you. Although we've only worked briefly together, I know you're good. You're well respected at Abel's by people who matter. I should also say that I'm no therapist, but I believe in saying things as I see them.' Michael wondered what was coming next. He knew that Jen was a straight-talker, but her caveat about not being a therapist flagged up that she was possibly going to say something personal. 'I'm going to start with another question,' she continued. 'What is it that frightens you?'

Michael hadn't expected this. 'What do you mean, what frightens me?'

'I may have got this wrong, but I see you constructing all these defences. It sounds as if there was an invisible barrier between you and your father. You've been determined to pursue your own path as a way of avoiding joining him on his. You refuse to have anything to do with your brother to the extent of not being able even to bring yourself to talk to him about this huge decision that has significant implications for both of you. I'm not saying this as a criticism, but as an observation. Are you okay with me saying this?' Michael nodded. He knew there was truth in Jen's words, but he had never been confronted with it before.

Jen continued, 'It's interesting that you've chosen to become an accountant. It's almost as if the structure and the rules of the profession provide a safety net for you. You seem to me to be a precise person who always wants to do the right thing. I reflected, last night, why that might be. The thing about rules is that they offer guidance on what is right and wrong. I have to say that I, as a second-generation Chinese immigrant who doesn't always know the unwritten rules of behaviour here, also find the prescribed way of doing things in our profession to be a comfort. It's much less scary when you know what you have to do than it is not to know. So this is what leads me to ask what you're frightened of, because it seems to me that you're putting up barriers against perceived threats and taking refuge in something that feels safe and secure.'

Michael felt a swirl of emotions. Jen had, in just a few short minutes, explained his life, in a way that had never previously occurred to him. 'That's a big question so early in the morning. I don't know what the answer is. I would probably need more of your therapy sessions to get to the bottom of it. But what you say strikes a chord with me. I hadn't thought about it before, but the world does feel quite scary to me. I do feel quite small and alone at times.' Michael couldn't believe he was opening up in this way and being so honest. The shock of the last few weeks had shaken the very foundations of his being. He found himself saying things that previously he wouldn't even have admitted to himself. Not only that, but his confessional was taking place over a Formica table with, if not Mother Superior, certainly a superior of his at work. 'I worry about being exposed. And so I suppose I do try to make myself safe by not putting myself in the path of danger. Please don't ask me what kind of existential threat I think my brother poses…' Michael smiled. He was beginning to feel self-conscious about revealing too much and had tried to lighten it with a joke.

'Maybe you're right to be wary. History has plenty of examples of brothers that want to kill each other. Funnily enough, it's less of a problem in China because the one-child policy has meant we now have little experience of sibling rivalry. I'm afraid I can't offer you the benefit of personal experience, as I'm an only child. However, I do have a Chinese proverb for you. "When the winds of change blow, some people build walls, others build windmills."'

Michael thought about this before saying, 'So you think I should go for it? Give up my career and accept the terms of my father's will?'

'It's not for me to say. You need to do what feels right for you.'

'Yes, but what do you think. What would you do?

'Okay. Let me tell you a story. My father was a

government official in China in the 1960s. He had a good job and was well respected in the community, but he became increasingly uncomfortable with the Cultural Revolution and the kind of duties he was asked to carry out. He could easily have thrived there then, as government officials had all the power and privileges, but he has a strong moral barometer and didn't like what was happening. My father gave me that proverb. He says he could have built walls and turned a blind eye to what was going on – or, as he put it, he could build a windmill by giving up absolutely everything except his wife and leaving for another life. I hesitate to describe it as a "better" life because my parents went through hell to get first to Hong Kong and then on to England. They came here in the late seventies not speaking a word of English and with very little money. They arrived with nothing, and then spent everything they earned from their dry-cleaning business on my education.'

'So does your father believe it was a windmill worth building?'

'Absolutely. He and my mother sacrificed everything, really suffered and worked unbelievably hard, but they are so proud of what they have achieved, or, more to the point, what *I* have achieved.'

Michael didn't say anything for what felt like a few minutes but was probably only a matter of seconds. He chewed his bacon while thinking about what Jen had said. He felt comfortable sitting in silence with her. He hadn't expected such a response. He had thought she might encourage him to stay with Abel's. He had sought her professional opinion because he knew that he was being unduly affected by his feelings for Marianne and feared he might make the wrong decision for the wrong reasons. Part of him had wanted Jen to support his desire to build his career at Abel's and walk away from the will. It seemed to be the sensible course of action, and so he had thought she was likely to endorse it. He had hoped her professional opinion would provide him with the reassurance and courage to do what his head was telling him was the right thing to do. That she seemed to be suggesting the opposite was unsettling.

'But what about the fact that I struggle with the whole business of undertaking? Don't you think the owner of a business needs to be passionate about its product?'

'I thought about that while walking here this morning. I agree with it in an ideal world, but then it occurred to me that my father never really loved dry cleaning itself. It was simply a means to an end for him. He loved the business he built but had no great affinity with its product. And then I thought about our work. As accountants, we never really get involved in the products of our clients, and yet we can make a significant difference to their business. Many of the financial directors I deal with are quite removed from the frontline of their business. In theory, it wouldn't be impossible for you to construct your work so that you focus on the business and the numbers and not get involved in its operations. Your role could be very different from your father's, whom I'm sure was a hands-on manager. Presumably, the business already has some competent undertakers who know the product inside out. From what you've said, it sounds as if the missing bit is professional strategic financial leadership. Undoubtedly it would be a challenge, but I don't think it would be insurmountable. I often think the secret of any business is to make sure you have the right people in place and then give them the room to get on with it.'

'Are you suggesting I could delegate the bodies?'

Jen smiled. 'Absolutely. That's the joy of having your own business. You can do what you want to do and employ others to do what you *don't* want to do.' She let this sink in before continuing. 'It also struck me that there might be an opportunity to be had from your revulsion about the whole thing.'

'Go on.'

'Well, death is such a taboo topic in Western culture. You're not alone in feeling queasy about it. You could make it your mission to help transform the whole experience by focusing on the concept of a "good death". You would be well placed to drive this because you would know what it would take to change your deeply held negative perceptions about it all. There was that advertising campaign for razors that had the owner saying, "I loved the product so much that I bought the company." In your case, it could be more like, "I hated the product so much that I changed it."'

'What? Changed death? I may be good but I'm not that good.'

Jen laughed. 'No, not changed death. Immortality would be a tough promise to deliver. If you pulled that one off, two million pounds would quickly become small change. No, I meant changed the experience of death and dealing with undertakers. As you said yourself, it's all so dreary and depressing. What if it wasn't? Why does it have to be that way?'

'Wow. That's quite a thought.'

'Which leads me to the other thing I wanted to say to you.' Jen took a big breath and added, 'This may be presumptuous, but I thought that maybe I could join you in this venture.'

CHAPTER FOURTEEN

Boating lake incident

South London. August 1998

'This was a bad idea.' Michael was sitting at a circular table by the boating lake in Battersea Park on a warm Saturday afternoon. He was highly agitated. Having arrived in the park fifty minutes previously, and despite walking its full circumference to kill time and calm himself, he still felt on edge when Cat appeared. She had suggested Battersea Park because it was close to home for her and neutral territory for the two brothers. She had thought very carefully about where might be the best place for Michael and Jack to meet. Battersea Park because it offered good walks should the nervous tension of the occasion need release. It also had a café with tables sufficiently far apart to provide a degree of privacy while also being public enough to discourage a shouting match, should things descend in that direction. Cat was herself beginning to question the wisdom of the meeting, and feeling increasingly tense, especially now that Jack was ten minutes late. Just as she was starting to fear that he might have bailed, he appeared.

Jack gave Cat a quick hug and then turned to his brother. 'Hello, Mike, long time no see.'

Michael grimaced a little. 'It has been. If you don't mind, I'd prefer it if you could call me by my name. I hate Mike, but I think you know that.'

'Oh yeah, sorry, mate – of course, I forgot. I'm a bit nervous. Hey, hello, Morty, what are you doing here?' Jack bent down to cuddle Morty, whose tail was wagging furiously.

'You know about Morty?' Michael was surprised.

'Yeah, Dad got him a year or so ago. What's he doing here?'

'Dad bequeathed him to me. I knew nothing about him until I met Wilfred Owen. Mind you, there was a lot I didn't know about Dad until I met Wilfred. I returned from Swindon a rather reluctant dog owner and with a load of shocking revelations. I have to say, though, Morty's been great.'

Jack laughed. 'That's funny. So what conditions did Dad attach to Morty?'

'None, other than the life-changing responsibility of having to look after a bloody dog. I suppose you want me to call you Jack, rather than Jonathan?'

'Yes, please, if you want me to respond. No one calls me Jonathan.'

'And you can call me Cat.' Both brothers laughed. Well, that's something thought Cat, maybe this will be okay after all.

Jack said, 'I was going to offer to get you both a coffee, but on second thoughts it's far too nice a day to sit around. Shall we walk and talk?' He was shuffling from foot to foot with nervous energy.

'That's a great idea,' said Cat. 'We can walk all the way round the park, it's especially nice along the river.'

As Cat and Michael got up from the table, Jack turned to Michael and said, 'So what prompted this? I guess it's related to Dad's will.'

'It wasn't my idea. It was Cat and Marianne who persuaded me that we should at least meet.'

'Oh.' Jack frowned. 'Marianne didn't say anything about that.' His cheery bonhomie briefly slipped. Cat was quick to notice this potential minefield and jumped in by explaining, in a monologue long enough to shift the focus of the conversation, that yes she had engineered the meeting. Fairly much repeating what she had said to Michael when they last met, she shared her thoughts about their father and the business he had built. She recalled her mother's recollections of Mrs Merriweather, the importance of the firm within the community and how she found it hard to understand why the two brothers couldn't put their differences aside.

As she talked, Michael watched Jack. His brother had bulked out from the weedy, stick-thin teenager he remembered. Michael had been pleased to notice when they shook hands that he was still the taller by an inch or so. Jack seemed as keen to please as ever; whenever they caught each other's eye, he gave a nervous ingratiating smile. Pathetic, thought Michael. It occurred to him that were they to work together, he would easily be able to dominate his little brother. Michael also thought that Jack would be a liability. He'd never held down a successful job and had pretty much failed at everything. Putting aside his animosity to him as a brother, Jack would pretty much be the last person on earth that Michael would choose as a business partner. He watched Jack hanging on Cat's every word; it was obvious how much he wanted this. Michael felt nauseous.

Jack was pleased that Cat was talking at length. It gave him time to think. Michael's mention of Marianne had thrown him: he sensed something was going on beyond his awareness. But Cat's heartfelt comments about his father and the business were helping calm his nerves. And God, did he feel nervous. He was late because he had been in such a state that he had initially gone to the wrong part of the park. There was so much at stake in this meeting. As he had joked to his friends the previous evening, it was literally a two-million-pound meeting. He cursed his slip of the tongue in calling his brother Mike. It was an unfortunate reflex. It felt strange to Jack that this was his brother. He knew him but didn't know him. He was connected to him, but also completely disconnected. Walking through the park with Michael and Cat, Morty at their heels, Jack felt entirely alone. He wanted to find a way to establish a rapport with his slightly cold, austere and terribly serious older brother but felt intimidated by the prospect.

Cat finished her little speech with, 'Sorry, I'm talking too much, but I felt all that needed to be said.'

Michael said, 'No, that was helpful, other than it seems to me that you're talking about a completely different person than the man I knew as my father.'

Although he had no intention of admitting it then, Michael had begun to entertain the possibility of accepting the terms of his father's will. The evening with Cat and Marianne in the wine bar had weakened his resolve to oppose it. And then Jen had shown him a way of making it work that had previously not occurred to him. The thing that had most surprised him was Jen volunteering to join. She had explained that she was struggling to cope as a working mother with a ten-month-old baby at Abel's, which, she said, didn't do work-life balance. When Michael had mentioned that Abel's had offered some of their people to support him in the first year, she had seen a window of opportunity. Michael had argued that there was no way that Abel's would agree to it because they valued Jen too highly. Jen thought they would have no choice if she threatened to resign if they didn't agree to a one-year secondment at Merriweather's.

The prospect of working alongside Jen put a completely different complexion on the opportunity. Michael almost felt excited about it. (That is until he remembered the fat dead body of his nightmares.) But if he was honest with himself, Michael knew his biggest motivation was Marianne. Put simply, walking away from the deal would be to walk away from Marianne for ever. And he just couldn't do that. He didn't know if agreeing to the will would create any realistic chance of him getting together with Marianne, but it did at least represent a better chance than if he walked away. There was, of course, the minor complication of his brother; but Michael didn't see any serious competition walking alongside him in Battersea Park.

Michael had no intention of revealing his hand. Although he was already beginning to contemplate how it might work, he wanted to make Jack suffer by giving the impression that he was still opposed to the idea. That way, he would be at least two steps ahead of his brother if it did come off. He said to Jack, 'So Cat persuaded me we should at least talk about it. It is, after all, a pretty big decision that affects both of us. But I have to say, I think it would be a disaster.' Michael enjoyed seeing Jack's face drop with disappointment and noticed how his brother brought out the worst in him.

Cat spotted this too. This was a very different Michael to the one she knew, but she decided to hold her peace and see how it played out. She had said enough already. They needed to work it out between themselves. Or not.

'Why?' said Jack. 'It doesn't have to be a disaster. As Dad said in his letter, we have the talent to take the business to another level.'

'Remind me, Jack – what exactly are your talents?' Cat felt her heart drop at Michael's cruel question. She could see its impact on Jack.

'Okay, fair enough. I don't have your experience or

skills, but I'm good at advertising, although I admit I still have a lot to learn.'

'How long have you worked in advertising?'

'Ten months, but already they're giving me a lot of responsibility.'

'That figures. Advertising agencies are so flaky. How can anyone with so little experience be given any responsibility? Anyway, I don't see what relevance that has to a small local undertaker's business.'

'I disagree. All businesses need to position and promote themselves. And anyway, Dad had no experience of undertaking when he took over the business. He did all right. Where there's a will, there's a way.'

'Yes, but that's it. There isn't a will. Well, I suppose, technically, there is a will – Dad's will, but as far as *I'm* concerned there's no will. As you'll well remember, I always told Dad I wanted nothing to do with the business. I don't see why that should change just because he's dead and has dangled four million pounds in front of us.'

Jack was reminded of the helplessness he felt as a child when Michael bullied him. 'If you've decided, then I don't see the point of this meeting,' he said sullenly.

'Well, I suppose there's no harm in us at least meeting face to face to avoid any possible misunderstanding.' Michael was enjoying Jack's palpable disappointment and decided to turn the knife a little by asking his kid brother if he had thought about what it would be like to become a millionaire. 'Hypothetically, of course, because it's not going to happen.'

At this point, Cat decided to intervene and suggested the three of them take a rowing boat out on the lake. 'We could be like three men in a boat. Morty could be Montmorency.'

Michael said, 'Unfortunately they don't allow dogs.'

'Maybe we could tie him up by the hire shop. He seems well behaved.'

'No, let's take him with us. It would be much more fun.' Jack, spotting an opportunity to turn the tables on his brother, suddenly cheered up.

'We can't. It's clearly stated in the rules.'

'Fuck the rules. It's only a poxy little pedalo company.'

'The rules will be there for a good reason. And anyway, they won't allow us on with him.'

'What good reason? Morty's hardly going to sink the damn thing. You and Cat could get the boat and row it round to that spot over there where Morty and I could jump on. No one will notice.'

Cat, feeling they needed to do something different and wanting to support Jack, said, 'I suspect the rule exists because of the Canada geese that are often here, but as there don't seem to be any around at the moment I can't see that it would do any harm. What's the worst that could happen?'

Even though it went against his every instinct, Michael reluctantly went along with the plan. Initially all went well. The two extra passengers successfully boarded the boat, unnoticed by the busy handlers on the other side of the lake, and the earlier tension briefly dissipated. Cat, who was a Jerome K Jerome fan, couldn't resist asking about

Morty's ambition in life. Her literary reference passed the brothers by, but the consensus was that Morty's aim in life, unlike Montmorency, was to be good. Jack resisted the temptation to comment that such an obedient dog was a perfect match for his control-freak of a brother.

And then all hell broke loose. The worst did happen.

They rounded a quiet corner of the lake and found themselves face to face with a couple of swans and a cygnet. One of the swans started hissing at them. Morty, perhaps stung by the observations about his compliance, decided this was the moment to show that he was a real dog. He rushed to the bow of the boat and started barking loudly at the swan. The threatened bird rose as if to attack. The boat handlers, alerted by the commotion, started shouting at the stricken vessel while running around the side of the lake. It wasn't clear if they intended to rescue the occupants or to rebuke them for their breach of the rules. The commotion drew a crowd of spectators. Michael, mortified to be publicly witnessed in the act of committing a crime, angrily shoved Jack while yelling, 'You idiot. I said this was a bad idea.' Jack was trying to control Morty, and thus already slightly off-balance when he was pushed …

As Cat remembered it afterwards, he toppled over in slow motion, making a desperate and ultimately futile attempt to stay in the boat. As he hit the water, horrified screams mixed with raucous laughter from the crowd amassed at the edge of the lake. Fortunately, this caused the swan to change tack, deciding it was one thing to intimidate an overexcited dog but that a graceful retreat was a more prudent course of action when confronted by a six-foot human torpedo. The swans glided away as if it was nothing to do with them. Jack surfaced, and, much to Cat's relief, started roaring with laughter. Michael wasn't sure how to react; he just wanted to get out of there and away from the angry pedalo people, who were shouting at him as if it was his fault. He was, though, relieved that the swan hadn't hurt Jack and that his brother was reacting with apparent mirth rather than anger. Jack spluttered from the water, 'Mike, Mike, you've got to admit we make a great team. Just think what we could do together with Dad's business.' Even Michael had to laugh at that.

'I need to stay out of it,' Cat confided to a friend afterwards. 'Everything I do to try to help ends in disaster. I encouraged Michael to meet with Marianne and now I have a bad feeling about where that might lead. Then I persuaded Michael to meet up with Jack and it was terrible. I couldn't believe the change in Michael; he became a real bully. I've never seen that side of him before. Then I had the bright idea of suggesting we go out on a boat. What was I thinking?'

'Well, at least you now know you're not cut out for relationship coaching,' joked her friend.

Cat continued, 'The weird thing, though, is that Michael called afterwards to say he thinks they should both meet with the lawyer. I honestly don't know what he's playing at. He was adamant that it was a bad idea that he wanted nothing to do with, but then two days later seems to be agreeing to proceed. I don't know what he wants. I

113

asked him why he had gone all Mr Hyde over Jack. He just said he's hardwired against him and there is nothing he can do about it.'

'Like you said, probably best to stay out of it. Let them sort themselves out. What about Jack, what does he make of it all?'

'I think he's a bit confused, but ultimately he's excited that there's a chance it may now happen. Jack lives in the moment and tends not to get too defeated by past disappointments. The main thing he can't stop talking about is the incident on the boating lake. He thinks it was so funny. Jack was crying with laughter when he recounted how Michael prostrated himself in apology in front of the burly Latvian boat handler. Whatever happens, he said, that moment alone was worth two million pounds. Then again, it was interesting to see how he allowed Michael to walk all over him beforehand. I'm now inclined to agree with Michael that it would be a disaster if the two of them end up working together.'

'Particularly,' Cat's friend added, 'if Michael ends up shagging Jack's girlfriend.'

'Don't. Just don't go there.'

CHAPTER FIFTEEN

Magic roundabout

_____

Central London. July 1998

There was a limit to the amount of small talk available on the advantages of living in Swindon, and Wilfred had said it all. He and Michael were killing time while waiting for Jack in the members' lounge of Wilfred's London club. The one cultural landmark in Swindon that interested Michael was its magic roundabout, which Michael thought didn't sound very magic at all. 'On the contrary,' said Wilfred, 'it's a superb piece of design. Unappreciated, but brilliant. It's one of the scariest junctions in the country yet has an almost perfect safety record. Why do you think that is?'

'It's safe because people are scared shitless by it? Everyone avoids it. There are no accidents because it has no cars?'

'Not exactly, but you're right that it's safe because it's scary,' said Wilfred. 'Drivers *and* pedestrians think twice about what they're doing before they do it. Lack of attention causes most accidents. The magic roundabout forces people to concentrate and, as a result, avoid accidents. It's a useful metaphor for life. I sometimes wonder if we've got it all wrong with our desire to make society easier and more convenient. Like lemmings jumping off the cliff without thinking what they're doing, we're all sleepwalking to disaster.'

'So you think all our problems could be solved if we had more of Swindon's magic roundabouts?'

'Exactly, we need more complexity.'

'It feels as if I've got more than enough complexity in my life at the moment, thanks very much. Talking of which, here finally is the antithesis of complexity.' Michael and Wilfred, along with everyone else in the lounge, turned to watch Jack as he hurried towards them. 'So embarrassing. My brother always has to make a statement.'

When Jack reached them, Michael asked, 'What the hell are you wearing? You look as if a parking attendant has dressed you at a car boot sale.'

'Yeah, sorry,' said Jack, 'and sorry for being late. I'm not normally late.'

'The evidence suggests otherwise. Second time this week. But why on earth are you dressed like Fido the Clown?'

'I came from work…'

'This is your *work* attire?' Michael was genuinely astonished. 'I thought advertising agencies were supposed to be cutting-edge and fashionable. You look as if you've come from a homeless shelter.'

'I normally wear jeans and a T-shirt to work.'

'That figures. Advertising agencies are playpens for toddlers.'

Jack ignored Michael's dig. 'Unfortunately, I forgot about this meeting when I went to work this morning. I arrived here half an hour ago, but they wouldn't let me in because I wasn't appropriately attired. I had to rush over to the nearest shop to get a shirt. This rather natty yellow checked number is all they had in my size. I then had to borrow the jacket and tie from the doorman. Bizarrely, they're okay with my combat trousers because they're full-length.' Jack started laughing. 'It does all rather clash, doesn't it?'

Wilfred said, 'Well now that we're all here, I suggest we adjourn to the meeting room I've reserved.'

For all his bonhomie, Jack was berating himself for arriving late and making a spectacle of himself. Yet again, he had created a great story, but this was the one occasion he had wanted to impress upon Michael that he could be taken seriously. How had he fucked up to the extent of looking like this? His baggy yellow checked shirt only passed the dress code of Wilfred's club on account of having a collar but was otherwise clearly intended for colour-blind teenagers at a paintballing party. It was at least cheap. It was so bad, in fact, that Jack thought he might conceivably be able to wear it again at a grunge festival; but it certainly didn't go with the bold pink-striped jacket that had been left in the doorman's cupboard. The doorman said that no one had returned to claim it in the five years since it had been left behind. He supposed, rather sniffily, that it had belonged to one of his *American* guests. It was difficult to imagine the jacket going with anything, least of all an orange polka-dot tie and a pair of khaki combat trousers. Jack wondered why he couldn't get his act together when he was with Michael. It was as if his subconscious was determined to sabotage him and always present him to his brother as an infantile idiot.

Once the three of them – the accountant, the lawyer and the pantomime clown – were settled in the meeting room, Wilfred asked the two brothers to say what they both thought, having now had a few weeks to reflect, about their father's proposition. Michael gestured to Jack to go first. Jack had thought beforehand about what he might say, but in the moment completely forgot his carefully prepared words and lapsed into what he was sure came across as incoherent babble. When he finished, Wilfred summed up. 'So you would like to accept the terms of your father's will. Is that correct?' Jack nodded. Wilfred turned to Michael. 'And what about you, Michael? You expressed some reservations when we last met. Have you changed your mind?'

Michael said, 'I've given this some considerable thought. Yes, Wilfred, you are correct. I did have plenty of reservations. I still do, if I'm honest – but I think there might be a way of making it work. If you don't mind, I would like to share a short presentation I've prepared to help articulate my thoughts.' Jack woke up at that point, realising that whatever else he had thought this might be about, it was, in fact, a straightforward battle of sibling one-upmanship. Cat had warned him, when they'd spoken after the boating lake incident, that he needed to be careful not to get trampled all over. Jack now knew what she meant. He was going to have to up his game. Michael's presentation was impressive. It tackled every one of his earlier concerns, outlining the pros and cons of each, before proposing a suggested course of action. It had been well researched and professionally prepared. Jack wondered if it was all Michael's work or if he'd had help with it. When Michael proposed hiring Abel's to be the company auditors and seconding Jen Ng as Head of Finance and Operations, it became clear who had helped him with the presentation.

Jack had to admit that Michael's points were well made and well argued. He was particularly impressed that Michael was so open and honest about his underlying antipathy to the business of burying the dead. The adman in Jack liked the thought of turning this negative into a positive by using it as an opportunity to provide a different kind of funeral experience. Michael also presented a persuasive argument that, although the business was making money, there was still room for improvement in terms of its profitability. Michael said he suspected that, although their father had done a reasonable job of bringing costs down, there were further economies to be achieved by upgrading the firm's financial and operational systems. In this respect, he felt Jen could be a valuable asset, as this was what she was known for being so good at with Abel's clients. Jack was also interested to hear from Michael's analysis that the number of deaths per year was currently down. 'Surely that can't be right,' he said. 'The population is growing, and so, with more people, there must be more deaths.'

'You might think so, but one of the reasons the population is growing is that we are all living longer, i.e. not dying. Or rather, we're postponing our deaths. But the biggest reason that death rates are currently down is that the current cohort of the population who should now be dying are already dead.'

'What do you mean?'

'The War generation, who would now be in their seventies and beginning to die off, died prematurely. What that means for the business, in the short term at least, is that the only way of growing it is by taking trade from its competitors. We would need to become more attractive to the bereaved than any of the other funeral homes. That may be possible, but by all accounts it's becoming an increasingly cut-throat business. I suspect the quicker win, at least in the five years we would be involved, would be to improve profitability through increased efficiency.'

'Okay, that makes sense – but I have to say I like the sound of the competitive challenge. One thing you haven't addressed yet is our roles in the business. What are your thoughts on that?'

Michael, who had anticipated this question, said with relish, 'Well, I would be CEO. Obviously.'

'Why "obviously"?'

'Well, as I hope I've demonstrated, not only do I have some solid business experience, but I've also got a vision for the business. Who else could be CEO? I don't know if there are any other appropriate internal candidates, and the whole point of us taking it on is to continue as a family firm, which means it needs a family member at its head. It has to be me.'

'Why not me?'

Michael looked with disdain at Jack, in his pink-striped jacket, his yellow checked shirt and his orange polka-dot tie, and said, 'Seriously?'

'Yes, seriously. Why does it automatically have to be you?'

'I can't believe you're even asking. One, I'm the eldest. Two, I have proper business experience under my belt and know what I'm doing, and three, you've never held down a job for more than a year. You have no real business experience. You don't know what you're doing.'

'You've got no more experience of running a business than I have. What did you think my role would be, then?'

'I thought you could be responsible for the advertising. I thought maybe you could be the Advertising Manager.'

'Fuck off. Are you serious? You the CEO and me the Advertising Manager? I might as well be the bloody tea-boy.'

'I'm perfectly serious.' Michael was being deliberately provocative, but he also genuinely believed that he was better qualified to run the business than his brother and couldn't see that Jack would be anything but a liability. Michael had, though, seen this meeting as an opportunity to strike the first blow. His extensive preparations were a bid towards asserting pre-eminence.

'I think perhaps I should intervene at this point,' said Wilfred. 'I'm delighted to hear that you both seem inclined to accept the terms of your father's will. There's still a lot of detail we need to work through together. We can come to that later, but first I would like to say a couple of things about your respective roles in the business. The first is that you both need to keep sight of your father's ultimate intention, which is to bring you both together. This has to be an equal partnership where you have an equal share in the business and an equal say in the key decisions. I appreciate that you might not agree with this, but your father believed that you both have something significant to bring to the business. Rightly or wrongly, he felt you have complementary skills.'

Michael snorted. 'Well, that's ridiculous. Dad wasn't of sound mind.'

'As I said: rightly or wrongly. The fact is, though, these are the terms. It's your choice whether you accept them or not. Your father wanted you to work together to bring your respective talents to bear for the benefit of the business. And I have to say that, in my judgment, he was very clear-headed. The second thing I need to say is that one of the many conditions of this arrangement is that I take a non-executive role in the business. I will have no responsibility, or say, in the running of the firm; I will simply be there to mediate between the two of you as required, and to ensure that there's a reasonable standard of fairness in your working relationship. I can see from this afternoon that I may have my work cut out, but nevertheless I'm here to help try to realise your father's desire that the two of you work together.

Wilfred's intervention persuaded the two brothers to put their argument to one side and listen to what he had to tell them. The three men spent the rest of the afternoon poring over the details of the will and its expectations. Mr Merriweather's will set up a trust of which Wilfred Owen was the nominated trustee. The proceeds would be distributed in quarterly payments of £100,000 each. These were subject to the conditions of the will being met in that quarter. Any income the brothers chose to pay themselves from the business was additional. Jack found his mind wandering to the luxury car showroom.

Over the next few weeks, they met many more times, always at Wilfred's club. Jack dressed immaculately for each meeting, having overhauled his wardrobe after that first sartorial disaster. He was also always early. Once he even arrived before his brother. Soon, all their sessions were starting half an hour before the agreed time. For those few weeks, then, it seemed that Michael and Jack might indeed be able to satisfy their father's dying wish and work effectively together.

They were both now approaching that magic roundabout with due care and caution. Wilfred's concern was what might happen when they exited it.

CHAPTER SIXTEEN

As the dust settled

September/October 1998

Wilfred, who had now presided over several complicated family scenarios, had learned not to predict how they might turn out. He was confident in the planning that had gone into the will and believed its strictures were as watertight as could be. Still, the lawyer was less optimistic than Mr Merriweather had been in Michael and Jack's ability to work together for five years. He feared for the firm, having two inexperienced and warring leaders at its helm. He couldn't help but notice that in the last two months neither brother had taken the opportunity to spend any time in the business itself. His biggest concern was that it might all unravel three or four years down the line when the whole thing would be extremely challenging to unpick. The contracts the brothers had signed stipulated that they would need to pay back whatever they had received should that happen. Wilfred was under no illusions as to how hard that would be to enforce. He would be well remunerated for executing Mr Merriweather's will, but he knew he would have to work for it.

Michael's life had been turned upside down in the last few tumultuous months. All his carefully laid plans, and everything he had been working towards, had been thrown up in the air. He had gone from wanting nothing to do with the family business to committing his next five years to it. He had given up a promising and secure career to become a small business owner, a role for which he was utterly unqualified. For all his bullish assertions in front of his brother, Michael was acutely aware that he had no idea how to run a business. Rather than be a respected accountant, he was to become an undertaker, the prospect of which made his stomach turn. He took great pride in telling people he was an accountant, and couldn't imagine confessing – at his school reunion, for example – that he was now an undertaker. He hadn't told anyone about the family firm when he had been a pupil there, saying only that his father was a businessman. To come clean now would feel like revealing a dirty little family secret. And, having once successfully expunged his odious little brother from his life, he was now sentenced to work alongside him for five years. Convicted criminals get less, he told himself. Michael was determined to get the upper hand over Jack. After Wilfred's intervention, he had decided to hold fire and pay lip service to the notion of equal partnership. He was confident, though, and particularly with Jen at his side, that he would be able to run circles around Jack. He would call all the shots; he just had to be smart about it.

And then there was Marianne. She had been the catalyst for him changing his mind. Not through any argument she had made, but because of his desire to be with her. He had a gnawing anxiety about her absence. Ridiculous though it might sound, it would not be an exaggeration to say that he had done all this, given up everything he wanted, for her, someone he barely knew. What if it all proved futile? What if she never returned? Even worse, what if she stayed with Jack? Michael was at least pleased to note that she seemed to have disappeared from Jack's life as well. He had to trust his instinct – something he never usually did – that he and Marianne were meant to be. And when she did eventually return, it would be to him and not his brother.

Michael had serious misgivings about it all, but he had crossed the Rubicon. There was no going back. In the space of five short months, his father had died, he had fallen in love with a stranger who had then disappeared, and he had unfathomably changed the course of his life. To cap it all, Michael was now a dog owner. Before his father died, in the days when he was leading the life he wanted to live, Michael had envisaged growing into a comfortable family life in the shires, one that would inevitably have involved a dog. In his dreams, the family came before the dog. Morty's premature arrival symbolised the topsy-turvy chaos that had engulfed him. All he had ever wanted was a normal life. What he had ended up with seemed anything but.

Jack, meanwhile, was hyper. Unlike his brother, who as far as he could see seemed to crave a dull, boring life,

Jack thrived on unpredictability and spontaneity. It made him feel alive. Marianne had once shown him a quote from Voltaire that said that you could choose to live in either the convulsions of distress or the lethargy of boredom. 'That's no choice,' Jack had said. 'Who on earth would choose a boring life?' The quote had stuck with him, though, and provided some solace when things didn't turn out quite as he hoped. Bad things, he could rationalise to himself, were simply the 'convulsions of distress' that made life worth living. One of those things at that moment was Marianne. Having absented herself from Jack's life to concentrate on her dissertation, she now told him that she planned to go travelling around Europe with one of her university friends. She said that they should separate temporarily, at least while she was away. Jack heard the word 'temporarily' and closed his ears to any further talk of separation. Now, more than ever, he needed her calm presence by his side. He had tried to talk her out of it, but she had been insistent that she needed space. Jack, who could not conceive of a life without Marianne, felt a sense of foreboding about her increasing distance from him. But he convinced himself that everything would be okay 'in this, the best of all possible worlds', paraphrasing another Voltaire quotation that she had introduced him to because she felt it encapsulated his approach to life. Jack preferred the more prosaic 'It'll be all right on the night'.

He distracted himself from the pain of Marianne's absence by thinking about luxury cars, being a business owner, and how they might transform perceptions of death. He knew that he was going to need to tread carefully with Michael to avoid being marginalised, but, in his usual optimistic way, he also assumed he would be able to manage whatever was thrown at him. The one advantage he had over his brother was Michael's aversion to dead bodies. Jack decided he would need to immerse himself in the work of undertaking to capitalise on this advantage.

His friends at the agency didn't know how to react when he handed in his resignation. It was the first time anyone had ever left them to become a funeral director. They threw a wake for him, presenting him a tombstone-shaped leaving card with the inscription, 'Death of an Adman'. Jack was sorry to leave the agency. At just short of a year, it was the longest time he had held down a job.

Marianne was in a different place. For the last two months, she had lost herself in her dissertation and was pleased with how it had turned out. Apart from a few calls, she had had little contact with Jack. She now believed it might be possible for her to cut the cord of her relationship with him and sever links with the Merriweather boys entirely, at least until the dust settled. She was finding it harder now that she didn't have the distraction of her dissertation, but the opportunity to travel round Europe with her university friend Suzy had come at the right time. Jack had been the only boyfriend Marianne had ever had, and up until now she had never really thought about where their relationship might go. It just was. She couldn't believe they had been together for six years. It had flashed by. The space she had created for herself made her realise that she needed to broaden her horizons and live her own life. She had dreaded telling Jack that she thought they needed to separate, and she was relieved to have got the conversation over with even though he hadn't seemed to have heard her. He had kept reinterpreting what she said as 'only until you're back' and saying that he would stay loyal. Marianne hadn't pressed it, though; she felt she had said enough. At times she missed Jack terribly – he had become such a fixture in her life – but she also felt unusually liberated. She had tried not to think about Michael and had been mostly successful in this. That fateful meeting with him had helped her see that there were possibilities beyond Jack, but she had been pleased to have been able to keep the lid on any feelings she might have for his older brother. 'All we need do is find a couple of sexy Frenchmen,' Suzy had helpfully suggested. Marianne was also beginning to think she might try to look for work or study abroad.

As Jen had predicted, Abel's agreed to let her join Michael in return for the contract to audit the business. They assumed it would only be for a year and presented it as a paid sabbatical. Jen hoped it would become a one-way move, but that would depend on how it worked out.

While Abel's might have been understanding, Jen's father certainly wasn't. 'After everything we've done for you, everything we've sacrificed, you do this to us!' He was shouting in Mandarin, reverting to his native tongue, as he always did when he needed the vocabulary to express himself. Not that words were required, since his anger was so evident in his face.

'Dad, this isn't about you.' Jen also spoke in Mandarin. It was very much her second language, but she felt she needed to meet him on his level.

'Of course it's about us. We're family. Your mother and I came here to build a better life for you. We've worked so hard to give you the best. And you've taken that opportunity. You did well at school and now have a good job. We couldn't have asked for more. It was all we ever wanted. But now you tell us that you're throwing it all away. Think about it, please. This is not a respectable job. It's not professional. These are not good people. I didn't work every day and every night for my daughter to become an undertaker.' Jen's mother sat sadly in the corner and simply wanted to know why.

'Well, that went well,' said Jen when she reported back to Michael. 'It would be fair to say that my parents don't exactly regard this move as the pinnacle of everything they've ever strived for. In my father's world, being a partner of a reputable accounting firm is as good as it gets. And a job with an independent funeral home is just about as *low* as it could get. The notion of work-life balance is nonsense to my father. For him, work *is* life. They think I've gone from the best possible job in the world to the worst possible job. They can't begin to understand why. As far as they're concerned, I'm committing career suicide and taking their reputation with me. I'm sorry – insensitive of me to talk about suicide.' Her father's extreme reaction had given Jen pause for thought, but she was his daughter and, as she reminded him, he had once given up a well-respected job to follow his instinct. 'That's completely different,' he had said.

'No, it isn't,' she had replied.

On the one hand, Cat was pleased to hear that Michael and Jack appeared to have put their differences aside to make a go of it. On the other, she was deeply concerned about how it might work out. Having observed them together, she knew this would not be a harmonious working relationship. Cat just hoped they could get through the five years without killing each other. She had also been pleased to hear that Marianne was travelling, and hoped against hope that she didn't represent a ticking time bomb that might blow the whole thing apart when she returned.

Morty missed the original Mr Merriweather terribly, but was adjusting to his new life as the faithful companion of a London bachelor. He would have been delighted to know that a return to the funeral home was on the cards.

The staff at Merriweather's had mixed feelings when they heard that the two brothers would be running the business. The day after Mr Merriweather suddenly exited himself from the firm, there was an all-staff meeting. A very young-looking lawyer had told them that it had been their recently deceased boss's wish that the business should pass to his two sons. Some within the company wondered how they could have booked the town hall at such short notice, fuelling speculation that the whole thing might have been pre-planned. This rumour was quickly quashed, as none of Mr Merriweather's loyal team could imagine why he might have killed himself. In those early days, before the evidence had mounted up, they all supposed it must have been an accident. The lawyer had explained that Michael and Jack needed time to grieve for their father before they decided whether to give up their promising careers and join the family business. The lawyer was confident that they would do so, but thought it might take six months or so to sort out. In the meantime, he advised that Mr Merriweather had stipulated in his will that the business be run by Royston McGinty and Monica Moody. This was no surprise to anyone as these two stalwarts had effectively been running it in close partnership with their old boss for the past five years. It was to be business as usual for the interim, as far as the 'usual' was possible given the extraordinary circumstances of the figurehead turning himself into ash and dust.

PART TWO

Down to business

CHAPTER SEVENTEEN

Four fookers

Hertfordshire. November 1998

'We never had any fookin' board meetings before. I don't see why we need one now,' Royston McGinty growled. 'We never even had a fookin' board.'

The newly convened Merriweather's management team squeezed into the deceased Mr Merriweather's tiny old office. Royston McGinty, Jack Merriweather and Wilfred Owen stood, while Michael Merriweather, Monica Moody and Jen Ng occupied the only three chairs in the room.

'How did you discuss management issues and decisions?' Michael was feeling uncomfortable. For all his previous bluster about his business experience, this was his first ever board meeting. The enormity of his position was just beginning to sink in. He felt a tremendous pressure to impress and to do the right thing; only he had no idea what the right thing was. It was also the first time for six years that he had set foot back in his father's apartment above the funeral home. Disconcertingly, they were occupying what had, many years ago, been his bedroom. His father had converted it into his office when Michael moved out. Finding Royston McGinty in his bedroom would have been the stuff of nightmares when he was a teenager, and it didn't feel much more comfortable right now. The first thing he needed to do, he decided, was to get a proper office away from this hellhole. Michael hadn't spent his whole childhood plotting his escape only for it to become his place of work a few years later. There were too many ghosts, too many bad memories. He tried not to think of the bodies in the basement.

'If ever we needed to talk about anything together, we just did,' said Monica. 'Never needed to organise a meeting. But there's not much to discuss. We just do what needs to be done. Just get on with it, really.'

'Perhaps I should start this meeting,' said Wilfred.

'Jonathan will take notes,' said Michael, who felt his stomach lurch a bit as he saw Royston roll his eyes at Monica. Jack decided that now was not the time to fight and just nodded. He didn't even correct Michael for calling him Jonathan – but he did register it as another of those little put-downs to be avenged when the time was right.

'You might be wondering why I'm here,' Wilfred continued breezily.

'I'm wondering why we're all fookin' here,' muttered Royston under his breath but audibly enough for everyone to hear.

'Mr Merriweather asked me to act as chairman for

the five years that he wanted Michael and Jack to run the business.' Jen noticed that Wilfred referred to his client as Mr Merriweather, while always calling his two sons by their first names. The formality of it gave the dead man a patriarchal presence. 'My role is simply to ensure that the terms of the will are met. I'll have no say in the running of the business itself. I will, though, chair these board meetings, which I suggest we hold every month, at least for the first year.'

'What's the fookin' point?'

'It's good business practice,' said Michael, trying to sound assertive. He knew he needed to take control.

'Is it? Only two of us here know what we're doing. You four fookin' fookers have no fookin' idea.'

'Clearly, you and Monica know the business inside out and we don't. But what we – at least Jen and I – bring to the party is a track record of helping improve many different kinds of businesses. You and my father have done a great job building Merriweather's into what it is today; but I hope that we'll be able to bring our own professional experience to bear and help it grow into something even bigger and better.'

Royston folded his arms and harrumphed. Monica said, 'Well, it is what it is.'

Jack hadn't been planning to say anything, but realised he needed to ensure that his brother didn't completely airbrush him out. He had also decided that he would try to win over Royston and Monica over the next few months and let his brother take the heat of whatever battles needed to be fought with them. 'Can I just add how much we appreciate the way you've both kept the business running over the past few months. Dad always used to say that the success of the business had little to do with him and everything to do with you two. I can see what he meant.' Jack was pleased to see that Monica appreciated his flattery. Jack continued, 'For right or wrong; Dad wanted Michael and me to take over the family business. He believed that we might have something to offer. Now, he might have been mistaken, but we've decided to respect his wishes and give it a go. One thing's for sure, though: we won't be able to do it without you.'

Michael felt a flash of irritation as his brother scored points in the meeting. It felt as if battle lines were being drawn. He needed to take back control. 'I'll start by sharing some early thoughts that Jen and I have had about the business.' Jack was amused to see Michael starting to look around the room. He knew he was looking for an overhead projector for his presentation. He realised, with delight, that Michael must have assumed that every meeting room had an overhead projector.

Later that evening in the pub, Jack had his mates in stitches with his retelling of this little episode that highlighted the gulf between Michael's experience of the corporate world and the reality of running a small business. The punchline of his story, about Royston's expression when Michael had asked him where the overhead projector was, had one of his friends sobbing with laughter. Jen had come to Michael's rescue by suggesting that they just talk it through without the slides.

It was a similar presentation to the one Michael had shared at Wilfred's club, repackaged for the different audience. It was clearly mostly Jen's work, but Jack noticed that she was careful to let Michael take ownership of the presentation and its insights. She supported his lead by adding small points of explanation or elaboration. Jack was pleased to hear Michael promote him from Advertising Manager to Business Partner. It was interesting that Royston and Monica didn't say anything. They didn't even challenge Michael's assertion that there was an opportunity for more all-round efficiency. Jack supposed this was probably because a presentation of strategic thoughts was utterly unfamiliar to them. It was such a different language to them that Michael might as well have been talking Swahili. Jack saw, meanwhile, that Michael didn't realise this. He seemed so focused on what he wanted to say that he was failing to engage with his audience. Jack's brief tenure in advertising had given him plenty of experience of this: presenters who erroneously assumed they'd been heard, simply because they'd said what they had wanted to say.

Royston broke the brief pause after Michael finished talking by asking, 'So what do you fookin' want Monica and me to do?'

'Just continue doing what you are doing now.'

'And what are you fookers going to do?'

Seeing Michael hesitate, Jen jumped in. 'We need to get to know the business properly. Initially, we'll conduct a full audit.'

'What the fook's that?'

Jack wondered if Royston was being deliberately obtuse or whether he genuinely didn't understand a word of what Michael and Jen were saying. He thought probably the latter.

'An audit is a thorough review of the finances of the business. It will give us a full picture of what's going on and where the strengths and opportunities lie. As you rightly point out, we don't yet know enough. An audit will provide a good starting point.'

'What about the fookin' work itself? Don't you think you need to understand that?'

'How do you mean?' Michael said weakly.

'How to handle bodies. How to prepare them for fookin' burial. How to embalm them.' Royston slowly and deliberately spelt out what he saw as the job description for Michael as if he were throwing down a gauntlet. 'How to manage grieving relatives and all of the crap that comes with that. The finances can't teach you any of that.'

'You're right,' said Jen, assuming control of the meeting from Michael, who was beginning to look decidedly queasy. 'But while the numbers can't tell us any of that, you'll be surprised at what they can reveal.'

'Your dad always got stuck in.' Royston spoke directly to Michael. It was as if he wanted to test him by attacking what he knew to be his weakest point. 'He believed that any funeral director worth his salt should be able to embalm a body.'

Michael took the bait, raising his voice. 'Well, I'm not

my father. I'm going to do things differently.' This silenced the room. No one apart from Jack had seen Michael express his anger before. Jack chose to add a little fuel to the fire, by saying, 'I think Royston raises a good point: I, for one, would like you to teach me how to embalm a body.'

CHAPTER EIGHTEEN

Shit-faced

_____

Hertfordshire. November 1998

Jack woke with a jolt. The dark purple walls of his old childhood bedroom took him way back in time. For a brief moment of panic, he thought he was late for school. The apartment seemed uncommonly quiet. Usually, his father would be pottering around at this time, getting ready and preparing breakfast for the two of them. Jack had to remind himself that his father was dead.

Jack had decided to move back into his father's apartment, at least while he got the bearings of his new life. It made no sense for him to pay rent in London and commute out to work in Hertfordshire. When Marianne's back, he thought, I can use her place as a London base. He was feeling her absence and hoped a change of scenery might help. He didn't want to mope around in his London apartment waiting pathetically for her return, so he'd given notice to his landlord, packed up his meagre possessions in a few bags and decamped to the apartment above the funeral home. Michael had been shocked when Jack told him of his intention to move back into the family home. As far as Michael was concerned, Jack might as well have been setting up in Hades.

Jack was less bothered about departed souls that morning than where he could find a good breakfast. Settled in the greasy-spoon café around the corner, he began to think about the day ahead. As someone who lived in the present, Jack tended to react to situations he found himself in rather than plan ahead. He realised he hadn't given any consideration to the practicalities of his new job and had no idea what he was supposed to do. Yesterday was easy, the board meeting had taken up his time, but today and tomorrow, and indeed the days after that, were much less clear. In all his previous jobs, he had turned up and been told what to do. But now there was no one to tell him what to do. Not only that, but it also wasn't at all clear whether there was *anything* for him to do. The business didn't need him and hadn't asked for him. His co-owner didn't want him. There were no apparent tasks in the offing, and no one to instruct or guide him. His communications skills didn't seem relevant for a business that did no advertising. It occurred to Jack that he could get away with doing nothing. Literally. All he needed to do, to honour the terms of the will, was to attend Wilfred's monthly board meetings and not fall out with his brother. It was tempting.

But Jack had been stung by Cat's admonishment that he was only interested in the money. It was, he had to admit, partly true. He couldn't wait to get his first £100,000 in three months and had already spent most of it in his head. He hated the thought that he might be so superficial; what would his dead father think of him if he squandered his fortune on wine, women and fast cars, without a day's hard graft? Fuck that, he admonished, Dad's dead, it doesn't matter what he might think. More important by far was what Marianne would think, and to his surprise, Jack found himself concerned about what Michael might think, too. He didn't want to be seen as a wastrel. Far from it, Jack wanted to prove himself: to his brother, to his girlfriend and to himself. He wanted to be a hero in his own life. His challenge was how to fashion a heroic narrative as a provincial undertaker.

So Jack needed a plan. Michael, aided and abetted by Jen, clearly had one. Now Jack also needed to work out how to counter his brother's desire to sideline him into irrelevance. His instinct told him to bide his time when it came to Michael. There was no point in being drawn into a fight that he couldn't win. He decided to go along with his brother for the time being. Maybe Michael would come to value his support – although he very much doubted it. Leopards, as they say, don't change their spots, and this leopard was much more likely to have him for lunch, given half a chance. No, Michael wasn't going to change. If he was going to prove himself to his brother, Jack knew he would have to do so by becoming stronger, by becoming an adversary who commanded respect. And he knew his best opportunity lay in exploiting Michael's weakness. He would get to know the business from the bottom up and become the expert undertaker his father had been. Michael had admitted he was planning to do the opposite, almost act as an external financial consultant to the business. The combination of the two different approaches, Jack thought, could conceivably dovetail well. Alternatively, they could end up in disastrous disagreement. Either way, this gave Jack a plan. He strode out of the café full of purpose.

A couple of days later, he stood opposite Royston McGinty in the embalming room, a naked corpse laid out on the bench between them. Jack covered in a gown, wore plastic gloves and some special shoes that Royston told him to buy, because 'blood spatter and bodily fluids don't look good on your fookin' party shoes'. Jack was controlling an urge to vomit. Royston refused to believe that he had lived his whole life in a funeral home and never seen a dead body, but it was true. Michael had been so traumatised by the experience that their father had taken great care to shield the two boys from any further accidental encounters with corpses. 'A fookin' undertaker's son and you haven't seen a fookin' body? I don't fookin' believe it.' Jack wondered if Royston had engineered it so that he would lose his virginity, so to speak, with a particularly gruesome suicide. The lyrics 'blew his mind out in his car' came inappropriately to him, as Royston mused aloud how this was a 'fookin' tricky reconstruction'. He wasn't wrong: the corpse belonged to a forty-five-year-old former farmer who had ended it all with a 12-bore shotgun under his chin. 'Luckily, the gun must have slipped as he did it, as he only blew half his fookin' face off,' explained Royston. Luckily was not the word Jack would have chosen.

'Used to drink in the Bull,' said Royston.

'What? You knew him.' Jack was surprised. It seemed so incongruent that this lifeless form had been a living, breathing – and drinking – person.

'Yeah. Saw him there last week. Shit-faced.' Royston paused. 'Although nowhere near as shit-faced as the poor fooker is now.' He emitted a deep ironic chuckle.

'Why do you think he did it?'

'Fook knows. For some fookers it just all gets too much,' said Royston philosophically.

Jack was physically and emotionally exhausted at the end of the day. He had a new understanding of the term 'dead weight'. He couldn't believe that a corpse could be so heavy and so awkward to move. He also began to understand why his father had valued Royston so much. Jack had been amazed at the skill with which he reconstructed the blown-away jaw of the shit-faced farmer. And he was pleased to have made some progress with Royston, who appreciated Jack's commitment to learn the business from the bottom up.

Best of all, Jack had learned a stunning revelation about himself that he never knew before. In their one personal conversation, Jack had asked Royston how he came by his name. 'Me mam was a young Scottish lass. She came down south and found work as a fruit-picker round here. She got into a relationship with some other fruit-picking fooker. Happiest days of her life, she said. I was conceived in the car park at the back of a pub that's no longer here. I was made in Royston. She liked the name of the place and decided to call me Royston. God bless her soul.'

'What happened to your dad?'

'I don't know, picking fookin' fruit back in Romania, probably. Or somewhere around there. Me mam never was sure where he was from, even though she said he was the love of her life.'

'Made in Royston. That's some story.' Jack smiled.

'Yeah. But it's not as good as your fookin' story, is it?'

'What do you mean, "my story"?'

Jack had to verify what Royston told him with Monica afterwards, so improbable did it seem. 'Oh, he didn't go and tell you that, did he? He shouldn't have done. Are you all right, my love?'

'All right? I'm more than all right. So it's true, then? I think it's a brilliant story. Hard to believe, but brilliant.'

CHAPTER NINETEEN

Room with a view

Hertfordshire. November 1998

Michael's thoughts were interrupted by the ping of a new email.

> From: Jack Merriweather
> To: Michael Merriweather
> Date: 21 November 1998 at 10.34
> Re: Support
>
> Hi Michael
> Anything I can help with?
> Jack

Michael paused for a few seconds before replying.

> From: Michael Merriweather
> To: Jack Merriweather

Date: 21 November 1998 at 10.35
Re: Support

No.
Michael Merriweather

Michael was in a temporary office in Royston. Jen had found it for them at short notice when Michael made it clear he wasn't prepared to work out of his childhood bedroom. Jen had been shocked by the lack of infrastructure at Merriweather's and had to agree with him that it wasn't a practical option for them to work out of the funeral home. The board meeting earlier that week had been a revelation. Jen was thankful that her father hadn't been a fly on the wall: it would have destroyed him to see how far his daughter had fallen. She was beginning to question whether she had taken leave of her senses in her desperation to leave Abel's. Could her decision-making have been affected by all those sleepless nights and the overwhelming pressure of juggling single-motherhood with a high-powered executive job? Might there have been another, more sensible option available to her? The contrast between her old smart, glass-walled office, with fully-operational technology and a well-oiled support team, and her current circumstances could not have been more pronounced. Not only was Merriweather's lacking in even the most basic business structure and discipline, but her new colleagues also fell short of what she expected from the management team of a functioning business. Furthermore, they all already seemed to be at war with each other.

In Jen's experience, management teams often grew apart as a result of working together. This cobbled-together team of misfits, on the other hand, were miles apart from each other before they had even started. And yet despite this, Jen felt alive in a way she hadn't for a long time. She was in control of her time and free to give her daughter the attention she needed. If it didn't work out, Jen rationalised, she could, God forbid, always take the offer of a return to Abel's. Alternatively, she was sure she could find something else, assuming that her CV hadn't been irreparably damaged by the career equivalent of a bungee jump on an untested cord. Jen envisaged a future employer listening in disbelief as she tried to explain why she had chosen to join a provincial undertaking firm. It would certainly raise serious questions about her judgment and business savvy. But she was getting ahead of herself; she was only four days into her new job. She shouldn't be thinking like this, however bleak the outlook might seem from her cheap, characterless office in Royston; however out of his depth Michael was beginning to appear; however broken the brothers' relationship might be. It was a challenge, to be sure; but this was what she wanted. Jen was determined to do everything in her power to make a success of it. She could only do her best. It still wasn't entirely clear to her what her role was or how to go about it, but it wasn't in her nature to sit around and wait. Jen's strength was that she got on and dealt with whatever was in front of her. That was why, five minutes after Monday's board meeting, she had interrogated Monica to find whether she knew of any spare space in town for an operational office. And why, three days later, she and Michael were in a Portakabin in the car park of the train station, only a few minutes away from what currently passed as the headquarters of Merriweather's.

Jen wheeled around in her chair. 'So, Michael, what do you think of your nice new office?'

Michael glanced around the beige room and said, 'It's perfect. We've even got our very own table, not to mention our very own walls. More than I had at Abel's.'

Jen said, 'And a window with natural light. More than I had before. It's even got a view.' They looked out at the car park and the unremarkable office block beyond. 'We've clearly both gone up in the world.' They both laughed.

'But seriously, Jen, how do you feel about all this? I'm worried I might have ruined your career. You must be wondering what the hell has happened. Don't you regret it?'

'Of course not. This is exactly the kind of challenge I needed. Remember, it was my decision. If anything, I persuaded you to go for it. How do you feel about it all?'

'If I'm honest, I'm not sure. Our meeting on Monday in my old bedroom with that psychopath Royston and my clueless brother made me question what the hell I'm doing. I can't believe that everything I've ever strived for has brought me to this point.'

'Think of it as a detour. We've departed the beaten track to explore a scenic route. If we don't like it, we'll rejoin the highway.'

'The problem is I've no idea what I'm supposed to do. None of my training has prepared me for this.'

'I'm your guide.'

'Do you know which way to go?'

'I got you here, didn't I?' Jen smiled.

'What, to a Portakabin in Royston? Is this our destination? This is it?'

There was a rumble of a train arriving in the background. One of its passengers glanced into the Merriweather headquarters as he walked past on his way to the car park. The commuter's expression suggested to Michael that the Portakabin may have been lying dormant for some time, such was the man's apparent surprise to see signs of life within.

Jen said, 'No, this is not the destination; it's our launch pad. This is where the journey starts for real. I suggest that initially at least, we treat this as if Merriweather's is a client of Abel's and we're external accountants conducting an audit. Over the next few weeks, we should interrogate the books and talk to all the key people. That way, we stick to what we both know and we get to properly understand the lay of the land. Deadlines help focus the mind, so we should set ourselves one. I suggest we aim to complete this in three months. We can draw on Abel's to help us. They'll want a proper audit on us anyway as we're a new client of theirs.'

'Okay, that makes sense.'

'It seems to me that the business operates as a federation of different groups each with their own accounts. The three original Merriweather homes are reported in one set of accounts and the Dyer's business, as far as I can make out, is separated into three or four different groups.'

'Why do you think that is?'

'I've no idea. Monica might be able to tell us. I suspect it's because the business has grown by acquisition and no one ever thought to amalgamate the separate accounts. It might be because your father didn't have the know-how to do it. We should aim to bring them all together as one coherent business with a single set of accounts.'

'I knew there was a reason why I invited you to join. Thank God someone knows what to do.'

'Most importantly,' Jen continued, 'we need to always keep in mind the vision we outlined in our plan to Jack and the board. Our immediate focus is to get the business in good shape and improve profitability through increased efficiency. Then we will be in a better position to reposition the firm to focus on the concept of a good death.' Jen paused. 'You won't like this, but I think Jack could have a part to play in the repositioning work.'

Michael raised an eyebrow. 'Seriously? I know he's my brother, but he's an idiot. He's got no business experience and has failed in everything he has ever done.'

'Michael, I know it's going to be hard, but you are going to have to reframe your perceptions of your brother. The reality is that you are now equal partners in the business. You have to find a way of working together. Jack's not stupid. And you don't have any experience of repositioning. You and I are accountants, we're not marketing people. In my experience, if you give people the opportunity, they often surprise you.'

'Give Jack any opportunity, and I guarantee you he'll fuck it up.'

Jen gave an exasperated sigh. 'Michael.'

'Okay, I know. But just wait. You'll see.'

Back in London that evening, Michael took Morty for a long walk around Regent's Park. Despite Jen's reassuring presence and her showing him a way forward, he still felt unsettled. He couldn't shake the feeling that he'd made a huge mistake in giving up everything he knew for something he never wanted. Michael couldn't find a way to get excited about the family business. Jen seemed energised by the challenge, but he could only see insurmountable obstacles. He knew he had to find a way of working with Jack. He felt he could probably control him, but he didn't want to appear a complete bastard in front of Jen. And Royston frightened him. He didn't know how to handle his antagonism. He was also worried about Monica, whom he'd ignored when he lived in the family home many years ago.

Michael sat down on a bench while Morty befriended some other dogs in the park. He watched people walk past, most, he presumed, on their way home after working late, or perhaps after a post-work drink with colleagues, as he often used to enjoy. He missed the camaraderie of working in a large office, the banter and the letting off steam in the bar after work through the sharing of stories of how awful everyone's respective bosses were. His thoughts drifted to Marianne.

CHAPTER TWENTY

Velvet linings

Hertfordshire. November 1998

'It's true. I really was conceived in a coffin,' said Jack to his disbelieving friends. Jack's friends had all had known Mr Merriweather, and struggled to reconcile their memory of a strait-laced pillar of the community with such a radical act of fornication. Jack was holding court in the Bull. Immediately after finishing his first day as an assistant embalmer, and having verified Royston's story with Monica, he had called a number of his old local friends to meet in the pub that evening. They were the academic underachievers that Jack used to hang out with and, like Jack, had all drifted into jobs that required no qualifications after escaping school at sixteen. Unlike Jack, though, who had gone in search of opportunity in London, they had stayed at home. They were a close-knit group who met regularly.

Jack felt comfortable in their company, but as his horizons broadened, he was becoming increasingly con- scious that they all seemed to be settling for unexceptional lives. He was intrigued by their apparent lack of ambition and wondered what drove him to want more from his life than they appeared to want from theirs. His closest friend, Dale Kemp, whose blonde crewcut and mischievous grin he had been drawn to in their first week at primary school, was now a farm labourer who had already fathered two girls, one with his current wife. Dale, more than anyone else, had been responsible for Jack's undistinguished school record. Jack loved Dale to bits; they bounced off each other and, depending on your perspective, brought out the best or worst in each other. Clayton Hutchins had always been the straight guy, the more sensible of the three musketeers (as they had once liked to think of themselves). He was now a fully qualified plumber and also married, although not yet with children. Clayton was nothing if not methodical, and he wanted the security of his own home before starting a family.

Julia Bristow had always thought herself as one of the boys. Jack wasn't surprised that she was unmarried. Julia was never that big on commitment and too much of a party animal to settle down before she had to. She and Jack had always been slightly flirtatious with each other. Marianne was suspicious of Julia and, after an unfortunate episode at Clayton's wedding, Jack had tended to try to avoid situations where the two women were in the same place at the same time. 'Poor you,' Julia had said when she heard that Marianne was out of the country, stroking Jack's arm in mock consolation. Julia worked at a local estate agency, which she said gave her an inside track on some of the more salacious local gossip because she got to go to the houses of couples who were in the process of separating. They were part of a bigger group of friends, but the four that met in the Bull that evening were the heart of the troop. They were also the only ones who were available at short notice. Dale had encountered some resistance from his wife, who had expected him to help put their one-year-old daughter to bed, but the opportunity of a drink with his old mucker took precedence.

Jack had always been the raconteur of their gang, and now his material was getting better and better. His stories about life as a London adman were highly entertaining, albeit slightly other-worldly and harder to relate to than those about people they all knew. They had loved Jack's updates on the negotiations with his brother. The Battersea Park boating incident, which had been recited with gusto to everyone who happened to be in the lounge bar of the Bull one Sunday afternoon, had brought the house down. Clayton had to apologise afterwards for spraying a stranger with the beer he had chosen to quaff at just the wrong moment. Jack did briefly wonder if he should be a little more careful about denigrating Mike so publicly, given his new determination to try to build bridges with his brother, but, as always, such consideration lost out to the chance of telling a good story.

'How could Royston possibly know that you were conceived in a coffin?' asked Clayton.

'Apparently he was there.' Jack delivered this revelation deadpan, controlling his urge to laugh at the horrified reaction of his friends.

'*No*' was all Julia could say. Dale and Clayton were speechless. Jack didn't say anything as he let his friends picture the scene. A local undertaker, who presented himself at all times with the utmost decorum, in coitus with his wife was a shocking enough image, particularly for his friends, who remembered Mr Merriweather as being stiff and uncomfortable in their company. That the act should have been committed in the company of his heavily tattooed embalmer, let alone that it was taking place in a coffin, turned it into a scene of unfathomable debauchery.

'The coffin had a velvet lining.'

Julia started laughing. 'I can't believe your dad would do such a thing.'

'What? Have sex? You think I'm the product of immaculate conception?'

'Well, yes, I have to say I find it hard to imagine your dad having sex. I'd rather not think of it at all. Anyone's parents, for that matter.'

'So your dad fucked your mum in a coffin?' Dale finally found his voice.

'Yes, Dale.'

'Why?'

'Why did he fuck her, do you mean? I have to say I'm not entirely comfortable talking about my parents in this way.'

'No, you klutz, I mean why did he fuck her in a coffin? Or if you want to be all prissy about it, why did they engage in sexual congress in a velvet-lined casket?'

'I want to know why Royston was there,' said Julia. 'There are a surprising amount of threesomes around here, you know.'

'Shut the fuck up Julia, Royston did not participate in a threesome with my parents.'

'Maybe Royston's your real dad.' Dale gave Jack a playful push.

'I'm no fookin' bastard child of a fookin' embalmer.' His friends laughed at Jack's impersonation of his employee. Jack glanced around the pub to double-check Royston wasn't there. 'By the way, you'll never guess who I embalmed today.'

'Who?'

'I don't know him, but you will. Royston said he was a regular here. A local farmer who topped himself last week.'

'Bloody hell,' said Dale, 'that'll be Norman. Fuck, what was that like?'

'Pretty gruesome, to tell the truth. I nearly threw up. Amazing how Royston patched him up, though. Do any of you know why he did it, why he killed himself?'

'No one knows, not even his wife,' said Dale. 'There are some rumours that he got into financial difficulties, but his farm seems to be doing okay, so I'm not sure that's right. He did start spending more time here over the past few weeks, and always by himself.'

'Royston said he was shit-faced last week. Made a good joke about it, saying he wasn't as shit-faced then as he is now.'

'I dunno about that. Whenever I saw Norman here, he

only seemed to have a couple of pints before slipping off quietly.'

'Can we get back to your parents' sexual proclivities?' said Clayton. 'I want to know what happened and how you came into being.'

'Okay, but I need another pint first. Who wants another drink?' Jack had noticed that since learning about his imminent fortune, his friends were more willing to let him get in the rounds than they had before. Not that he minded. Once he returned from the bar, he filled them in on what Royston and Monica had told him.

His parents had apparently had a long and boozy lunch to celebrate a special occasion. Monica wasn't sure what they were celebrating, but thought it might have been their wedding anniversary. To take time out of the working day and to drink at lunchtime was, needless to say, highly unusual and completely out of character for Mr Merriweather. So Monica supposed it must have been a significant event.

'Maybe he was plucking up courage for his threesome with Royston,' Dale suggested.

Monica, who had only recently started working for Mr Merriweather at the time, remembered being shocked to hear her boss slurring his words when they returned late-afternoon. Mr and Mrs Merriweather were in high spirits, so Monica had left work on the dot at five o'clock, so as not to be in the small building with the obviously drunk and disturbingly playful couple. 'I'd never seen your dad let down his guard before. I could hear them upstairs and didn't know where to put myself, so I left as soon as I could.'

Royston, who had been out that afternoon collecting a body, let himself into the home early that evening to drop it off in the embalming room. Hearing some unusual noises from the casket selection room, he pushed open the door and was confronted with the naked buttocks of his boss, who was prostrate in, as he put it, a Heartwood Veneer. 'They heard me,' Royston had told Jack, 'because Mr Merriweather jumped out of the Heartwood. It was only then that I realised fookin' Mrs Merriweather was in there as well. I then had an unclothed Mr Merriweather standing to attention next to a Heartwood Veneer containing a naked Mrs Merriweather. I didn't know where to fookin' look. Nine months later, you were born.'

'Wow' said Julia.

Over the next couple of hours and many drinks (all paid for by Jack), the old friends kept returning to his not-so-immaculate conception. However hard they tried, they could not shake the vivid scene that was now seared into their minds. 'Where was Mike in all this?' asked Clayton at one point.

'I dunno. God, I hope he wasn't there as well.'

Eventually, Dale decided it was time to face up to his parental responsibilities. 'A bit late for that, mate: it's ten o'clock.' Clayton said, 'I reckon Karen will be well on her way to becoming the second ex-Mrs Kemp.'

Dale shrugged by way of response as if he didn't disagree with Clayton's assessment of his fragile marital status. 'Anyway, I need to be back at work on the farm in less than eight hours.' This was a much more plausible excuse for leaving before closing time.

Clayton decided he should go home as well. 'Clearing clogged drains on a hangover is never a good idea.' It occurred to Jack that embalming a messed-up corpse on the back of five pints of Abbot Ale was equally inadvisable, but decided to stay for a final drink with Julia. They were the last to leave the pub an hour later. Jack's place was en route home for her, and so the two of them stumbled together along the high street. When they reached the funeral home, Julia said, 'I'd love to see your velvet linings.' Jack was under no illusions about what she was suggesting, and while he had no desire whatsoever to recreate the scene he had described a few hours earlier, he did at that moment want Julia. The cumulative effect of their years of flirtation; that stolen kiss at Clayton's wedding; the loosening influence of the alcohol and the continuing, and never adequately explained, absence of Marianne all combined to make him think *what the fuck*. But then he thought of Marianne again. 'I'm sorry Julia, I can't do it. I'd love to, but I can't.'

Julia didn't even try to hide her frustration. 'She's not coming back, you know Jack. You need to move on.'

CHAPTER TWENTY-ONE

Train set

Hertfordshire. March 1999

The fourth board meeting, like the second and third, took place in the Portakabin. Three of the four fookin' fookers who, according to Royston, had no fookin' idea three months ago, all now felt slightly better informed about the business. Wilfred was the only fooker who still knew nothing more than that he gleaned from these meetings. As he drove through the countryside of Wiltshire, Oxfordshire and Hertfordshire, he reflected on how much he was enjoying his time as non-executive chairman of a provincial undertaking firm.

Wilfred chose the scenic route, rather than the quicker, motorway option, partly because it made for a more pleasant drive, but also because it felt more appropriate. The meandering lanes, shaggy hedgerows and unexpected obstacles he encountered along the way were appropriate metaphors for his experience of the Merriweather board meetings, which were equally unstructured, lacking in clarity, and always contained at least one underhand or cutting comment. For Wilfred, they were a light diversion from the mundane bureaucracy that tended to occupy most of his working days, but he was under no illusion that these early days of calm would last. As the two brothers were not yet up to speed on the business, not to mention both of them being palpably out of their depth, and as Royston and Monica were unversed in the ways of formal business meetings, the sessions were, as Royston remarked every time, *a bit of a fookin' waste of time*. Wilfred, though, was confident that, over time, they would become essential. For now, if nothing else, they allowed him to ensure that the bothers complied with the conditions of his client's will. Three months down, fifty-seven to go.

Michael and Jack seemed to be observing an uneasy truce, primarily by keeping out of each other's way. Wilfred had noted, though, that Jack now had a desk in the Portakabin, as well as in the funeral home. It also helped that they hadn't yet had any decisions to make. Michael was occupied with the audit, and, as far as Wilfred could see, had fallen into his old familiar role as auditing assistant to Jen. Thank God for Jen. She had been an inspired and lucky hire. It didn't bear thinking how the brothers might, or might not, have coped without her there.

Jack was focusing on learning the trade. He had signed up for a funeral director's course that took two days a week over six months and spent the rest of his time soaking up as much as he could learn from Royston, Monica and others within the business. The highly-entertaining stories Jack shared at their board meetings even occasionally managed to produce a grudging smile from Michael. Although not always. Michael had once rather pompously objected to Jack's story about the removal of the corpse of an eighty-four-year-old man from a local brothel. The pensioner who despite advanced dementia had had sufficient wits about him to slip out of his care home and find his way to said brothel. 'You know how people with Alzheimer's remember the words of songs they used to sing,' Jack explained, 'well, the homing instincts of this old gentleman must have been similarly deep-rooted. He suffered a heart attack in the brothel, sadly not, though, "in flagrante delicto". His carers only realised he had gone AWOL when they received a call from the Madame, asking them to remove the body of their partially clothed and completely deceased resident from her hallway.' Michael didn't think such a story was appropriate for a board meeting.

The fourth board meeting marked a step change, as this was when Michael and Jen presented their audit. It signified a shift from learning about the business to beginning to have an impact on it. Jen explained that this was primarily a financial audit, and that a full-scale operational review would also be required, although that would take longer. She was also at pains to emphasise, as tactfully as possible, that because the business had only filed fairly rudimentary accounts in the past, there were inevitably some gaps in their analysis. Jen let Michael take the lead in presenting the audit even though she was clearly its primary architect and often interrupted to translate for their financially illiterate audience.

At one point, Michael said, 'The business has a strong cash position with nine months' cover.'

Jen explained, 'In other words, the business is secure because it has good cash reserves. Nine months' cover means that if revenue completely dried up, we could continue in business and cover our costs for another nine months. Generally, businesses need to have at least three months' cash cover. Having as much as nine months' cover might suggest that the business hasn't invested as much in its development as it might have done.'

'Mr Merriweather always preached prudence,' Monica observed. 'Three months doesn't sound very long to me.'

Michael said, 'It is, for a business like this, where there are guaranteed sales.'

'By sales, you mean fookin' deaths.'

'Well, yes, not to put too fine a point on it. By way of comparison, a dog food manufacturer can't rely on future sales in the same way.'

'A fookin' dog's got to fookin' eat, hasn't he?'

'Yes, but there are more variables in play, such as competition, changing tastes…' Michael felt his analogy slipping away from him, and, for once, was grateful when Jack jumped in. 'Dog food. There's an idea. We could diversify by offering dog food. We've got the raw materials, after all.' And then, upon seeing the expressions of his fellow board members: 'Sorry.'

Jen broke the silence. 'Michael's right. Undertaking

is a predictable business. What's the saying? "There's no such thing as a sure thing, except death and taxes." This means we can be reasonably confident in reducing our cash cover and reinvesting in the business. And I can assure you, as an accountant, I don't often say that. Monica, Mr Merriweather was right to be cautious, but only to a point. Another saying is that you need to speculate to accumulate. I think deep down Mr Merriweather knew this. In his letters to Michael and Jack, he wrote that he had taken the business as far as he could. I think he realised that it now needs investment and that his two sons might be better able to manage that than him.'

Michael resumed his presentation. He navigated his way through profit and loss statements, a preliminary balance sheet, debtor analysis and just about managed to explain the concept of margin. His confidence grew, and he felt in command. To his horror, he also sensed the beginnings of an erection. Power goes to the head, as they say. To quell his excitement, he focused on Royston, which did the trick. He concluded by asserting the business now needed to formally consolidate all its different accounts into one.

'What does that mean?' asked Monica.

'It means that, from a financial point of view, we bring the business together into a single set of accounts. But the implications go beyond the accounts. Jen and I think it should all be brought together into a single, more coherent business.'

'Me too,' said Jack.

'So, what does that mean in English?' asked Monica.

'It means, for example,' continued Jack, 'that we might bring all the homes under the same brand umbrella.'

'She said fookin' English.'

'So that all the homes are called Merriweather's.'

'Is that sensible?' asked Monica, 'The Dyer's name is well known in many of the towns around here.'

'If I may,' said Jen, 'we're not saying we will change the name of all the funeral homes, but we should consider it because there are a lot of arguments for it. And by the way, it doesn't have to be Merriweather's, we could rename them all Dyer's. But I think Merriweather's probably makes more sense particularly because the next generation of Merriweathers are taking it on. I think the whole issue of branding and promotion is one that Jack should probably lead.' Jen glanced at the brothers as she said this, noticing a slight grimace from Michael and a smile from Jack. 'But it's more than an issue of branding. If we properly put the business together, it will have implications for our operations, our people, our suppliers, and the whole way we organise ourselves. It's a big decision that we should consider carefully to be sure we are all in agreement, but there is certainly a powerful argument for doing it.'

'There's another big opportunity,' Michael said. 'The mortgages have been paid off on our buildings. That means the business is sitting on a goldmine of property assets. Our cost–benefit analysis shows we have several underperforming assets. We could sell these and reinvest the money both in the more profitable parts of the business and in the infrastructure that it badly needs.'

'What the fook does that mean?' Although the jargon was gobbledegook to Royston, he understood enough to know that he didn't like the way this was going.

'Four or five homes are barely profitable. We could sell those homes and reinvest that money to strengthen the rest of the business,' said Michael.

'Like pruning a tree to help it grow,' added Jen.

'Which homes?' asked Monica.

Royston exploded when Michael listed them. 'There's good fookin' people employed in all of them homes.'

Seeing Michael recoil a little at Royston's outburst, Jen stepped in. 'Everyone would be offered other jobs within the business. Remember, this would be to help the business grow and get stronger.'

'Surely selling homes would make us a smaller business?' said Monica.

'It would mean we would have fewer homes, yes, but it would allow us to invest in improving and enlarging our remaining homes, as well as building a decent infrastructure and start promoting the business more aggressively. These homes are underperforming because they're each relatively close to another of our homes. If we increase the capacity of the nearby home, we should be able to transfer the business of the old home and manage it more profitably.'

'I don't like it. I don't fookin' like the sound of it.'

Once everyone else had left the Portakabin, Michael and Jen conducted a post-mortem on the meeting. Michael was on a high. His only complaint was with Royston's negativity. Jen counselled him not to worry too much about it, pointing out that this was all entirely new for Royston, that he was naturally resistant to change and that he didn't yet trust the brothers. 'Doesn't trust me, you mean. He seems okay with Jack.'

'Well, Jack's making an effort to work with him.'

'There's more to it than that. Anyway, it's our business, not his. We can do what we want with it.'

'Hey, that's the first time I've heard you say that.' Jen had caught Michael's more defiant tone and punched him affectionately on the arm.' I think you might be on the way to becoming a proper business owner.' Little did she know then how prophetic this was to prove.

Michael had a spring in his step as he walked home from King's Cross. He had turned a significant corner and was finally feeling more positive about his new circumstances. His confidence had grown immeasurably through the audit. He felt less lost and was starting to see a path for the next few years. It was as if a switch had been flipped when he'd said to Jen 'We can do what we want with it.' Michael now knew what he needed to do and, more importantly, was beginning to believe that he could do it. All his life, he had sought refuge in the security of structure and established rules, but it dawned upon him that he was now in a position to create his own structure. *He* could set the rules. Adrenalin coursed through his veins; he felt powerful. As soon as he got back into the apartment, he put on The Stone Roses at full volume. Morty, not being a great fan of guitar-led Indie rock, took refuge in the bedroom.

That evening Michael met with Cat and Richard at

their favourite North London bistro. Cat said, 'Hey, you look different. What's happened?'

'Yeah, undertaking suits you, it seems,' said Richard.

'Nothing much, I just had a good day.' Michael enjoyed telling his friends about his ideas for the business. He regaled them with some of the stories he had heard over the past few months, even repeating some of Jack's. He found himself painting Royston as a bit of a villain, bigging up his tattoos – his fookin' tattoos. Cat knew Royston and his intimidating presence from their childhood, and didn't disagree with Michael's exaggerated caricature of his new colleague.

'Well, it sure as hell makes my week seem pretty dull,' said Richard.

'Actually,' said Michael, 'all I've been doing is what I used to do every day at Abel's: an in-depth audit. The only difference is that this time I get to act on my recommendations. At Abel's, you do the audit, give the presentation and then walk away. It's up to your clients whether or not they take your advice.'

'And mostly, they don't,' said Richard glumly.

'What struck me only this afternoon is that this is my train set. I get to make the decisions.'

'And Jack, too,' said Cat. 'Doesn't he get a say?'

'Well, technically, yes, but…'

'But what?'

'He's got no experience. He doesn't know even know what a balance sheet is. Anyway, I get to make the decisions, and you know what, I like that feeling.'

'Good on you, mate.' Richard clapped Michael on the shoulder. 'And, by the way, you played a blinder getting Jen to go with you. You can imagine the speculation that has caused back at Abel's. No one can believe she's given it all up to go and shovel a few graves. Everyone's convinced you must have blackmailed her or something.'

Later that evening, out of earshot of the others, Michael asked Cat if she had heard from Marianne. Cat groaned and told him he shouldn't be asking about her. Michael protested that it was an innocent enquiry. Both of them knew this wasn't true. Cat did eventually say that she had heard Marianne was taking a year off in Paris. 'Apparently, she's got a job at the Picasso Museum.'

CHAPTER TWENTY-TWO

The art of war

Hertfordshire. March 1999

Jack was surprised to find Michael by himself in the Portakabin. It was the first time in their four months as co-owners of the business, and in the preceding three months of negotiations, that the two of them had been alone together in the same room.

'Hi, what are you doing here?' Jack asked as he walked through the door.

'It may have escaped your attention, but this is my office. I work here.' There was an edge to Michael's reply. Just as Jack would have expected: there was always a sharpness to Michael's tone with him.

'Yeah, sorry. I thought I'd work here today for a change. Where's Jen?' Jack had become so accustomed to seeing Michael and Jen as a banded pack that it was odd to find one without the other.

'Not in today, she's got some appointment with her daughter.' Michael didn't look up. He gave every impression of wanting to dispense with conversational niceties so that he could continue his work. Unusually, his desk was covered with piles of paper, although being Michael, they were neat piles, symmetrically aligned. Despite Michael's body language, Jack felt compelled to try to engage his brother in conversation. 'What are you working on?'

'If you don't mind, I need to concentrate on this,' Michael said with obvious irritation. Jack grunted acceptance and went to make himself a coffee. He had noticed a fresh mug on his brother's desk. At least Morty was pleased to see him. Jack was delighted when, once settled at his desk, the Labrador got up from beside Michael and crossed the floor to rest beside him. He wondered whether Michael noticed this act of betrayal, before concluding he might be reading too much into what was undoubtedly a non-political gesture. The dog was just being friendly, for God's sake. It was a sorry state of affairs that he was mentally scoring points over canine affection, but it had always been thus. Michael seemed to make every encounter between them adversarial. Remembering Cat's wise words from his father's memorial service, that he didn't have to be a victim, that it was in his power to change their relationship, Jack decided to give it a go. He needed to keep his emotions in check and be careful not to antagonise his brother, but he did want to take this opportunity for a proper conversation.

'Michael, can I have a word?'

'Not now.'

'When, then?'

'For fuck's sake. Can't you see I'm trying to work?'

'How about when you've finished that?'

'When I've finished?' Michael sounded exasperated. 'This is days and days of work. Some of us have a business to run around here.'

Michael's unprovoked barb hit the mark. So much for remaining cool, calm and collected. In five short sentences, Michael had rebutted him, dismissed him and insulted him. Jack felt an adrenalin surge. 'That's completely unfair. You do everything you can to exclude me and fob me off with meaningless tasks. It's as much my business to run as it is yours.'

'You've no idea how to run a business. You don't know the first thing.'

'I'm learning. And, by the way…' With that, the gloves were off, and he was fighting back. 'As far as I can see, you don't seem to know what you're doing either.' You're just Jen's stooge.' The punch hit its mark. Some might say it was below the belt. Michael jumped out of his chair, causing it to fall noisily on its back. Morty, assuming they were under attack, sprang up and started barking loudly. For a brief moment, Jack thought Michael was going to hit him, but instead he issued a string of expletives and stormed out of the door. Morty stopped barking and looked at Jack as if to say, 'What the fuck was that about?' Jack said to Morty, 'Well, that went well.'

Michael had left his jacket on the back of his chair. Jack wondered what compelled his brother to wear a suit to work. No one else did, not even Jen. He wondered why

Michael was the way he was. It was difficult to comprehend that they came from the same gene pool.

Michael returned twenty minutes later and snarled, 'I can't work with you here.'

While his brother was out Jack had resolved not to rise to the bait, whatever the provocation. He said, in as measured a tone as he could manage, 'I'm afraid I'm not leaving.' Michael glared at him. There was real venom in his expression. He went to his desk and started to put the piles of paper into his briefcase. Jack said, 'What are you doing?'

'I'm going home. I can't work with you here. You say you're not leaving, so I have no option but to go and work at home.'

'Michael, that's ridiculous.' Too much. As soon as he'd said it, Jack realised he was fanning the flames of his brother's anger.

In his haste and anger, Michael knocked one of his piles. Sheets of paper fell to the floor. 'Fucking hell. Look what you've made me do now.'

Jack, poker-faced, said, 'It wasn't me guv, it was 'im,' and pointed at Morty. The accused was not sure how to react. His tail swayed cautiously and slowly as he waited with trepidation to see what happened next: Labradors don't do anger. Michael tried to suppress a smile; Jack's wit had punctured his ballooning rage. He gathered his papers from the floor and then sat back heavily in his chair. He knew he needed to control his anger, or at least keep it from view, but there was something about Jack that always set him off. They sat in silence for a few minutes. Morty got up and walked over to Michael in a gesture of solidarity.

Another long silence.

Jack took a sip of his now cold coffee. He became aware of various sounds from outside the Portakabin, the tweets of birds mingling with the distant rumble of a train. The tenor of everyday life outside felt at odds with the palpable tension within. The Portakabin was situated in a slight depression off the road, shielded from the noise of the traffic. It was also blocked from the sun's rays for most of the day and often seemed a little gloomy, with a slight chill to its unheated air. All this gave the metallic cabin a heightened atmosphere that Jack couldn't help thinking would make for a perfect crime scene in a B-rated movie.

Eventually, Michael spoke. 'I appreciate this is difficult for you, but you have to understand that it's not what I wanted. I don't think I could have been any clearer to Dad that I wanted nothing to do with the business. Or, for that matter, with you.' Michael paused. Jack wanted to respond but had an instinct that it might be better to stay quiet. Michael got up and turned on the kettle. 'The thing is, I'm finally beginning to see a way of making this work. I had a bit of a revelation the other week after our board meeting. It struck me for the first time that this is my business. It's not Dad's *now*. *I* get to decide what to do. And there's a lot that can be done with it.'

Michael poured himself a coffee, without, Jack couldn't help noticing, offering him one. He resisted correcting his brother on who owned their business. He sensed Michael knew what he was saying and that he wasn't just saying it to provoke. Jack wanted to hear where this line of thought might take them.

'You're right, Jen is currently leading this, but only because she's got more experience of conducting audits than me. I'm finding my feet and am increasingly feeling ready to take the lead.' Jack was beginning to feel uneasy. In previous discussions, Michael had either corrected himself, or been corrected, to acknowledge co-ownership rather than sole ownership of the business. Now he seemed to be deliberately emphasising that it was his.

'Once we've completed the audit and set the strategy, I want to take quick, decisive action. We need to make some big changes and do so quickly. Change programmes often fail because they're watered down and the management team loses their nerve. Fortune favours the brave, as they say. The big advantage of an owner-managed business is the opportunity of decisiveness.'

Michael had regained his composure and found an air of authority that Jack had never previously seen in him. It was unnerving. He couldn't hold it in anymore. 'What about me? Where do I fit in with all this?' He did everything he could to moderate his tone. He didn't want to sound like the trampled-upon little brother.

'Do you want an honest answer? Or do you want me to say what you want to hear?'

'I'd like an honest answer.' Jack wondered if he really did. The fragile peace that had held for the past seven months between the two brothers was built on loosely disguised falsehoods and the holding of tongues.

'Okay, then. The truth is you don't fit in.' Michael said this as if he was reading the shipping forecast. The thought crossed Jack's mind that his brother might well be a sociopath. Michael continued, 'In my opinion, businesses can only be successful as a collaborative enterprise when they have established procedures and proper governance. Abel's is a good example of that. Alternatively, businesses that have a visionary, decisive leader at the helm can succeed. Where it goes wrong is when there's an ill-advised attempt to combine the two. So many small companies are successfully started by entrepreneurs only to mess it all up when they get to a certain size and start getting run by committee. Merriweather's' success has, although I'm loath to admit it, been all down to Dad.'

'What about Royston and Monica? Haven't they had something to do with it?'

'As good lieutenants, yes, but Dad made all the decisions. I bet they did everything he told them to do. Even, incidentally, abetting his final departure.'

'What do you mean?'

'He couldn't do it all by himself. Royston had something to do with it.'

'Do you know something I don't?' Jack sensed that Michael was withholding something, so assertive was his allegation.

'I don't want to go into that now. The point I want to make is that our business – and note that I'm calling it *our* business – needs singular leadership. If I'm perfectly frank, the best thing would be for you to let me get on with it. You need to attend the board meetings to meet the conditions of the will. If you want to have some involvement, then I'm sure we can carve out some token role for you. Jen thinks you should lead the branding and promotion, which, if you remember, was what I suggested right at the beginning.'

'You proposed that I should be the fucking Advertising Manager.' As always, Michael knew how to push those buttons. And, as always, Jack found it next to impossible not to react.

'As far as I'm concerned, you could have the title of Global Marketing President, so long as we're clear that I'm running the show and making the decisions. Hell, we could even call you Chairman, I don't mind, but the important thing is that one person is in charge, and that person should be me.'

'Why should it be you?'

Michael exhaled. 'We've been through this before. You don't have the experience.'

'So? Dad didn't have any experience when he started.'

'You don't even know what a balance sheet is.'

'So? You don't even know what an OTS is.'

'A what?'

'OTS. Opportunity to see. The currency for measuring advertising media.'

'What the fuck has that got to do with a funeral business?'

'About as much as a balance sheet has to do with embalming a body.'

'Well, that's where you're wrong and why you're unqualified to run this business. The disturbing thing is that you can't even see it yourself. If the finances aren't in good shape, then there's no business. The bodies will rot.'

'I don't see why we can't work together as Dad wanted. The ad agency I worked for was run by two guys who disagreed with each other on absolutely everything. Despite all their arguing, they believed their opposing perspectives led to better solutions in the end.'

'What's that got to do with it?'

'They built a successful business, a top-twenty advertising agency.'

'Advertising agencies aren't proper businesses. Everyone knows that.' Jack realised their argument was going nowhere. He wanted to tell his brother that he was a narrow-minded, arrogant, self-righteous prick. Michael was so rigid and unyielding in his views, not to mention often being wrong. But he was nothing if not consistent. Jack knew it was pointless to try to change his opinion and even more useless for him to try to do so. He was the last person in the world to whom Michael would listen. Jack was more concerned about Michael's strident and assertive tone. It was as if he had made a conscious decision to dispense with any pretence in his bid to assume absolute control. Stay calm, he told himself.

'This is a futile argument,' said Jack. 'Can we get back to the point? As I understand it, you want me to let you run the business as you see fit.'

'Yes.'

'What's in it for me?'

'You're free to do whatever it is you want to do. You get the two million pounds from Dad's will as well as the dividends as a shareholder in a successful business. You could live the life of Riley, which as far as I can see is pretty much what you've always done, only this time you would have money. You could even go and set up your own advertising agency. Given your experience and talent.'

'You really can't resist taking every opportunity to make a snarky comment, can you?' Jack felt his temperature and his voice rising. 'Why do you always have to be so vindictive? Am I that much of a threat to you?'

'I'm simply being honest. You asked me to be honest.'

'You know you're being more than honest. You're doing everything you can to crush me.' Jack was almost shouting now.

Michael simply shrugged.

Jack lost control. The bullied child in him came storming to the surface. 'I hate you. I fucking hate you.'

Michael made a show of returning to his work as if his little brother wasn't there.

Jack exploded. 'Okay, then. If that's how you fucking want it...' He was so angry he couldn't think how to complete the threat. 'If that's what you want, you'll regret it. I'll make fucking sure of that.' And with that he stormed out of the Portakabin.

Mortuary Merriweather wasn't a political animal. Labradors, by nature the canine equivalent of Switzerland, are avowedly neutral. Morty didn't take sides, and he especially didn't want to be seen to favour either Michael or Jack. Already feeling uncomfortable about his initial involvement in the argument, he lay as still as possible: equidistant from the brothers until their conversation ended. Avoiding even a tentative tail thump for fear of any false suggestion of partiality, the only movement was in his eyes, which had tracked from brother to brother as each spoke. Morty sensed, from the tone of the conversation, that all was not well in the family of Merriweather. He hadn't heard Michael speak in such a forceful, monotone way before. It carried a hint of menace. It sounded to Morty as if Michael was staking a territorial claim. It occurred to him that Michael could have communicated his message much less ambiguously by pissing in all four corners of the office, as Morty himself would have done had he needed to assert top-dog status. Morty also noticed something in Jack's body language that signified he had had enough. He suspected that Jack might not even be aware that he had reached a breaking point, but Morty's extrasensory perception told him that whatever he might be saying, the younger brother was not at the point of acquiescence. In short, Morty felt a sense of foreboding for the future. He prayed he would not have to choose sides.

Michael, meanwhile, smiled to himself.

Jack marched directly into town and bought himself a copy of *The Art of War* by Sun Tzu. 'Have you got anything else like this?' he asked the bookseller. 'If so, I'll take the lot.'

CHAPTER
TWENTY-THREE

Two tigers

Hertfordshire. April 1999

As Jack walked through the entrance to his office, a small bundle of energy barrelled out from the neighbouring room and hit him with full force, knocking him back into the corridor. He lost his balance and found himself sprawled on the floor, trying to protect himself from further assault.

'You bastard, you fucking bastard.'

'Monica, please. Please, stop,' Jack tried to shield himself from her blows. He was surprised at her strength. As he lay prostrate on the swirly purple carpet, straddled by his furious general manager, a thought flashed through his mind that this was not the kind of employee interaction he had envisaged when he took on the business. He'd always assumed he would be a benevolent boss, popular with his staff, yet here he was being beaten up by one of his long-standing and most highly valuable employees. He managed to extricate himself from her and escape outside, slamming the door behind him. 'Monica, what have I done? Why are you so angry?' He jumped back as something, a coffee cup by the sounds of it, smashed against the other side of the door. 'Monica – please.'

'Fuck off.'

'Monica, what have I done?'

The door swung open. A demonic-looking Monica glowered at him. Jack stepped back, fearing she was going to hit him again. 'Royston's been arrested.' She slammed the door shut.

'Monica, that's nothing to do with me.'

An accusing voice from behind the door. 'So you knew about it?'

'No, of course not. C'mon, please calm down.'

'Don't you fucking tell me to calm down.'

Jack sat down, in shock, on the pavement outside. He was reminded of his childhood. Cast as the miscreant on the naughty step, any notion that he was in charge seemed ridiculous now. No one took him seriously. And no one, not even Monica, had any respect for him. He doubted she would have attacked Michael like that, even though he was the true target of her fury. Then again, maybe she would. Jack would have loved to see that. He remembered his father mentioning that she had a volcanic temper, but he had never seen anything like this. He decided to sit it out until she calmed down. He wondered why Royston had been arrested and why Monica blamed him. He couldn't believe how powerful she was. She must be in her fifties, he thought, not a tall woman, but sturdy. To Jack, she had always been a model of restraint. Not only was this outburst entirely out of character – or at least it was for the Monica that Jack thought he knew – but it was all the more surprising given that he was now her boss. Recovering from the shock of her attack, Jack chuckled to himself at the absurdity of it all. He was already looking forward to warning Dale never to mess with Monica.

After twenty minutes, the door opened. Jack walked in. Cautiously. He found Monica sitting quietly in the kitchen. 'Jesus Christ, Monica, what was that about?'

'I'm sorry, Jack, I lost it.'

'No shit, Sherlock.' Jack could tell from her pursed expression and clipped tone that, although the rage had gone, she was still angry. He decided to hold his peace. Now was not the time to make a witty observation about a future as a rugby number eight.

'Royston's been arrested,' Monica said flatly.

'Yes, so you said,' replied Jack. 'What for?'

'Something to do with your dad's death. It appears the police have some new evidence.'

'New evidence about what?'

'Something that implicates Royston.'

'They think he killed Dad?'

'I'm not sure. Maybe not killed, but had something to do with it.'

'What, aiding and abetting a suicide?'

'Something like that.'

'Where is he now?'

'In a police cell.'

'Bloody hell. The poor fooker.' Monica even managed a slight smile at Jack's impersonation. 'What's changed? I thought the police interviewed him at the time and decided he had no case to answer.'

'They did, but apparently they've got new evidence from an anonymous source.' Monica paused and glared at Jack. 'Royston is convinced the anonymous source is Michael.'

'You've spoken to him?'

'Yes, he called me from the police station to ask me to find him a lawyer.'

'Did you?'

'Did I what?'

'Find him a lawyer?'

'I called Wilfred. He was a bit off actually. I thought he said something about conflict of interest at first, but then he corrected himself and said that he wasn't qualified to help with this kind of situation. He did then give me the number of a Cambridge lawyer, who I think is now representing Royston.'

'We should cover his legal costs,' said Jack quickly.

'Are you sure you know nothing about it?' Monica stared at Jack as if to force a confession. He thought back to the moment the previous week when Michael told him that Royston had something to do with their father's death. He hoped his face didn't betray him. 'No, absolutely nothing. This is the first I've heard of it.'

Monica put her head in her hands. 'Everything's gone to shit. I don't know what your father was thinking. How could he ever think that you two could run the business? I'm sorry I attacked you, and I'm sorry I've messed up the office, but I was so angry. Royston's in serious trouble.'

Jack called an emergency meeting the next day with Jen and Monica. 'Does anyone know where Michael is?' he asked. Jen told them that Michael had said he was taking a few days off, but hadn't said where he was going. 'Unfortunately, he's not answering his phone. I presume he'll be back on Monday.'

Jack said, 'I went to the police station first thing this morning. Royston is likely to be charged with aiding and abetting Dad's suicide. They wouldn't let me see him, but, hopefully, they'll release him on bail later today. I said to Monica last night that we should cover his legal costs. We should support him in whatever way we can. We also need to think about how we can cover his workload while he's out.'

'Don't worry about that. I've sorted it,' said Monica. Jack was surprised at how quickly she had reverted to her old, efficient self. Neither of them said anything about their fight. It was as if it hadn't happened.

'I'll set up an extraordinary board meeting for early next week,' said Jen.

Monica's mobile rang. 'Sorry, I need to take this,' she excused herself as she walked out of the office. She came back a few minutes later. 'That was Royston's solicitors. The police are going to keep him in for another twenty-four hours. They're considering changing the charge to manslaughter.'

'What?' Jack found himself raising his voice. 'That's outrageous.'

'The solicitor said it could be worse: it could be a murder charge. The only reason it isn't is that they seem to accept that your father was probably the instigator.'

'Probably? Of course he fucking was. They can't possibly think that Royston took it upon himself to kill him without his agreement.'

'I think they accept that, but the reason it might be a manslaughter charge is that the police appear to think Royston must have turned on the cremator. They're saying that Mr Merriweather couldn't have done so himself.'

'Fuck, what a mess. Presumably, Royston is denying having anything to do with it.'

'I don't know, but I guess so.'

Jen said, 'Do you know what the new evidence is?'

Monica shook her head. 'I don't. The lawyer said assisted suicide could be punishable by up to fourteen years imprisonment.'

'Fourteen years!' Jack was shocked. 'That can't be right. Fourteen years? Are these lawyers any good?'

'I don't know. Wilfred gave me their number but I don't think he knew them.'

'I need to speak to Wilfred. Have you got his number?'

It went straight to answerphone. Monica said she needed to go, as there was a lot to sort out in Royston's absence. When she was gone, Jack turned to Jen and said, 'Did you know anything about this?'

Jen, slightly taken aback by Jack's accusatory tone,

shook her head and said, 'No, of course not.'

'Monica said that Royston thinks Michael might have something to do with this. And something Michael said to me last week makes me think he might be right.'

'What did Michael say?'

'It wasn't so much what he said as *how* he said it. He stated with complete certainty, apparently, that Royston had something to do with Dad's death. I just wouldn't be surprised if he had something to do with this evidence, whatever it might be.'

'Oh God, I hope not.'

'This is all getting a bit out of hand, isn't it? It doesn't feel like a game anymore.'

'Did it ever feel like a game?'

'A bit.' Jack hesitated as he thought about it. 'But I had a wake-up call last week.'

'What happened?'

'Mike and I found ourselves together here. It was the first time we'd been by ourselves since all this began. Come to think of it, I can't remember the last time we were *ever* alone together.' Jack paused as he racked his brain. All he could remember were unhappy moments in his childhood when Michael was bullying him. He couldn't recall a single occasion when the two of them had played happily together. 'You know, now that I think about it, I'm an idiot to suppose that there's any chance of us working harmoniously together. We've always fought, or at least he's always fought me. But that's going to change. Anyway, that's pretty much the conclusion I reached last week. After our meeting, if you could call it that, I went out and bought *The Art of War* by Sun Tzu.'

Jen raised an eyebrow. 'Have you read it yet?'

'I have. Cover to cover.'

'Was it useful?'

'Very. It advises to only enter battles you know you can win. I know I can't beat Michael yet. It says that if your enemy is superior in strength, evade him.'

'Is Michael your enemy? Really?'

'You tell me.'

They both sat in silence for a while, Jack waiting for Jen to answer his question; Jen thinking how best to answer it. Eventually, Jen spoke. 'It's difficult for me to understand, given I'm an only child. But I've worked with several family businesses. It's certainly true to say that infighting between family members almost always destroys both value in the business and the dignity of the participants.'

'So what can I do? I'm not the one who's picking this fight.'

Again Jen took her time to respond. 'Well, if I were advising a client, I would probably suggest keeping a low profile; find trusted managers who can run the businesses under your supervision, and be patient.'

'Evade your enemy. Exactly what Sun Tzu advises.' Jack took a sip of coffee. 'But, not to put too fine a point on it, Michael appears to have shopped our trusted manager to the police.'

'Maybe he doesn't trust him.'

'That's very likely true, although totally unfair. Royston has given everything to this business.'

'The question posed by family businesses,' said Jen, 'is whose benefit are they for? Public companies are supposed to be for their shareholders. A private company exists, first and foremost, for the interest of its owner.'

'What about its employees and customers? Don't they count?'

'From an accountant's perspective, both are just a means to an end. They simply exist to help make money for the business owner. That's capitalism for you.'

'What's this got to do with Royston?'

'There's a proverb that says two tigers cannot share one mountain. A leader has to be able to trust a key manager.'

'Does your proverb recommend that the dominant tiger pushes the other off the mountain? Because that's what Michael has done by shopping Royston to the police.'

'*Might* have done, we don't know.'

'I think it's pretty fucking obvious that he's done it. It's very mafioso. He's even got the name for it. Have you seen *The Godfather* and what Michael Corleone does to his enemies?'

'Perhaps I shouldn't say this, but there's another Chinese saying that advises killing a chicken before a monkey. The monkey can then take the message as a warning.'

'You and your bloody proverbs.' Jack smiled.

'I'm sorry, but I've been brought up with them. My dad loves them. I think they remind him of happier times back in China and help him make sense of the sometimes bewildering world he finds himself in.'

'So how does the monkey one apply?'

'Decisive action can be an effective way to signal who's in charge.'

'Jesus. So Michael is getting Royston jailed for manslaughter simply to satisfy his ego. Are you sure you know nothing about this? You seem very matter-of-fact about it.'

'I know nothing about it. I don't even know if there is anything to know. We're just speculating here. As an accountant, I prefer hard evidence. All I'm saying is that a business leader needs to be able to trust his team. The most successful businesses are often brutal.'

'How many of your clients have resolved a power struggle by getting their adversary arrested?'

'None that I know, but you'd be surprised. That kind of thing is more common than you might think. Suspicious deaths, white-collar prison sentences, trashed reputations can often be traced back to petty rivalries.'

'Wow. I've underestimated you. You're tough.'

'I'm just realistic.'

'Going back to your tigers: didn't you say that two tigers can't share the mountain?'

'Yes.'

'So where does that leave Michael and me?'

'That's an excellent question.'

'What's the answer? Have you got a good proverb? Preferably one that doesn't involve me being thrown off the mountain or eaten.'

'How about "Good things come to those that wait".'

'I've heard that before. Who said that?'

Jen laughed. 'Guinness; it's from their new TV commercial.'

'Of course it is. Guinness – that's an oracle I can believe in. So are you saying I should just wait?'

'Give me a minute.' Jen jotted down some notes on her pad and then said, 'I think there are five options. The first is that you both align on the strategic direction of the company and all key decisions.'

'Well, that's not going to happen.'

'Don't discount it. For all your differences, I suspect you're closer than you may think on the task at hand.'

'On putting our key employee behind bars, for example? I don't think so.'

'Okay, well, maybe not that, then. I was more thinking about the overall direction. But maybe there is too much personal history between you both for this option to be viable right now.'

'What's the second option?'

'For you both to accept and respect your differences, to clearly define your respective areas of responsibility and to develop a workable decision-making process. There are plenty of successful businesses that thrive through healthy conflict and disagreement between their leaders, but it needs mutual respect and a clear set of ground rules.'

'Well, that's the problem, isn' it. Mike doesn't respect me; he makes that pretty bloody clear all the time. This is the option I hoped might happen. It's what I thought we had agreed with Wilfred, and indeed it is, I believe, what Dad wanted. The problem is that Michael hasn't signed up to it. He told me last week that he thinks the business, in fact any small business, needs singular leadership. He believes he should lead and I should just suck it up.'

'Well, that's the third option.'

'What's the fourth?'

'The opposite of that. You assume total control and Michael takes the back seat.'

At this, Jack broke out into laughter. 'What are the chances of that?'

Jen nodded, 'I have to agree it's unlikely. But don't rule anything out.'

'You said there were five options. What's the fifth?'

'You go to war.'

CHAPTER TWENTY-FOUR

Extraordinary meeting

Hertfordshire. April 1999

Unusually, Michael was the last to arrive at the board meeting. Equally uncharacteristically, he wasn't bothered about keeping his colleagues waiting. He had caught up with his messages on his return to London the previous night and felt a little irritated to be summoned to an urgent board meeting straightaway. His first reaction to hearing that he needed to attend an extraordinary board meeting the next morning had been: *Who are they to tell me what to do?*

He entered the Portakabin to the sight of four board members sitting around their Formica boardroom table, all looking expectantly at him. 'Where's Royston?' said Michael. No one answered. He repeated his question while he hung up his coat. 'So, where is he?'

'I think you know where he is,' said Jack.

'I'm sorry, I have no idea. I assumed he would be here. Anyway, what's this all about? Why do we need an extraordinary board meeting?'

Jack scrutinised his brother, who seemed uncharacteristically buoyant. It had been five days since their showdown in which Michael had made it crystal clear that he intended to take control of the business and expected his brother to back off. Since then, he had mysteriously disappeared, Royston had been arrested, and Monica had assaulted Jack. Five long days. Jack decided to hold his peace. He was consciously playing a tape over in his head that said 'Evade your enemy, evade your enemy…'

Michael, either not noticing the atmosphere in the room or choosing to ignore it, continued to press for an explanation. 'Wilfred, what's going on? Why do we need an extraordinary board meeting?'

The lawyer shrugged his shoulders and said, 'I'm sorry, I'm afraid I'm as in the dark as you.'

Jen then said, 'I called the meeting. And to answer your other question, Royston has been arrested on suspicion of aiding and abetting your father's death. He's possibly facing a charge of manslaughter. I called this meeting to discuss what we should do.'

'Did he?'

'Did he what?'

'Did he aid and abet my father's death?'

Monica, who had been glowering at Michael, said in a slow and deliberate tone laced with controlled anger, 'Do you know anything about this?'

'About what?'

'About Royston's arrest?'

'Of course not, I've been away for the weekend in France.'

'You don't seem surprised.'

'I'm not.'

'The police say they've got some new and incriminating evidence from an anonymous source.' Monica held back from accusing Michael directly of being that source. She didn't need to verbalise it; her whole demeanour made it clear what she thought.

'Okay – but why the extraordinary board meeting?'

Jack could contain himself no longer. 'One of our key managers has been arrested. We need to agree on how we support him and what action we need to take to cover his absence.'

'Support him?'

'Yes, we've put him in touch with some lawyers who Wilfred recommended. I think we should cover his legal expenses.'

'That's interesting. You think we should cover the legal expenses of a man accused of killing our father, the founder of this company?'

With that, the room exploded, or at least Jack and Monica exploded. Wilfred and Jen were stunned observers. Jen, who had seen it all before and thought she now had the measure of Michael, was amazed at his transformation from an inexperienced, slightly nervous manager into she wasn't quite sure what. Jack and Monica were both shouting at the same time: Monica, to accuse her boss of shopping her colleague to the police: and Jack, to describe his brother as being a fucking psychopath. Meanwhile, Michael sat there, impassively. Wilfred tried to restore order, which was only successful when he stood up and banged on the table loudly. 'Please, calm down.'

But Michael had no intention of losing his moment. He waited for everyone to quieten down before casually throwing more fuel on the fire. 'Jen, you said we need to discuss what to do. It's clear to me. If Royston has done what he's accused of, then he needs to be relieved of his duties. Not that he would be able to perform them while detained at Her Majesty's pleasure. But until this is proven, he should be put on indefinite leave.'

'What the fuck do you mean "until"?' Jack was finding it impossible to evade his enemy.

'I'm sorry. Innocent until proven guilty. Of course.'

'So why put him on indefinite leave? We should support him. We can't deprive him of his work.'

'I repeat my previous question. Do you think we should support a man accused of killing our father, the founder of this company?'

'Yes, as a matter of fact, I do. It's what Dad would have wanted.'

'Well, I'm sorry. I couldn't possibly work with Royston under such circumstances. No business could afford to have someone accused of manslaughter continue in a managerial position, least of all when the man he's accused of slaughtering is the founder of that business.'

Jen put her hand on Monica's shoulder to stop her from rising as she said, 'Michael, you're using quite intemperate and inflammatory language.'

'I'm sorry, but surely you agree it's not an option for

Royston to be involved in the business while this is going on. Imagine what the media would make of it, for a start.'

'Why do the media need to know about it?' asked Jack.

'C'mon, Jack, you're not that stupid. Do you think the very same media who splashed every detail of Dad's death across their front pages would somehow miss a story like that? And what about our customers? How are they going to feel about their recently departed and dearly beloved being tarted up by a heavily-tattooed man accused of manslaughter?'

Monica said, 'Did you do it? Are you the anonymous source?'

'Of course not. What information could I possibly have that would incriminate Royston?'

Jack was surprised at such an emphatic denial. He was pretty sure that it must have been his brother, but the brazenness with which he brushed off the accusation unnerved him. If Michael was lying, he was doing so very effectively. Jack caught Jen's eye, but found it impossible to read what she was thinking. Monica decided not to press it.

A brief silence ensued as everyone tried to process what had been said. Wilfred, remembering his responsibilities as chairman, proposed they take a vote on whether to put Royston on indefinite leave. 'This is not a voting matter,' said Michael.

'With all due respect,' said Wilfred, 'I think it is. If any board member is to be voted off or put on indefinite leave, it has to be with the agreement of the board.'

'We're a private company, so it's the owner's decision.'

'Well, the articles of association that we drafted and agreed after our first board meeting specified that all operational matters are subject to board approval.'

'Except for the appointment of directors. Jack and I, as owners of the business, have the ultimate say on that.'

'Well, it's a grey area because we're not deciding on the appointment or dismissal of a director. We're simply determining whether or not to put Royston on indefinite leave until this difficulty is resolved. And anyway, your father was clear in his instructions that Royston and Monica should, initially at least, continue to be actively involved in all decisions concerning the business.'

'With all due respect, Dad is dead. Also, I want to make it clear that it is not an option as far as I'm concerned for Royston to remain in the business unless and until he is cleared of these charges.'

Wilfred held his ground. 'That may be so, but I'm afraid I am going to put this to the vote. All those who think that Royston should be placed on indefinite leave raise their hands.'

Michael's arm had been resting on the table. He raised it, with what to Jack's eye looked like an extended middle finger in a contemptuous gesture at all of them. After a brief pause, Jen followed suit by putting up her hand and saying, 'I have to agree with Michael that it would not be tenable for Royston to be involved in the business while all this is going on.'

'And those against?' Both Jack and Monica raised their hands immediately and defiantly. Wilfred gulped. 'Then I suppose, as chairman, the casting vote falls to me, although I don't think I should be deciding this.'

Monica interrupted. 'What about Royston's vote?'

'He's not here,' said Michael, 'and anyway he can hardly vote on an issue that affects him personally. Even if he were here, he would have to abstain. Look, Wilfred, this is pointless. I'm not working with Royston. I refuse to work with someone who's accused of killing my father.'

'Hold on a minute,' said Jack, 'aren't we're jumping the gun a bit here? Royston hasn't yet been charged with any crime.'

'He will be.'

'What makes you so sure, Michael?'

Wilfred jumped in before Michael had the opportunity to inflame the situation further. 'Hold on, I haven't yet cast my vote. Jack raises a good point. Maybe I was premature in putting this to the vote. I don't think we should take action until Royston is charged.' Wilfred paused before adding, 'If he's charged. If indeed he is charged then I would vote to grant him leave until he goes on trial. If it comes to that.' The way Wilfred added his little proviso caused Jack to wonder if he too knew more than he was letting on. It felt like a game of poker, one where everyone was holding their cards close to their chest.

Jack then asked for a vote on whether the firm should cover Royston's legal fees. Much to Michael's chagrin, this was passed four to one. Yet more battle lines drawn between the two brothers.

Then, just as the meeting was winding up, the door

burst open to reveal who else but Royston himself. He stood imposingly in the door frame; his attention lasered in on Michael.

'You fookin' fooker.'

CHAPTER TWENTY-FIVE

Facing the music

Paris. May 1999

Back in Paris, and having spent twenty-four hours thinking it all through from every conceivable angle, Marianne finally put pen to paper.

3 May 1999

> *Dear Jack,*
>> *I'm writing this letter with a heavy heart*

Marianne then had second thoughts and tore what she had written into tiny pieces. A letter was the coward's way out. She owed it to him to tell him in person.

Meanwhile, Michael was facing an entirely different proposition. Royston, after a lifetime of restoring bodies, now appeared hell-bent on wrecking one. At least, that was how it seemed to Michael, confronted by the apoplectic embalmer in the doorway of the Portakabin.

'You. Fookin'. Fookin'. Fooker,' Royston repeated

slowly and deliberately. Michael suspected, and prayed, that Royston was more bark than bite. But he wasn't entirely sure. He couldn't help noticing that no one else in the room appeared to be coming to his defence. No one was jumping up to pacify Royston. No one, that was, except Morty, who pulled himself up and sauntered over to Royston with a wagging tail. As he bent to pat the dog, Royston somehow appeared less threatening. But he was still fookin' angry. 'You fookin' stitched me up with the fookin' police.'

'I'm sorry, I don't know what you're talking about.' Michael hoped he sounded calmer than he felt.

'The police say they have evidence that I received money from Mr Merriweather's death. They think this proves I had something to do with his fookin' suicide.'

'I'm sorry, I know nothing about this.'

'Bollocks.'

Jack said, 'Did you receive money?'

'Yes, but it had fookin' nothing to do with Mr Merriweather's death.'

'What was it for?' Jen asked.

'I'm not going to say. That's between him and me. But obviously I had nothing to do with his death: I fookin' loved the man. I owe him everything. Why would I fookin' kill him? You think I would have wanted to swap him for this fookwit?' Royston pointed at Michael.

'Are the police charging you?' Wilfred asked.

'Yes, they fookin' are. They're charging me with aiding and abetting Mr Merriweather's suicide. They've released me on bail.'

Michael, who had regained his composure now that the immediate threat had passed, and keen to regain the upper hand against his adversary, said, 'Wilfred, could you let Royston know what we've just agreed.' At that moment, Jack thought Wilfred looked as young as he did when he first met him: less the composed lawyer carefully pulling strings and more like an intern horribly out of his depth. He thought he detected a slight stammer in Wilfred's response. 'Do you think now is the moment? Perhaps we should let things calm down a little.'

'Royston needs to be informed immediately.'

'Okay, then.' Wilfred composed himself. 'Royston, in your absence, we, the board, have agreed two things. The first is that we will cover any legal costs you incur in defending yourself; we'll support you to the best of our ability.' Wilfred paused in anticipation of an expression of gratitude from Royston. None was forthcoming. Royston was still glaring at Michael and hardly seemed to be listening to Wilfred. 'Second, we've agreed that you should be granted indefinite leave from work to give you every opportunity to defend yourself.'

Royston heard that part. 'What does that fookin' mean? Are you fookin' saying that I can't work?'

'Well, yes. At least until this issue is cleared up.'

'You fookers. What the fook will I do? My work is everything.'

'I'm sorry, Royston,' said Michael, 'but it would be untenable for you to continue working here given the charges you're facing.'

Monica, who had been quiet since Royston's appearance, said, 'I want you to know that I disagree with this. And that Jack also voted against it.'

'Thank you, Monica,' said Wilfred. 'Royston, it's honestly in your best interests. Look, I'm going to speak to your lawyers. Hopefully, we will be able to clear up this little misunderstanding quickly, and you'll be able to return to work.'

That evening Wilfred, following the agreement of his dead client, took it upon himself to write to Royston's lawyers. His letter contained irrefutable evidence that the money paid by Mr Merriweather to Royston just two months before his death was related to the repayment of monies owed from an investment that he had made on behalf of Royston a couple of years previously. Wilfred wrote that his involvement in this matter should remain entirely confidential, citing attorney–client privilege. Wilfred asked Royston's lawyers to pass the information on to the police, and said he was confident that when they did so the charges against their client would be dropped. He was under no illusions that it would lead to complications in the business, as it was difficult to see how Michael and Royston could possibly maintain a working relationship. Still, Wilfred knew what Mr Merriweather had wanted. The undertaker had taken extraordinary steps, when preparing his will, to avoid any possibility of his trusted colleague being implicated in his death.

The following Saturday, Jack was surprised to hear his doorbell ring. Assuming it must be the postman, he threw on a T-shirt and opened the door expecting to have to sign for something or to take an oversized package that didn't fit through the letterbox.

It wasn't the postman; it was Marianne. It was the first time Jack had seen his girlfriend in nearly nine months. Nine long months during which he had remained faithful to her and refused to believe that she wouldn't one day come back. Standing in the doorway of the funeral home, dressed in nothing more than a pair of distressed boxer shorts and an old Oasis T-shirt, this was not the reunion that he had envisaged. All he could say was, 'Marianne, what are you doing here?'

After a few seconds he managed to compose himself. 'Marianne, I'm sorry, that was a crap welcome. I wasn't expecting you. Let me do it properly.' He moved to hug her. He couldn't help but notice that she seemed to step back – almost imperceptibly, but enough to signal that she had no desire to resume their old familiarity. Jack then felt her stiffen slightly in his embrace. In a matter of a few short seconds, her body language had told him everything he needed to know and confirmed all his worst fears. Jack realised that his world was about to be turned upside down.

Extracting herself from his hold, Marianne said, 'Jack, we need to talk.'

'What about?' He was conscious of how forced and unnatural he sounded. He tried to lighten up. 'What am I saying – we've got loads to talk about. I want to hear all about you and your travels. You look great, by the way.' It was true, she did. Jack had always thought Marianne looked great, but he had forgotten just how beautiful she was. 'I love that jacket. You look like a proper grown-up person. As you can see,' Jack pointing to his boxer shorts, 'I've also dressed for the occasion.' A flicker of a smile crossed Marianne's face. 'I've gone up in the world since you last saw me: I've become an undertaker. I'm sorry I'm babbling; c'mon in for a coffee.'

'Thank you, Jack, but I think it's best that I don't come in.'

Jack was unable to maintain his false jollity in the face of Marianne's flat perfunctory tone. 'What do you mean it's best that you don't come in?' He tried to stop his voice rising. 'Are we strangers now? Are you going to tell me it's all over? Out here? Is this how it all ends? Me standing here in my boxer shorts on Baldock Street?'

'Can we talk about it in that café around the corner?'

'So you are ending it?'

'I'm not sure there's anything to end. Remember we agreed to separate when we last talked?'

'That was temporary, and as I remember it I didn't agree to anything. You basically told me that was how it would be. I told you then that I would wait for you, and I have.'

'Jack, please let's not fight on the street. I'm going to the café to let you get changed. Please come, I owe you an explanation.'

Jack watched her go before closing the door. He sat down on the stairs and buried his head in his hands. He couldn't believe what had just happened. He knew what she was going to say: that their relationship was over. That their six years together and his nine months of waiting now counted for nothing. Why couldn't she have told him then, instead of leaving him in limbo for so long? He had been loyal to her in these last nine months, staying steadfast and refusing Julia's not-so-subtle advances. What an idiot. He was angry with her for treating him this way. It wasn't like her. He contemplated not going to the café, but was also desperate to know what she wanted to say to him. If she was going to end their relationship, it would be better to know than to be left hanging. He got dressed and walked slowly to the café.

Marianne was sitting at a table facing the door, looking as if she was waiting to conduct an interview. The small café was nearly full. The weekend clientele, a mix of families with children and couples, gave the place a different atmosphere from when Jack breakfasted here before work. He took the seat directly in front of Marianne. The waitress appeared and asked him what he wanted. 'Nothing, thank you,' he answered. What he wanted to say was, 'Marianne, I want Marianne.'

Jack had dreamed of this moment almost every day since Marianne had left. In his fantasy it was the kind of reunion that inevitably plays out in the final scene of a movie, when absence has made the heart grow stronger and the lovers live happily ever after. They would hold hands and tell each other that never again would they be apart. He would ask her how she was and where she had been. He would tell her how much he had missed her... He had imagined sharing the stories he had been storing up to tell her, stories such as the boating incident and his not-so-immaculate conception. But this was not the reunion of his dreams. And so all he said was, 'Okay, what is it you want to tell me?'

Marianne took a deep breath. 'I'm sorry, Jack. I'm so sorry.' There were tears in her eyes.

It suddenly all became horribly clear to Jack. 'It's Michael, isn't it?'

Marianne was thrown. 'What? Michael? No, this is nothing to do with him.'

'Bullshit,' Jack spat with venom. 'You've slept with him, haven't you?'

'Of course I haven't, Jack.'

'I don't believe you. Michael spent a weekend in Paris last month. He was with you, wasn't he?'

Marianne looked helpless. 'Jack, please calm down. You've got this wrong. It's not what you think.'

'He was with you, wasn't he? Tell me the truth. You owe me that at least.' Some of the other customers turned at the sound of Jack's raised voice.

'I did see Michael in Paris,' Marianne said quietly. Jack had an immediate, visceral reaction, a tightening in his stomach. He felt his whole body tense as he clenched his fists. 'But it's not—'

The anger surged up inside of Jack – hurt, humiliation, betrayal, embarrassment, but above all, anger. He grabbed a glass of water from the table. Something stopped him hurling the glass at the wall, but that was the limit of his restraint. Keeping his grip on it, he chucked its contents all over the floor and then pushed back his chair, which fell noisily to the floor behind him. The café went silent. Everyone turned to watch him. Without another word or even a glance at his ex-girlfriend, he stormed out.

CHAPTER TWENTY-SIX

Hitting the fan

June 1999

The shit had well and truly hit the fan, as they say.

Surveying the wreckage of the business, Wilfred reflected on whether he could have done anything differently. It had been his first assignment that had involved a family business, and as he swilled his whisky in its tumbler he hoped it would be the last. He cut a lonely figure that evening in his local. In response to the barman's, 'Tough day at the office?', Wilfred nodded and murmured, 'You could say that.' His intervention with the Cambridge lawyers had done the trick; the police had dropped all charges against Royston.

Michael remained implacably opposed to Royston returning to the business, insisting there was no smoke without fire and that he must have got off on a technicality. To everyone other than Wilfred, Royston's sudden release was a mystery. All anyone, Royston included, knew was that the police had new evidence that explained that the payments had nothing to do with Mr Merriweather's death. Wilfred was intrigued that Royston appeared genuinely bemused by it all. He didn't even seem to know much about the payments, even though they had swelled his bank account significantly. 'I don't pay attention to that sort of fookin' stuff,' he had said.

It proved impossible to convene a board meeting to discuss Royston's future because Jack had disappeared. Michael had applied for a restraining order against Jack after he had turned up outside his London flat, threatening to kill him. Michael called the police, who arrested Jack for disturbing the peace, using threatening and abusive language, and smashing a communal flowerpot outside the apartment block. When he first heard of the incident, Wilfred assumed the disagreement was to do with Royston, improbable though it seemed that Jack would have got quite so worked up about his embalmer-in-arms. Monica put him right. 'Jack thinks Michael fucked his girlfriend.'

'Oh fuck,' said Wilfred. 'Did he?'

'Who knows,' said Monica. 'I wouldn't put it past him.'

As it happens, Michael hadn't fucked Marianne, although not for lack of trying. As soon as he heard from Cat that she was working at the Picasso Museum in Paris, he booked himself on the Eurostar, intent on seducing his brother's girlfriend. He was to be thwarted in this attempt. Marianne had successfully broken the spell of the Merriweather brothers, was happily settled in Paris and very much in love with her newish French boyfriend. She had been surprised when Michael appeared one morning unannounced at the museum. Once she had composed herself, she invited him to join her and her boyfriend for dinner. Michael had been left in no doubt that evening that his opportunity had passed; his only not insignificant consolation was that Jack had lost the love of his life. It took all of Marianne's powers of persuasion to get Michael to promise not to break the news to his brother. The following morning Marianne started to write to Jack before deciding she needed to tell him in person.

On returning to London, Michael found a shoulder to cry on in Cat. The shoulder quickly turned into a hug. Before they knew it, Cat and Michael became, much to their surprise, a couple. Cat told her friends that she was a rebound girlfriend, explaining in her self-deprecating way that only she could be a rebound from a relationship that had never existed. As is the way of things, Cat then became pregnant.

As for Jack, no one knew where he had gone. He had disappeared off the radar.

With his sibling out of the picture, Michael argued with Wilfred that they should proceed with business as usual. 'We can't just shut everything down and wait for my little brother to get his head together. We need to make some decisions. If Jack can't be bothered to turn up, we must move on without him. And as Royston is still suspended because we need a board resolution on whether to readmit him, we must also proceed without him.'

Wilfred disagreed; he argued that the four remaining board members were an insufficient quorum. He was particularly mindful of Mr Merriweather's insistence that the business should be an equal partnership between Michael and Jack. In the absence of a board meeting, Michael went ahead and fired Royston.

Royston, meanwhile, talked Monica out of resigning. He told her that he would be fine, there were plenty of other opportunities for him with his specialist embalming skills, and anyway, he had recently been made aware of a small windfall from his former boss. 'Besides,' said Royston, 'I need someone on the inside because one day I'm going to get even with that fookin' fooker.'

Wilfred had called Jen to ask for her advice, support, or indeed anything. Any hopes he had entertained a few months ago that Michael and Jack would be able to find a way to work together had been well and truly dashed. Wilfred was shocked at how quickly Michael had evolved from an uptight junior accountant into a destructive dictator, seemingly unconcerned about the consequences of his actions. Feeling that things had spiralled beyond his control, Wilfred needed to speak with someone who still had some semblance of sanity. 'Have you got a Chinese proverb that might help?' he asked her.

'*Que sera sera*,' she said. Jen seemed remarkably sanguine about it all, explaining that rifts in family businesses happened all the time.

'I'd hardly describe this as a rift,' said Wilfred, 'it's a little more than a family tiff.'

'Maybe,' said Jen.

Wilfred asked, 'Whose side are you on, anyway?'

'I'm on my side,' Jen had said.

It was quiet that weekday evening in the Distressed Lamb. Wilfred nodded at a couple of locals at the bar. He rarely visited the pub, even though it was only just around the corner from his home, so he knew these men's faces, but not their names. On the few previous occasions Wilfred had come here, it had been in the company of his wife, but she was out tonight, and he felt the need to take refuge in the comfort of the pub, with its glowing fire, low lighting and quiet conversations. The whisky helped, too. He began to think through the ramifications of what appeared to be an irreconcilable breakdown between the Merriweather brothers.

He remembered that Michael had proposed right at the outset that he should lead the business and Jack be a sleeping partner. At the time, Wilfred had advised that such an arrangement would not be in keeping with their father's wishes, but now he wondered if, perhaps, it was the only option left. Could Michael have intended to engineer such an outcome all along? If so, Wilfred was impressed. When he first met him, he would never have guessed that Michael had it in him to be so Machiavellian. Wilfred considered whether he could reinterpret the will to cover the scenario that Michael had engineered. It certainly wasn't what Mr Merriweather had wanted, but maybe there was an argument for it. If nothing else, it would buy some time. Given what had happened in these seven short months, it wasn't inconceivable that the pendulum would shift in the other direction in a year or two... But who was he kidding?

They say nothing is certain in life other than death and taxes, but Wilfred could now add a third certainty: the eternal enmity of the Merriweather brothers.

He decided not to rush into any decisions but thought he should probably begin to explore what might be needed should the nuclear option in the will need to be invoked. Were that to happen and the financial incentive removed, he doubted that either brother would choose to remain in the business. God only knew what would happen to it; presumably, he would have to sell it. Wilfred wasn't entirely sure who would be the beneficiaries of such a sale. He needed to check. And then he would need to get the brothers to return the money they had already received. What a mess.

Wilfred finished up his whisky and walked out into the summer evening, praying for a miracle.

Michael was relieved to be rid of Royston and felt it worth the subsequent fallout. Jen had provided wise counsel during this time. She had made it clear that it was a decision she wouldn't have taken because Royston was a cornerstone of the business, but she could see the merit of Michael asserting control and removing any dissenting voices on the board. She was less forthcoming about how they should respond to Jack's disappearance – no one knew how that would play out. She managed to mollify Monica, who had resigned from the board in protest, but then agreed to continue doing her job to help hold the business together. Monica made it clear that she was doing so for her old boss and her colleagues, for whom she felt responsible, and not for 'his little shit of a son'. Jen thought that, despite Monica's evident anger, they could probably trust her.

Managing Royston's departure had been much harder. He had sued for constructive dismissal and, according to the lawyers on both sides, had a watertight case, despite Michael's argument that it was unreasonable to expect him to employ a man suspected of killing his father. Jen came up with the solution of allowing Royston to front up a management buyout, on highly favourable terms, of the five homes they wanted to prune. There was some risk in creating a competitor, but Michael was dismissive of any threat Royston might pose as a business adversary. 'I'd be much more worried about letting him stew in his resentment and then him mugging me in a dark alley than in any damage he could do to the business. I'd back us in a battle of profit and loss sheets with Royston any day. Besides, you always say it's better to keep your enemies close. This way he's in our sights.'

For all her apparent calm, Jen had some anxiety about the business and, more particularly, her role in it. She was fascinated by Michael's reinvention as a despotic leader. While there was a certain logic to his decision, he was making some pretty high-risk moves. Jen had no choice but to throw herself into it, but she was already finding it harder to maintain the work-life balance that had been fundamental to her decision to change her job in the first place. Mindful that her subsidised placement had another five months to run, she resolved to keep an open mind on her future and do her best to enjoy the ride.

There was now, finally, equivalence in the brothers' relationship. Michael blamed Jack for their mother's death, something that was hardly Jack's fault. And Jack blamed Michael for stealing Marianne, something Michael hadn't done. Over such misunderstandings, wars begin.

PART THREE

Endgame

CHAPTER
TWENTY-SEVEN

Man of importance

Hertfordshire. November 1999

'I love it,' Cat whispered in his ear. Michael loved it too. It was ridiculously extravagant. Neither of them had ever bought property before, and yet here they were contemplating the purchase of a six-bedroom Grade II-listed Queen Anne country house. Michael didn't know what questions he should be asking. The house was spectacular, with its long gravel drive, lined with mature oak trees, and its beautifully proportioned frontage. The rooms were more than a decent size, too, each at least three times as big as his London apartment; there was land, twenty acres of it; and it all seemed to be in good shape. How else to judge a house? Michael didn't have a clue. At least Cat seemed to be asking sensible questions about electric sockets, damp-proofing and water pressure.

Their agent, a senior partner at Boyle, Boyle and Boyle, clearly sensed they were a soft touch and for all his superficial charm and obsequiousness, couldn't disguise either the envy or contempt in his patronising comments. Michael guessed he was from old money: in other words, living off an inheritance that had steadily lost value over the generations while retaining all its sense of entitlement. The agent gave every impression that this was the kind of house he thought he should be living in, rather than this young undertaker who, rather humiliatingly, was his client. It was precisely the kind of home that his grandfather, or great-grandfather, had owned before the family descended sharply on the scale of social mobility, marooning him as a provincial estate agent struggling to cover the fees of a third-rate private school. He had been keen to impress upon his clients that he was top dog in the Baldock office of Boyle, Boyle and Boyle, and, now that he had the measure of Michael's lack of house-buying confidence, all his deep-rooted class consciousness rose to the surface in subtle but discernible ways. An impartial observer would have assumed that the man from Boyle, Boyle and Boyle owned the place and that Michael was a visiting tradesman. Not that Michael was bothered: he was too enraptured by the prospect of setting up home in a fantasy house like this with his soon-to-be wife.

In the eighteen months since his father had died, Michael had metamorphosed from a cautious accountant into an avaricious risk-taker. He was unrecognisable to his friends, who were transfixed by his changed personality.

Michael was rolling the dice in every aspect of his life. Each success, he told himself, was evidence that fortune favours the brave. With Royston out the picture and his brother gone walkabout, Michael was keen to press home his advantage while he had no opposition.

In the five months since the boardroom coup, Michael and Jen had forced through a significant cost-cutting programme. They had quickly transferred the five unwanted homes to Royston, who had incorporated them as a separate business. There had been some dispute over the name of his new venture. 'You can't fookin' stop me from using my name.' The lawyers agreed, and Merriweather's soon found themselves competing with Royston's Funeral Home in Royston and some of the surrounding villages.

Michael and Jen introduced some sophisticated new management reporting systems. They streamlined the business processes, which enabled them to cut headcount. Monica, the trooper that she was, faithfully and skilfully carried out her role as executioner. She did as she was told, even though it was pretty clear her heart wasn't in it. The monthly board meetings continued. Wilfred had relented and decided they were quorate, at least for the time being. As there were now only four of them in the meetings, they tended to be little more than an update for Wilfred on the state of the business and progress against plans.

'It's all good; we're making the right moves,' said Jen. 'But we need to be cognisant of the potential risks from the pace of implementation.'

'But aren't they just the kind of moves we always used to advise our clients to make when we were at Abel's?' Michael asked. 'And then got frustrated when they didn't take our recommendations or moved too slow.'

'Yes,' said Jen hesitatingly, 'but that's the great thing about being an adviser. You don't have to live with the consequences of your recommendations.'

'But they made sense. We made good recommendations. And as you just said, we're making the right moves here.'

'Yes, but I've got this little voice of caution that tells me that advisers tend to make their recommendations knowing that their clients will never quite be so foolhardy as to implement them.'

'You're joking, aren't you?'

'A little bit, yes, but there's a difference between theory and practice. Being an adviser is not the same as being the client. I'm only really beginning to appreciate that now that I've crossed sides.'

'We're doing a great job. We've streamlined the business, we've cut the dead wood and we've got a great management reporting system. We've brought the business out of the dark ages; we're turning it from a corner-shop enterprise into a properly structured and professionally run operation. What's the problem?'

'I agree that each decision we've taken makes a lot of sense; it's just a lot in a short space of time.' Jen was conflicted between urging caution and supporting quick, decisive action. She wondered if she was overcompensating for years of frustration with indecisive clients who hesitated to take her blindingly obvious recommendations. Michael was behaving as she had always wanted her clients to act, and yet she was worried about the risks he was taking in what was an increasingly high-stakes game.

'Yes, but it needed to be done. We've laid the foundations for a highly profitable business.'

'Yes, but to play devil's advocate, those foundations have cost a lot of money, and, although they're creating the conditions for longer-term profitability, they do contain some risks.'

'You keep talking about risks. What are these risks?'

'Do you remember that model, Johari's window? We used a version at Abel's to help assess risk.'

'Remind me.'

'It's the idea that there are some things you know and some that you don't know.'

'The unknown unknowns?' Michael was reminded of the time that Jen had talked their client through this on the project they had worked together on at Abel's. It hadn't been an especially successful intervention. The client, paranoid at the best of times, had been completely spooked by the notion that there were dangers out there that he hadn't even known about.

'Exactly,' said Jen. 'There are some risks we know about, such as the teething problems of introducing a new reporting system within a company for whom the whole thing is completely alien. That's a big known known. We have a number of those. Then we have some unknown knowns, such as the impact of Royston's new venture, or indeed how the remaining staff at Merriweather's will respond to the enforced departure of some of their colleagues. I'm worried about staff morale. We're also struggling to recruit against our vacancies. That's another known known that worries me. We don't know why we can't find the right people, so that's an unknown known. And then there's Y2K. Who knows what's going to happen to our new computer system at the turn of the century in a couple of months' time? The doomsayers will have us believe it will go into meltdown. And then there's your brother. I would say he's a known unknown.'

'A known bastard, more like.'

'I know you're inclined to dismiss him, Michael, but not knowing where he is, or what he's going to do, represents a significant risk, given that he owns half the business. And then there are the unknown unknowns. And we don't know about those.' Jen paused. 'We're also tight on cash at the moment. Our various investments have cost money. We should be okay providing everything runs to plan, but we're vulnerable should something unexpected happen.'

'Well, you're a bundle of laughs, aren't you.'

'I'm only preaching caution and making sure that we make decisions with open eyes.'

'I appreciate that – I do – but we'll be okay. The one thing this whole experience has taught me is to have the courage of my convictions. It's all too easy to agonise about what might go wrong and end up procrastinating, whereas I'm finding that things seem to fall in place if you just get on and do it. And if they don't, well then we can deal with that when it happens. After all, if I had never plucked up the courage to ask you to join me in this venture, we might still both be stuck at Abel's.'

Jen didn't correct Michael, but wondered whether it was a case of hubris creating a distorted reality. He hadn't plucked up the courage. *She* had suggested it. It worried her that he was rewriting recent history to suit his heroic narrative. She also needed to talk to him about her future. She had extended her placement from Abel's for another six months, but thought it unlikely that there would be a further extension and was beginning to consider her options. Now wasn't the time to discuss that with Michael, though.

Standing in the hall of the mansion he was contemplating buying, Michael turned to the man from Boyle, Boyle and Boyle and asked, 'How long has this been on the market?'

'Well,' the estate agent said slowly, 'that's not a factor for exclusive properties like this.'

Michael waited for him to elaborate. He didn't. 'Why's that?'

'It's only right for a small number of people.'

'You mean, not many people can afford it?'

'Yes, but it's more than that. We only show properties like this to the right kind of person: those who truly appreciate their beauty and quality. The owners have lived here for three generations. They don't want to sell it to any old Tom, Dick or Harry.' Had he said any old Delroy, Mohammed or Ravi, Michael might have believed him. The estate agent oozed prejudice beneath his veneer of mannered politeness.

'So how long has it been on the market?'

'Not that long. Given that it's such an exclusive property.'

'Yes, but how long. I would like to know.'

'Well, I suppose it might have been on our books for two and a half years.'

'Two and a half years!' Michael was shocked. 'Why?'

'It's not that long for a property like this.'

'It's a fuck of a long time. There must be something wrong with it.'

'Not necessarily. There aren't that many people who can afford it, for a start. There have been a couple of offers.'

'What happened to them? Were they from Tom, Dick or Harry?'

'No, they were good people with the right kind of credentials. One of them was an accountant. Like you.'

'I'm not an accountant. I'm an undertaker.'

'Yes, but you're an accountant really. Professional, not trade.'

'So why weren't the offers accepted?'

'Too low. The owner is insisting on the asking price.' Had Michael been a true accountant, he would never have contemplated paying the inflated asking price for such an extravagant piece of real estate. But he wasn't. He might have been an accountant by training and, less than two years ago, by nature. But now he was a changed man. He was an all-conquering warrior, a risk-taker who knew no limits.

Michael paid a £350,000 deposit to secure the £2,350,000 dream house. The additional costs of buying the property cleared out his bank account. However, he calculated that it was still within his means. He had received £400,000 of his inheritance and he took a small salary from the business. The security of his quarterly payments of £100,000 meant that Michael knew he would have little trouble covering the mortgage and the costs of furnishing their new home. If not exactly to the manor born, Michael felt it sealed their union and signified his arrival as a man of importance.

CHAPTER
TWENTY-EIGHT

The tapping foot

Swindon. March 2000

Eight months after he had last seen Jack, Wilfred received an unexpected call out of the blue. 'Hi, it's Jack. Can we meet? I'll come to Swindon.' They agreed on a time the next day. 'Oh, and one other thing, please don't let Michael know we're meeting.' As he put down the phone, Wilfred thought Jack sounded different. More clipped – but maybe that was just his imagination. He wondered why Jack wanted to meet. And he was curious as to where he had been all this time. Jack had moved out of his room in the funeral home and hadn't been seen since. There hadn't been space in their brief phone conversation to ask, but Wilfred supposed he would have the opportunity to find out when they met.

Wilfred felt some guilt that the business had continued in Jack's absence without his representation. He very much doubted Jack would have supported Michael's brutal cost-cutting programme. As far as Wilfred could tell, the business appeared to be on course to improve its profitability, although he did have some niggling concerns that Michael and Jen might be stripping it of its heart and soul. But what did he know; he was only a lawyer with limited experience of the machinations of business. It didn't feel right, though, that Michael was running the show unilaterally without any consideration whatsoever for his brother. Wilfred, through his lack of objection, felt complicit in this and hoped Jack didn't call him out for siding against him.

As he waited for Jack to arrive, Wilfred felt apprehensive. He hoped that Jack was going to tell him that he was ready to return to the business and let bygones be bygones. It was unlikely, but what other options did Jack have? The more he thought about it, the more Wilfred realised that, although he needed Jack to return to his position on the board, such an outcome would bring untold difficulties. Wilfred couldn't imagine that Michael would relinquish his power and share it with his brother, nor could he envisage Jack willingly sitting back and letting his brother get on with it.

At some point, it would fall to him to determine that the brothers had failed to comply with the wishes of their father. He would then need to unwind the arrangements of the will. He had undertaken some tentative steps towards exploring what this would involve, which had only brought home the undesirability of such a course of action. He had identified the whereabouts of Sheila, the second

Mrs Merriweather, and knew how to contact her if he had to. The two brothers had, to date, each received £400,000. Wilfred had no idea how he would retrieve this money and baulked at the prospect of having to take legal action against them. It was also far from clear what would happen to the business if they walked away from it. At this rate, Monica would be the last woman standing.

The doorbell rang. Jack was ten minutes early. Just like his brother, thought Wilfred. Seeing him at the door, Wilfred caught a glimpse of a family likeness. Funny that he had never noticed it before, but Jack's profile, with that pronounced jawline, bore a strong resemblance to his father. Perhaps it was because his hair was shorter, but for a brief flash Wilfred had the disorientating impression that he was facing his old client. Jack was less effusive in his greeting than his usual exaggerated bonhomie (which Wilfred had always assumed to be an advertising agency affectation). He sensed Jack might be nervous. He didn't appear in the mood for small talk, giving every impression in that fleeting moment on the doorstep of just wanting to be invited in so that they could get on with it. Whatever 'it' might be.

Jack declined the offer of a coffee, and, ignoring Wilfred's enquiry about his wellbeing, launched straight into the reason for his visit. 'Look, I've come here to say that this arrangement is not working, nor can it ever work. My brother has always made it clear that he doesn't want to work with me; and now, after how he's behaved, there's no way I'm prepared to work with him.' Wilfred tried to maintain his impassive lawyer's face. Jack continued, 'I realise this will cause some complications and I'm sorry about that. To date, I've received £400,000 in payments from the Trust. I can pay that back. You just need to let me know to whom. Presumably the Trust?'

Wilfred nodded. 'Yes, yes, it would be to the Trust.' He couldn't contain his curiosity. 'But what about the car and the money you've spent?'

'I returned the car within two weeks. The dealership was surprisingly good about it. I think they're hoping I'll be back.' Jack rolled his eyes. 'As if.'

'But what about everything else?'

'I hadn't touched the inheritance other than for the car. I'm assuming I won't have to pay back the salary I took from Merriweather's as that was for services rendered. Not that I was allowed to render any services. I have, though, saved the salary I've received over the past six months and can return that if required.'

'Is there any way I can persuade you to change your mind?'

'No way. Don't think I haven't thought this through from every angle. It's not easy to walk away from two million quid. And you know what, I would have loved to take on the business. It's such a shame that my father didn't talk about it with us before topping himself. I don't think my brother and I could realistically have ever worked together, but I now know that I could have taken the business on from my father.'

Wilfred couldn't help noticing how Jack avoided using

Michael's name. 'I think, deep down, I may have the undertaking gene.'

'All the more reason for sticking with it and finding a way of making it work.'

'You know that's not possible. Surely you can see that. I tried – you know I tried. But my brother has crossed a line. There's no coming back from that. I want nothing to do with him.' Jack struggled to contain the anger he so obviously felt. 'In that respect, he's got what he wanted.'

'But can you just walk away and leave him with your father's business?'

'I'm not sure he'll stick with it when he's no longer being bribed to do so. He hates it. But if he did happen to stay – yes, it would be tough to see him running it into the ground and destroying everything my father worked so hard to build. But what choice have I got? I need to move on. Before all this, I never expected to go into the family business. I didn't care one jot about it. And I'd never even thought about any possible inheritance. So I just need to wipe the slate clean and pretend none of it ever happened. It's been an experience, and I've learned a lot, but now I just need to get on with my life.'

Wilfred couldn't put his finger on it, but there was something about Jack that wasn't quite ringing true. He got the distinct impression that Jack wasn't being entirely truthful with him. For someone who had always been very open and worn his heart on his sleeve, Jack was unusually controlled today. They say that most communication is non-verbal. Although his legal training had taught him to focus on what was said rather than left unsaid, even Wilfred could tell there was more to it than Jack was letting on. He noticed that Jack was tapping his foot as he spoke. It was as if he had to release his nervous tension somewhere. 'So what are you going to do?' Wilfred asked.

'I dunno. I might go back to advertising.' It seemed improbable to Wilfred that, after eight months of soul searching, and having taken the momentous decision to walk away from two million pounds, Jack wouldn't know what he was going to do. But Wilfred decided not to press it. Changing the subject, he said, 'I'm sorry, but I need to ask this: can you confirm that you understand that your stepmother and her daughters will become the beneficiaries of your father's will?'

'Yes, I understand that.' Jack remained impassive, but his telltale foot told another story.

'And you're happy with such an arrangement?'

'I wouldn't say I'm happy, but I understand and accept this is as my father wished.' The two men then discussed the process of untangling the will. Wilfred outlined what he thought were the next steps, although there were several points he wasn't entirely sure about, and some things, such as the destiny of the business, that would depend on what Michael decided to do. Jack was disappointed that it couldn't all be resolved there and then; he just wanted to get it done and walk away from it all. He offered to make himself available to sign anything as required, but was adamant that under no circumstances was he prepared to be in the same room as his brother. He also requested that it all be processed as quickly as possible. Wilfred tried to caution against rushing it, but Jack said, 'Look, I just want this done and dusted. I need to put it behind me. Please do everything you can to execute this as fast as possible. I'd appreciate that.' And with that, he left. The meeting had taken a little over half an hour. He gave Wilfred a new telephone number and made him promise not to share it with anyone else.

After Jack had gone, Wilfred sat back in his chair and let out a big sigh. He remained in that position for some time as he gathered his thoughts. Then he picked up the phone and dialled Michael's number.

CHAPTER TWENTY-NINE

Ali Bongo magic

Hertfordshire. March 2000

Finally, they were out of the Portakabin. It had served them well, but it was always temporary and didn't accord with Michael's vision of turning Merriweather's into a twenty-first-century business. They were three months into the new millennium, and Michael was determined to consign the practices and processes of his father to the archives of a bygone age. Although he hadn't pushed the boat out to quite the same extent as he had with the purchase of his home, the new office – a renovated school building on Market Hill – nonetheless, constituted a significant investment. Jen had cautioned him on whether it was sensible to be taking on a new ten-year lease with so much other change going on. 'There's no time like the present,' said Michael, 'and anyway it makes sense to get the office sorted when we're implementing the new system.' Jen put her concerns to one side. Michael was a man on a mission and no longer as receptive to her counsel as he had once been.

It was on their second day in the new office that Michael took the fateful call from Wilfred. He had driven to work for the first time, from his recently purchased Queen Anne mansion ten miles away. Michael had kissed his pregnant fiancée goodbye that morning, before driving his new Jaguar slowly along their long drive. He savoured his surroundings. The car was so quiet that all he could hear was the crunch of its wheels on the gravelled drive. Michael felt the Jaguar was a classic marque befitting a man who had made it. New home, new office, new car; everything was coming together.

On the one hand, he couldn't believe his luck; on the other, he saw his present circumstances as just reward for his bold decision-making. What were the lines of that Rudyard Kipling poem? 'If you can keep your head when all about you are losing theirs…'? Well, he had certainly done that. And he had met with triumph and disaster, and come out of it just the same. Well, almost the same. Confidence was the difference. He had learned to believe in himself. Michael reflected on how his father had trusted his ability to take on the business. He wondered what he would think if he saw him now. He would be impressed, Michael thought, conveniently forgetting his father's wish to unite his two sons.

It was a perfect day in a perfect week in a perfect life. Nothing was going to ruin it. Not even Wilfred's call.

Wilfred, who had anticipated a completely different reaction, was thrown by Michael's response. 'Good,' was all he said.

'I'm not sure you've understood. I don't think it's in any way good.'

'I understand perfectly. Jack is now finally out of my life. What's not good about that?'

Wilfred was bemused. After the call, he paced around his office in a state of agitation. A disturbing notion had supplanted his concern about the challenge of sorting out the mess: Michael may have taken leave of his senses. He tried calling Jen, but it went straight through to her answerphone.

Jen was at that moment being debriefed by Michael. Like Wilfred, she was struggling to see the upside and similarly beginning to question the sanity of her colleague. 'But don't you see,' said Michael, 'I'm free of him. It's the first sensible thing he's ever done.'

'But Michael, what about the business?'

'What about it? I don't think this makes any difference, other than removing the minor complication of my brother. Wilfred seems to think I would be able to keep the business.'

'But without the safety net of your inheritance, the business is extremely precarious. Remember, you're only taking a nominal salary at the moment because you have other income.'

'With the steps we've taken, the business will soon be making good money.'

'And what about your inheritance?'

'I never wanted it. It's blood money.'

'You might never have wanted it, but you've done a

pretty good job spending it in the last few weeks. You'll have to sell the house.'

'I'm not doing that. Cat loves that house.'

'Michael, get real, there's no way you'll be able to keep that house.'

'I'm sure there'll be a way.'

'How?'

'Look, only this morning I was thinking about that Kipling quote about keeping a level head, whatever life throws at you. What was that proverb you told me when we first discussed this over breakfast in that café? The one about the winds of change?'

'When the winds of change blow, some people build walls while others build windmills.'

'What's this if not a wind of change?' Michael smiled.

'I would say it's a fucking tornado.'

'Jennifer Ng. That's the first time I've ever heard you swear.'

'And that's the first time I've ever heard you use my full name. Seriously, though, I can't believe your reaction to this. I'm not sure you're facing up to reality. Perhaps you're in shock.'

'Maybe, but what else can I do? We're on a journey. I'm damned if I'm going to let my brother destroy everything. I don't want to be dictated to by his little whims. Sure, this is going to be challenging – but no one's died.' Michael checked himself. 'Well, quite a few people have died and here's hoping that many more do, but you know what I mean.'

'Well,' Jen took a deep breath, 'on the basis that it never just rains, I should probably let you know where I am right now.'

Returning home that evening, Michael opened the heavy oak front door to hear Cat shouting from the kitchen, 'You're back earlier than I expected. I've got loads to tell you.' Greeting him in the hall, she embraced him and said, 'It's so good to see you. I've missed you. How was work, darling?'

'There's some good news and some not so good news. What would you like first?'

'Let's get the not so good news over with first. Then I must tell you some thoughts I've had about the house. So go on, what's your news?'

'We probably need to sit down – I need a drink.'

'That sounds ominous.'

They settled in the kitchen where Michael told his fiancée about Wilfred's call. 'So the bad news is that I lose the inheritance and need to pay back the £400,000 I've already received. Oh, and Jen has just handed in her resignation. Yes, that's the bad news.'

Cat was dumbfounded. She couldn't equate the enormity of what Michael was telling her with the impassive tone with which he was delivering the news. It was as if he was telling her the photocopier had broken. 'What about the house? There's no way we'll be able to afford it.'

'It'll be a challenge.'

'What do you mean a *challenge*?' Cat was getting increasingly agitated. 'The £350,000 paid for the deposit, and the quarterly payments from your inheritance covered the mortgage payments. How can we possibly pay for it without that?'

'I honestly don't know. I'll find a way.'

'How. You're not Ali Bongo.'

'Who?'

'"My name is Ali Bongo, and I come from Pongo, Pongo-tiddly-pongo land."' Cat let out a slight laugh, but more as a nervous release than anything else. 'My father used to say that whenever we wanted money. He was a magician who conjured it up.'

'Well, we might need someone like that.'

'You said there's some good news.'

'I'm free of my brother. I've won.'

Cat was stunned. 'You can't mean that.' The brief levity of Pongo-tiddly-pongo land was replaced with anger. 'Is that all this is to you? A battle with your brother? What about us? Is that all I am to you? The spoils of victory?'

'No, of course not. You know that. I shouldn't have said *won*; I couldn't help myself. I suspect Jack probably thinks that he's won, too, as he's shafted me so effectively. But the reason it's good is that we could never have worked together. That was my father's pipe dream. The whole thing was divorced from reality. So that problem's resolved.'

Cat was beginning to wonder if she had got Michael all wrong. At times there was a psychotic quality to her fiancé that unnerved her. She knew that he was pathologically opposed to his brother, but right now it occurred to her that he might just be certifiably mad.

The unpalatable thought crossed her mind that she might have made a huge mistake in allowing herself to be swept up by her emotions and the excitement of her new relationship. They say falling in love is the loss of all reason. She had been settled in London, but then she got swept up with Michael, got pregnant and – before she knew it – found herself in Hertfordshire. Cat was not one to bear regrets, and everything that had happened in the last year felt right, but when Michael talked as he was talking now she felt a shiver of dread run through her.

'What about the business? You said Jen has resigned.'

'Yes. That's the bad news.'

'You're joking?'

'No, I'm not. Jen's departure, if she leaves, would be a real body blow.'

'You seemed to be suggesting Jen's departure is bad, but the rest of it, the fact we might lose the house and be destitute, is not so bad.'

'I'm sure we'll find a way to keep the house. We're here now. They can't just chuck us out.'

'They bloody can. If we don't make the mortgage payments, the bank will have us out in no time.'

'We'll make the payments.'

'How? You're going all Ali Bongo again.'

'I'm going to make a success of the business. Trust me; I'll find a way.'

'And you're going to do this without Jen?'

'Yes, that's why it's terrible that she wants to leave. I need her. I refused to accept her resignation.'

'How did she take that?'

'Okay. We agreed to talk about it when things have calmed down a bit.'

'What, when we're out on the streets you mean?'

'We're not going to lose the house.'

'Why does Jen want to leave?'

'The extension on her placement with Abel's finishes in a couple of months. She says the business can't afford her salary and she can't afford to work for free. She said there's an opportunity for her to get involved in her father's business. It seems that her experience of working in a family business has led to her helping out her father over the past few months, and she thinks there's an opportunity for them to develop that business.'

'Enough to pay for her salary?'

'I don't know. Jen plans on supplementing it with some consultancy work. Abel's are quite keen to get her back and so she thinks she might be able to cut some kind of deal with them.'

'That sounds good for her. How will you persuade her to stay?'

'I don't know. Perhaps I'll use some of that Ali Bongo magic.'

Cat returned to something Michael had said earlier. 'You know you said that Jack probably thinks he has won.'

'Yes.'

'I doubt he thinks like that. I can't believe he would do such a thing out of spite.'

'Why would he do it, then? He could have found a

way to suck it up and just take the money. He had been so keen to find a way of making it work. I'm not sure what's changed, but he's gone off on one. I'm pretty sure this is an act of vengeance. That's why I'm so determined not to let it take me down.'

'Do you think he knows about us? Or even this?' Cat patted her belly.

'I don't know, but it's interesting that he's made his move now. It's almost as if he somehow knew that this week would be the worst possible timing for me, given that we've just taken on the house and the new office. It makes me wonder… But I don't want to think about him; I've got more than enough on my plate. As I said, the good news is that I don't have to worry about him anymore.'

CHAPTER THIRTY

Chrysanthemum assault

Hertfordshire. June–December 1999

At his father's funeral, Cat had accused Jack of being a wimp. Her exact words, which had stuck with him, were: 'At some point in your life, Jack, you need to stand up for what you want and not run away when you can't get it.'

Well, now he was doing precisely that. The moment he found out about Michael and Marianne was the moment he knew what he wanted. Revenge. And while it might have appeared to his brother that he had run away he was, in fact, doing precisely the opposite.

Admittedly, he had completely lost it after storming out on Marianne in the café. Foolishly, he had tried to break into Michael's apartment the next day to confront him. He hadn't given a moment's thought to what he would have done had he managed to get in. He wasn't, at that point, thinking at all. When his break-in attempt was frustrated by a locked door to the apartment building (for all his talents, Jack wasn't cut out to be a cat burglar), he had taken out his anger on a flower pot. Getting arrested for assaulting a pot of chrysanthemums wasn't his finest moment. A few hours in the police cell, though, had brought him to his senses. He needed to think it through properly: he needed a plan. By the time Julia arrived to pick him up, he was even able to smile when she said, 'Who's been a naughty boy then? Beating up chrysanthemums. The lads will be impressed.'

The first move in Jack's plan was to go underground. He had to get away from Michael and the business, which meant moving out of the funeral home. When he called Julia from the police station, Jack asked her, 'Can I stay with you for a few days while I get my head together? I'll sleep on the sofa.'

Julia had replied, 'Of course you can; you can stay as long as you want. But fuck the sofa.'

Despite liking her privacy, Julia was only too happy for Jack to move in for a few months while he sorted himself out. She was delighted that Marianne was now out the way, and that Jack, at last, felt free to sleep with her. She'd always known it would happen eventually. At his request, she didn't tell anyone, not even Dale or Clayton, that he was staying with her. On the one occasion that she bumped into Monica in Royston High Street, she breezily waved away her enquiry about Jack's whereabouts, saying, 'I've no idea. Last I heard, he was pretty upset about his brother stealing his girlfriend and just wanted to get away from it all.' For those first three months, Jack hardly left Julia's place as he diligently worked on his plan for revenge. Her small cottage on the edge of an out-of-the-way hamlet was a perfect hideaway, and, once she had adjusted to the relative lack of privacy, Julia found she quite enjoyed having a man about the house who had dinner on the table when she returned from work.

At first, all Jack could think of was how to destroy Michael and Marianne's relationship. Julia managed to coax him away from that by telling him that Marianne had gone and he needed to let go of any hope of getting her back. 'Quite why you're still obsessing about that little tramp after what she's done to you, I've no idea' was her way of saying it. As he began to put some distance between himself and Marianne's betrayal, Jack accepted that Julia was right and that his enemy was Michael, not Marianne. Jack lost himself in the teachings of Sun Tzu. He could almost recite the whole of *The Art of War* from memory and began to imagine himself as a medieval Chinese warlord. Time, and the comforts of both Julia and her cottage, were helping heal Jack, who paid particular heed to Sun Tzu's advice to 'ponder and deliberate before you make a move'. It was seven or eight months before he would meet with Wilfred to renounce his inheritance. He had plenty of pondering and deliberating to do.

Jack first needed to decide what he wanted. To borrow from the terminology of his advertising agency days, he needed *clarity on his desired outcome*. Once Julia had helped him shift his focus from Marianne's betrayal, he began to consider what revenge might look like. This led him to the realisation that he wanted to humiliate Michael by outwitting him at business. Nothing galled Jack more than Michael's arrogant presumption that he was incompetent. (Nothing, that was, other than that the bastard had gone and fucked his girlfriend.) He decided that he would prove beyond all doubt – to himself, to Marianne, to his dead father and everyone else – that he was a more capable businessman than Michael, and, by doing so, push him off his pedestal.

Once he knew what he wanted, everything else began to fall in place. He knew it wasn't an option to go back into the family firm while Michael was there. Either he had to get Michael out, which seemed impossible – or, not to be defeatist about it, challenging in the extreme – or he had to set himself up as a competitor. The prospect of starting a viable undertaking business from scratch with no apparent funding made this an equally unlikely option. But then something happened that made Jack think the gods might be on his side after all. Julia brought news from the local grapevine that Royston had left Merriweather's and was taking over five of their discarded homes. Jack jumped for joy on hearing this. He knew Royston hated his brother almost as much as he did and might therefore be a willing accomplice in creating a hostile competitor to Michael. Jack didn't know whether Royston would want to join forces, but at least the opportunity was there. The old Jack would have impulsively picked up the phone to Royston there and then. The new Jack knew he had to bide his time, carefully plan his moves and wait for the right moment to approach Royston with a proposition he couldn't refuse.

In the embers of the twentieth century, with people's thoughts turning to how they might celebrate the New Year's

Eve of their lifetime, Jack hunkered down. He spent days interrogating his father's will, trying to find a route through its carefully constructed conditions and caveats. There was no option, he eventually concluded, but to walk away from his inheritance. Once he reached this conclusion, he felt strangely liberated. Again, it was a decision that led to greater clarity.

Rather than wait for Wilfred, Jack chose to take the initiative in disinheriting himself. Not immediately – he had fully absorbed Sun Tze's teaching that, in war, timing is everything – but as soon as the time was right he would make this move. Months, and the turn of a century, would pass before he put his plan into action.

Jack's sacrifice would also have the benefit of depriving his brother of his inheritance. At the time, Jack didn't suppose this would be a body blow to Michael, who had always claimed he wasn't motivated by money – although having two million pounds taken away from him would surely test whether he was as unconcerned about it as he claimed. Jack wished he could engineer a situation where he could be a fly on the wall when his brother found out.

He was, though, less concerned about Michael's lack of inheritance than the implications of losing his nest egg. Once he had worked out how to repay what he had already received, it dawned on him that he would need another source of income. In fact, to compete with Michael, he would need access to some serious money. It was Julia who came up with the brilliant idea that would help all the pieces fall into place. Not that Jack thought it was brilliant when she first suggested it.

'No way. I'm not going to do that. Just don't go there.' He was appalled by the suggestion.

'But why not? What have you possibly got to lose?'

'She's a viper, that's why not. There's no way she would agree to it.'

Julia persevered with her idea. 'But surely that depends on how you present it. Right now, she has no idea she's in line to inherit anything. If you get to her first, you could strike a deal with her.'

'I couldn't possibly trust her.'

'I'm sure there must be a way. I bet your Chinese geezer would find a way. You could get a lawyer to write up a watertight contract.'

The more Jack thought it through over the subsequent days, the more he realised that Julia was right. He had found it hard to stomach the idea that his detested stepmother would be the main beneficiary of him walking away from the will. It was this that had given him most pause for thought before eventually resigning himself that there was, sadly, no alternative. But now Julia had shown him a possible other way out. Given that his stepmother knew nothing of her imminent fortune, even a proportion of it would constitute a significant windfall. He could present her an ultimatum with two options. The first would be that she got a portion of the inheritance, say a million pounds. The second option would be that she got nothing and the status quo remained as it was. She didn't need to know that Jack had already decided to disinherit himself, irrespective of whether or not she accepted his proposal. Julia was right:

the Chinese geezer did have something to say about it: 'All warfare is based on deception.'

And so, a few weeks later, after a considerable amount of sleuthing to ascertain her whereabouts, Jack found himself nervously knocking on the door of a small house in Great Dunmow. When he had discovered that the second Mrs Merriweather, now Mrs Cartwright, lived in a prosperous market town, and remembering his father's complaints that she had done well out of the divorce, he presumed she must be relatively well off. He was quickly disabused of such a notion when he found she lived on the outskirts of Great Dunmow on a nondescript estate. While not deprived, it certainly wasn't the kind of place anyone with money would choose to live. While he waited for someone to answer the door, a tabby cat rushed up to him and started brushing his leg. During the drive over, Jack had tried and failed to remember what his stepmother looked like. While she had loomed large in his childhood as a wicked-stepmother figure, he realised that he had precious few first-hand memories of her. Apart from the occasional random sighting in the years after the divorce, Jack had not seen her or his two odious stepsisters since he was around five years old. But he had decided to take the risk of making a surprise visit. He wanted to get a better idea of what he was dealing with before revealing his hand.

His intended subterfuge failed the minute the door was opened by a friendly-looking lady in her early thirties who said, 'Why, if it isn't young Jack Merriweather.'

CHAPTER THIRTY-ONE

Serial stepmother

Essex. January 2000

The tabby cat pushed past Jack and ran inside, tail up. The lady, whom Jack assumed must be his stepsister, turned to shout into the house, 'Hey, Mum, look what the cat brought in.' Turning back to Jack, she smiled and added, 'Only joking.' Jack, whose guard was high, wasn't sure whether or not to believe her.

'I'm sorry, but are you…' Jack hesitated, '… Jenny?'

'Good guess, a fifty per cent chance, but I'm afraid you got it wrong. I'm Karen. Do come in and say hello to Mum.' Jack had not been expecting such a warm, cheerful welcome. He had planned to pretend he was a lawyer following up family connections to the late Mr Merriweather. He hadn't counted on being recognised and cursed himself for such a rookie error. Perhaps he wasn't cut out for undercover detective work after all. Furthermore, his preconceptions about a frosty, unfriendly atmosphere also seemed wide of the mark. His stepmother was seated on a sofa in a cosy, almost too warm, lounge. She got up, a little uneasily he noticed, to greet her guest. Karen said, 'Mum, do you remember Jack Merriweather? Your stepson?' She supported herself on a walking frame and smiled at him. Jack was surprised at how frail she was. His father had only been in his early sixties, and so, even if she was older than him, she couldn't be any more than in her mid-to-late-sixties herself. And yet she appeared much older. Meanwhile, she seemed genuinely pleased to see him. 'Yes, Jack Merriweather. I do remember you, although you're much bigger now than when I last saw you. To what do we owe this pleasure? Please make yourself comfortable. Karen, put on the kettle.'

Jack realised he needed to recalibrate. Sun Tze's advice was to know your enemy: it was becoming all too apparent to Jack that he had badly misjudged his. For a start, they didn't come across as enemies at all. The two women were charming. Jack had expected his stepmother to be both distrusting and untrustworthy, and, on this assumption, he had set up a complicated scheme of watertight contracts and a web of bank accounts. His plan was for the inheritance to go first into a joint account that appeared to any outsider to be in his stepmother's name; the funds would then be diverted into their respective personal accounts, but only with both of their signatures. As they chatted, Jack felt that trust was less likely to be the issue than that his stepmother seemed so sweet and caring that she might object to being party to anything that cheated her other stepson out of his inheritance. 'I'm afraid I wasn't a good stepmother to you,' the old lady was saying. Jack refocused. He couldn't afford to let his mind drift. 'I don't remember. I was only young.'

'It's true. I wasn't. I got better at it later, although I'm not sure I ever made a particularly good stepmother.'

'I'm sorry, what do you mean, "got better"?'

'Mum's a serial stepmother,' said Karen.

'A serial stepmother?'

'Yes, she's done it five times.'

'Five times? I'm sorry I don't understand.'

'She has a weakness for widowers.' The second Mrs Merriweather nodded her head sagely in agreement with her daughter. 'It's true,' she said quietly.

Karen continued, 'She thinks she can rescue them, but it all tends to go wrong because, of course, no one can rescue a widower from his grief. He needs to rescue himself. Problem with Mum is that she has too big a heart and can't help herself.'

'It's true. I should have learned from my experience with your father. That was the worst. He completely shut down emotionally. But the real problem was your brother. He hated that I had replaced his mother. Even though he was only five or six at the time, he made my life hell and turned both your father and you against me. But it was my fault, really.'

'Yes, Mum, but that didn't stop you repeating your mistake a further four times.'

'I know, I know. I'm a silly old thing.'

'You wouldn't guess it, would you,' said Karen, 'but my mother, your stepmother, has had six husbands.'

'Just like Henry the Eighth,' chuckled the second Mrs Merriweather, 'well, not that he had husbands, but you know what I mean.'

'Six husbands, two daughters, eight stepsons and five stepdaughters.'

'But I've stopped now. My gallivanting days are over.' She gave Jack a conspiratorial wink. He reciprocated with an admiring smile. 'But that's enough gossip about me. Tell us about yourself. You haven't said why you're here.'

Jack wanted to be truthful as possible, but he also needed to find the best possible way to present his proposal. He told his story by airbrushing his brother out it as much as possible. He explained how he had recently lost his long-term girlfriend, whom he had thought was the love of his life. He did reference his brother when he said that they had both gone to work in the family firm after their father's death, but skated over the reasons for his subsequent departure. Jack wanted to maximise the impact of when Michael, in his full Machiavellian glory, was shown to be the evil villain of the piece. He needed them to ask him about Michael. When they did, he wanted to give them the facts as unemotionally as possible so that the gravity of Michael's 'crimes' would reveal themselves without his embellishment. Jack was deploying his talents as a storyteller to full effect.

'How's Michael? You haven't said much about him.' Karen was the first to rise to the bait.

'To be honest, I don't have too much to do with him now. I haven't seen him for a while, but I think he's happy. He's got a new girlfriend.'

'That's nice. Have you met her?'

'I have, yes.' Jack paused for dramatic effect. Having laid it on thick when describing how Marianne had been seduced by an immoral older man who showed no concern for breaking up a beautiful relationship, he was now free to let them connect the dots. 'She was my girlfriend that I was telling you about.' Jack was pleased to see the second Mrs Merriweather's hand go to her mouth in shock.

'No,' said Karen. 'He stole your girlfriend?'

'I'm afraid he did.' Jack gave a helpless shrug of his shoulders. 'But what can you do. *C'est la vie.*'

'That's terrible, but how can you work with him after that?'

'To be honest, that was part of the reason why I left the family firm, although only a small part.' Jack paused.

Karen couldn't wait. 'What was the other reason?'

'We had different ideas about how to run the business.'

At the mention of the business, Jack's stepmother said, 'Is dear Royston McGinty still working there? He was a strange old stick, but I liked him. He and your dad were as thick as thieves, you know.'

'I did know that. And yes, I love Royston. My dad always credited him for the success of the business. To be honest, he's one of the reasons I left.'

'How come?' Karen was eating the story from his palm.

'Michael fired him.'

'No.' The second Mrs Merriweather let out a little gasp. 'Why, for the love of God, did he do that?'

'I don't think he likes him.'

'You can't fire someone just because you don't like them,' said Karen.

'Michael can.'

Jack then went on to explain, in as dispassionate a way as he could, that Michael was asset-stripping the firm and had fired many other long-serving staff as well as Royston.

Finally, the second Mrs Merriweather could hold back no longer. 'Ooh, he's wicked, that one. I hate to say it, but he's a bad 'un. He made my life hell when he was a little boy. I was always inclined to forgive him because he had lost his mummy, but now I think that maybe he was just a bad 'un all along. There's good 'uns and bad 'uns, and he's a bad 'un. It's as simple as that.'

Jack couldn't have put it better himself and was inwardly delighted that she had reached this conclusion herself, without the need for him to spell it out.

Without exactly saying as much, Jack successfully presented Michael as a cold-blooded accountant whose only interest was money and who was ruthlessly destroying everything that his father had built up. By comparison, and not entirely untruthfully, Jack presented himself as being primarily motivated by the wish to continue to build upon his father's legacy. He touched on some of his ideas for transforming the business and talked movingly about his revelation at his father's memorial service, when he came to appreciate, for the first time, just how interwoven the undertaking business was in the fabric of the community. By the time he had finished, his stepmother and stepsister were converted. Primed for his proposition, they were more than ready to join him in his fight against evil: the good 'uns against the bad 'un.

'I thought she was going to have a heart attack,' Jack told Julia when he got back home. 'She went completely quiet and looked as if she had stopped breathing when I told her that she stood to inherit a million pounds. In the end, she refused to take that much, saying that it was far too much money and she likes her simple life.'

'What about Karen, presumably she was less inclined to walk away from such a gift horse?'

'Yes, but like her mother, she was concerned about having too much. It was actually quite moving how humble they both were. But Karen could see the benefit of inheriting a certain amount of money. She thought it could be a good nest egg to cover the costs of providing care for her mum if she needed it. Needless to say, her mum thought such a suggestion was ridiculous, but we settled on half a million.'

'Wow. And they're okay with you having the rest.'

'Yes, mainly because they see that it's going to the noble cause of saving the business. They were embarrassed to inherit anything. They didn't feel they had any legitimate claim to it and so were absurdly grateful that I should have engineered a situation whereby they got anything at all.'

'I can't believe it. That's so different from what you feared might happen. So different from what you expected.'

'I would say this, wouldn't I, but I honestly think it's Michael's fault. It seems he completely poisoned the relationship and managed to turn both me and my father against them. It shows what he was capable of, even at such an early age. Obviously, it's not *all* down to him, though. As Karen said, marrying a widower while they're still grieving is not the most sensible thing to do. All my stepmother's subsequent marriages also failed to stay the course, although I got the impression that none of the others were quite so uncomfortable.'

Julia had loads of other questions for him, but she was also bursting him to tell him about something she had heard at work through the Boyle, Boyle and Boyle grapevine. 'The pompous ass who runs our Baldock office has just sold the most expensive house on our books.' Jack usually loved Julia's gossip on the domestic goings-on in Hertfordshire, but his head was full of his success in Great Dunmow, and so he was only half-listening to his girlfriend now. In fact, he wasn't listening at all. 'Do you want a glass of wine, love? I could do with one.'

'Did you hear what I said?'

'Something about pompous asses.'

'Jack, you need to hear this. Your brother has just gone and bought himself a two-million-pound house. Not only that, but it sounds as if Marianne is pregnant.'

'Fuck. How do you know that?' Jack felt as if he had been punched in the stomach. It was the 'Marianne is pregnant' bit that got him.

'As I said, one of my colleagues sold the house.'

'But how do you know Marianne's pregnant?'

'I don't know for sure, but it sounds like that's why they're in a hurry to buy a family house. Not quite sure why that means they need to buy a six-bedroom Grade II-listed Queen Anne country house, but there you have it.'

'I don't know what to say.' Jack poured two large glasses of wine and slumped down on the sofa. 'I don't know what to think. Fuck. Marianne's pregnant. I can't believe it.' He felt a wave of rising anger swell inside of him. 'Fucking bastard. How could he do that? I'll kill him.'

'It's not all bad news, you know.'

'Oh yeah? Tell me what's good about my ex-girlfriend bearing my bastard brother's child.'

Julia, who had had all afternoon to think about it, said, 'Well, I imagine it won't do any harm to your little revenge play.'

'In what way?'

'You've always said it won't necessarily be too much of a problem for Michael to lose the inheritance because he's not that bothered about money. I guess he'll be a little more concerned about it now, after buying a two-million-pound house.'

'Gosh, you're right, you're so right.'

'Presumably, he'll have to mortgage himself to the hilt. Not only that, but he'll have to put down a substantial deposit, which will presumably wipe out anything he's already received. Furthermore, this house has been on the market for two and a half years. It's a stunning house, but there just isn't much of a market for that kind of property at that price. He's paid over the odds for it.'

Jack felt his mood lift as his excitement about Michael's increased stakes in the revenge game displaced his anger about Marianne's pregnancy. 'Jesus Christ, Julia, you're right. He'll be completely shafted if he loses the inheritance. Stuck with a house he can longer afford and is unable to sell. What a day.'

CHAPTER THIRTY-TWO

Funeral wars

Hertfordshire. February 2000

Royston was struggling. It had been a few months since he had taken over the five homes. He'd never been in charge before. His entire working life had consisted of being a pawn in the army's hierarchy, followed by doing whatever Mr Merriweather or Monica asked him to do. Although he grew to be a real presence in Merriweather's, he had never actually initiated any action. Royston simply embalmed bodies and did as he was told. He only began to appreciate the limitations of his experience when he found himself responsible for twenty employees and all decisions relating to his new business. The one decision he felt particularly proud of was the naming of his new enterprise – Royston's Funeral Service. But even that decision had encountered dissent. The funeral director of the Guilden Morden home objected that his patrons wouldn't want to be buried by, as they saw it, the townies of Royston.

The newly-fledged business owner protested, 'But it's me. I'm fookin' Royston.'

'It's more complicated than that. You're Royston of Royston. My customers will think of the town, not the man.'

'Well, fook them, then.'

'That's all very well, but I don't want to lose yet more customers to Merriweather's of Steeple Morden.'

'Well, fookin' don't then.'

'I'm just saying I think the name could be a problem,' said the funeral director of the soon-to-be Royston's Funeral Home of Guilden Morden.

'How about you put a fookin' picture of me in the fookin' window? Then they would know which Royston it means.' The thought of his brooding, bald, tattooed boss glowering at the villagers of Guilden Morden from the window of his funeral home shut the recalcitrant director up pretty quickly. He decided to cut his losses and accept the name change.

That was the easy bit. Royston's chief difficulty was that he had no idea what to do next. At one level he didn't need to do anything because the five homes were autonomous self-managing units. But there was a reason why Michael and Jen had shed these five homes. They were all failing businesses in need of investment and steadily losing custom to the Merriweather homes in neighbouring villages. Royston was fiercely loyal to all his employees, but even he could tell that the funeral directors he had inherited were not the best. Furthermore, they were all feeling beaten down by the stress of their circumstances. It had been a relief for them to escape the strictures of Michael's increasingly stringent cost-cutting regime, and now they looked to Royston as their salvation. But while Royston was an exceptionally good embalmer, he was no saviour.

And he certainly wasn't a businessman. This much quickly became clear in his first meeting with his accountant. 'What do all these fookin' numbers mean?' Royston had a single O-level to his name. He was disproportionately proud of his C grade in metalwork, not least because his mam had burst into tears when he got the result. She told him that he was the first McGinty ever to get an academic certificate. But it wasn't in maths, and, despite having sat through Michael and Jen's financial presentations, Royston didn't have a fookin' clue what any of it meant. His accountant explained that it said the business was fundamentally unprofitable, and that either Royston needed to cut costs or increase revenue. 'It's as simple as that,' said the accountant.

'How the fook do I do that?' Royston couldn't understand why the money he had put into the business was not enough. His accountant patiently explained that it might help, depending on what he did with it. He said that he needed to invest it to grow revenues, 'such as through advertising or tarting up the homes, for example', or in 'cost-saving systems that will help improve the productivity of your employees'.

'That's what that fookin' bastard Michael Merriweather is doing. He's replacing people with computers.'

'Well, maybe that could present an opportunity for you,' suggested the accountant. 'If your competitor is getting rid of people, their standards of service might drop. You could make personal service your point of difference.'

'Fookin' right.'

'But the problem is that your employees are currently underperforming from a financial perspective. Revenue per employee is way below what it needs to be. Either your staff need to get better, or you need better staff.'

Royston put his head in his hands.

It was therefore a particularly opportune moment for Jack to call. Royston, distracted by his issues, hadn't paid much attention to what had happened to Jack. He had, though, heard from Monica that Michael had stolen his girlfriend and that Jack had disappeared. He was initially wary when he heard Jack's voice on the other end of the phone, because, as far as Royston knew, Jack was still the competition.

'I'm not sure I should be speaking to you. You're the fookin' enemy.'

'I'm not your enemy, Royston. Far from it. If you can meet me tomorrow, I'll explain. I've got a proposition for you that may be of interest.' Royston was intrigued by the clandestine nature of their meeting. Jack made him swear not to tell anyone, not even Monica – *especially* not Monica. Jack suggested meeting at the Silver Ball transport café on the A10 and said he would be at the table in the far corner. If Royston happened to see anyone he knew in the café, they should abort their meeting without acknowledging each other and rearrange for another time and another place.

'What is this? Fookin' corporate espionage?'

'Sort of. And by the way, I'll be wearing a woolly hat and shades, so you might not immediately recognise me.'

Royston laughed. 'Fook me. This sounds like the fookin' funeral wars. Am I going to be safe? Are you going to fookin' knife me to get rid of the competition?'

As it was, the Silver Ball was very quiet when the two would-be conspirators met the next morning. There was a smattering of long-distance lorry drivers and a couple of bikers, who might have identified Royston as a kindred spirit, had they not seen him arrive in his decidedly uncool little red Ford Fiesta. Royston didn't initially recognise the shadowy figure in the far corner until he raised his hand.

'So what's all this about then, matey? What's with all this secret stuff?'

'I need to swear you to secrecy, Royston. If any of this slips out, it will ruin it.'

'Ruin what?'

'My plan to destroy my brother.'

Royston snorted. 'I like the fookin' sound of that.'

'Can I trust you, Royston?'

'Probably, but I don't fookin' know what this is about yet.'

'I'll have to trust you – I do trust you – but this is sensitive shit that I'm about to tell you. I'm afraid I'm going to have to ask you to sign this.' Jack passed a legal document to Royston.

'What the fook is this?'

'It's a non-disclosure agreement. If you sign it, you're

legally bound not to tell anyone about this conversation. I trust you, but I can't take any chances. When I tell you what I'm going to tell you, you'll understand why. I'm happy for you to think about it first, maybe take the advice of your lawyer. Not Wilfred, though. Definitely not Wilfred.' Royston's curiosity got the better of him, and he agreed to sign the NDA without checking it. His instinct told him he could trust Jack, whom he saw as his father's son more than his brother's brother.

Jack took Royston through the plan he had meticulously pieced together over the last few months. He explained how he'd tried to work with Michael as his father had wished, and how he had swallowed his pride as his brother had become increasingly despotic and dismissive of his role in the business. Eventually, he had accepted that it was never going to work. The final straw was when he found out that Michael had stolen Marianne. He wanted to kill him, but over the past few months his burning fury had abated and he had decided instead to destroy his brother at his own game. Jack explained how he wanted to join forces with Royston. He proposed to use the money he hoped to get from the diverted inheritance to fund their new business to compete with Michael's. 'As you said earlier, it will be the funeral wars. It'll be tough, but I think we can do it. After all, David beat Goliath, and we're going to have one helluva slingshot if the inheritance money comes through.'

Royston felt a surging sense of relief. He knew he was out of his depth with the business, and floundering. The prospect of a partner who would assume responsibility for strategising, and all the other stuff that Royston couldn't do, lifted a huge weight from his shoulders. He was also totally aligned with Jack's mission to destroy Michael. Overcome with emotion, Royston leaned over the table to hug Jack. 'I'm in. I'm fookin' in.'

Jack shared some of his thoughts about how they might differentiate their business from Merriweather's and how they could promote this difference through advertising. Royston had no idea what Jack was on about with all his talk of repositioning and branding, but he liked his enthusiasm and energy. Jack finished his monologue by saying that he thought this was the kind of thing his father hoped his sons might do with the business. He pulled out his father's letter and pointed to the bit that read, 'I don't know what you will do with it, but I would love to see it. I've taken it so far, but I can't take it any further. I just don't have the ability.' 'You see,' said Jack, 'he had the wisdom to know that the business needed more and the humility to realise he didn't know what it was.'

'He was a fookin' great man.'

'But all that's for the future. We mustn't run before we can walk. We need to take one small step at a time. Knowing where we're headed means that we can start to move in that direction. Our immediate priority is to make sure that we beat Merriweather's in our territory.' Royston shared his accountant's thought about competing on service. Jack agreed. 'I think that's right, and it chimes with my longer-term vision. And we have several other potential advantages. We're smaller and therefore quicker. We have the element of surprise; they won't be expecting this. We have communications expertise, which they don't have. And, most importantly, we have the best fookin' embalmer in town.'

Royston smiled. 'Too fookin' right.'

'Fingers crossed, we'll have a war chest at a time when Michael is going to be tight on money. Getting that inheritance is essential. I don't think we should move on this until that's confirmed, but we should prepare to move very quickly once we get the money. That could be another six months or so. Maybe more. Are you on for that?'

Royston nodded his head vigorously.

'Are you up for going into partnership with me? I know I'm young and inexperienced, but I'm the same age as Dad was when he took on the business. I've had a good grounding through my few months at Merriweather's, thanks to you and Monica; also, I've now completed my funeral director's course – graduated with honours – I'll have you know,' Jack smiled and rubbed his chest in mock boast.

'Hey, well done, matey. We should frame your fookin' certificate and put it up alongside my metalwork one.'

'I want you to think about this. Give it twenty-four hours at least; there's no rush. You need to be sure.'

'I'm fookin' sure. I don't need more time.'

'That's brilliant to hear, but do think about it. Call me tomorrow, having slept on it. I've had this draft partnership agreement written up; it covers all possible eventualities. You do need to read it, and I strongly advise you to get legal advice on it. Once we press the button there'll be no going back. Once we're ready, my first step will be to tell Wilfred that I'm renouncing my inheritance. That will then take a few months to work through. I'll need to remain undercover in that time. We can work through our plans together, but I must still seem to have disappeared as far as everyone else is concerned.'

'I never had no fookin' contract with your dad. I'll sign this if you want, but I don't need to pay no fookin' lawyer to tell me about it. I'll fookin' trust you. That's all there is to it.'

'I know I can do this. I know *we* can do it.'

'Of course, we fookin' can.'

CHAPTER THIRTY-THREE

A shot across the bows

Hertfordshire. October 2000

'Oh fuck,' Michael said to himself as he was greeted with a full-page ad on the second page of the *Royston Crow* with a bold deep red headline that read: 'Buried by an Accountant or by People Who Care? Your Choice.' Michael devoured the copy, which argued for a new kind of funeral service. The lozenge-shaped logo in the bottom corner featured the words 'We care' engraved on what looked like a wooden tablet, with the name 'Royston's Funeral Service' round its edge. It made no mention of Merriweather's, although it was clear to Michael that he was the target of this shot across the bows.

The second shot, he realised with a sinking feeling, was on the opposite page of the local newspaper. Its lead story was a profile on Royston McGinty. To Michael's astonishment, Royston was pictured in a tweed jacket, no tattoo in sight, and looking every inch the trustworthy gentleman rather than his usual scary, unemployed navvy look. The article quoted Royston as saying he had become increasingly disillusioned with the funeral business's focus on the bottom line at the expense of giving people the send-off they deserved. Although not mentioning Meriweather's by name, he explained that the firm he used to work for changed when it was taken over by the accountants. For those in any doubt, though, the article helpfully named Royston's previous employer later in the piece. Michael couldn't believe how fawning it was. It explained how Royston had taken it upon himself to do something about this unforgivable drop in standards. 'Because we don't want to go back to the days when they used to throw the corpses of paupers into pits,' he was quoted as saying. 'Mark my words, that's where the funeral business is headed, because accountants don't care about a dignified death. All they're interested in is making money.' Royston's Funeral Service, by contrast, the article explained, started and finished with the needs of its customers. Michael was horrified to read that as part of his commitment to put customers first, Royston was slashing the base cost of his funerals. 'Because what kind of society are we if we put people in debt simply to bury their loved ones?' Michael put the paper down and started breathing heavily. This can't be true, he thought. How can Royston possibly afford all this? I can't believe he's done all this by himself.

Michael then noticed that the end of the article directed readers to the paper's editorial. He turned to page eight and a headline that read, 'Dignity in Death'. The leader was little more than a manifesto for Royston's Funeral Service.

It concluded by saying that 'Mr McGinty, Royston by name and Royston by nature, has the *Crow*'s support in his battle against the money-men who seek to strip us of our dignity in death.'

Michael slammed the paper down in anger. Is this legal? he questioned. How can they do this? Most of all, he was dumbfounded that Royston could have pulled off such an audacious move, let alone afford it. Michael knew how much money Royston had received from his father and how little money his troubled homes were making. It just didn't compute. 'Cat,' he shouted from the breakfast table. 'Come and see this.' Silence. Michael cursed the downside of living in such a big house. It was impossible to communicate with each other. It seemed at times as if they inhabited different worlds within the same universe. It would be possible to go for days in this house without seeing one another. It struck Michael that if ever he tripped and knocked his head in his study, he could bleed to death over two days before anyone even realised he was at home. Ever since Amelia had arrived, Michael had felt he was a bit-part player in Cat's life. He adored his two-month-old daughter and loved being a father, but there were times when he felt usurped. Right now, with every other part of his life falling apart and feeling under enormous strain, he needed Cat's support and comfort more than ever. But she wasn't there for him. Well, thought Michael ironically, at least we'll soon be rid of the problem of too much domestic space.

Over the past seven months, since Michael took

Wilfred's call about Jack renouncing the inheritance, reality had started to bite. Michael's initial reaction had been to brush it all off and deny that it made any difference to anything. He had been quickly disabused of this notion by Wilfred, Jen, his accountants and, finally, his bankers. Michael had reluctantly come to accept that there was no way they could afford to stay in the house he had thought they were moving into for life. They had been given a stay of execution by the bank, who wanted to minimise their losses. Cat's parents, concerned for the wellbeing of their first granddaughter, had also helped out by contributing to the mortgage payments. And Michael had substantially increased his salary from Merriweather's to help cover his rocketing personal costs. But it was unsustainable in the long term. The bank held off from foreclosing, but insisted the house be put back on the market. Figuring that it would be easier to sell with the young family still in residence, they had also provided some temporary relief on the mortgage payments so that Michael could just about make ends meet. But there was nothing to spare. Michael knew that the best he could hope for would be to lose his £350,000 deposit, possibly more.

Realising Michael was unable to pay back the money he had taken out, Wilfred had managed to package it as a debt within the total inheritance, to be repaid as and when the beneficiary required. Having met Mrs Cartwright, Wilfred was confident that there would be no immediate pressure to return the money but advised Michael to prepare a repayment plan to pay it back over the long term. The other complication Wilfred had had to resolve was whether Michael could remain in the family business. Surprisingly, given all his meticulous planning, Mr Merriweather hadn't envisaged this scenario. With the benefit of hindsight, it seemed evident that the relationship with the two brothers might break down and that one might want to stay in the firm and the other leave. As it was, Wilfred was helped out enormously by Jack saying, 'He can have it. I just want out.' Wilfred thought this unbelievably naïve of Jack, as the business itself still had value. The most equitable thing to do would be for Jack to force a sale and for the brothers to share the proceeds, but Jack wasn't interested. Wilfred supposed that Jack must have had some form of a breakdown, so wholly did he seem to have taken leave of his senses.

Michael left for work without having had the opportunity to speak to his wife about the reinvention of Royston McGinty as a local hero and himself as the villain of the piece. He had found Cat curled up in bed with Amelia, both dead to the world. He left them in peace to recover from their own sleepless night, as he wrestled alone with the various demons crowding his sleep-deprived mind. His drive to work along the A505 often allowed him to order his thoughts for the day ahead, but not today. He made the mistake of turning on the radio, only to find Royston McGinty pontificating, surprisingly lucidly and without a single *fook*, about how he was on a mission to fix the shortcomings of the funeral business. Michael wanted to scream. His nemesis was coming at him from all angles. Then, as he entered the boundary of the town, he was confronted with a large poster that read 'Buried by an accountant or by people who care? Your choice.' There was no branding, but with the accompanying media blitz, there was no need for any: it was crystal clear to Michael and, he was sure, the residents of Royston, which firm the poster was promoting. Then, to add salt to the wound, as Michael turned the corner into the car park, he saw, to his horror, the same poster on the hoarding outside his office.

Michael stormed into the building and screamed at his secretary, a temp who had only joined two weeks ago. 'I don't care what it takes, but get that fucking shit off that wall now.'

'Jen, please call me as soon as you can. I'm having a terrible day and need some advice.' Jen had left five months ago. Michael had tried his damnedest to persuade her to stay, but they both knew that, once the arrangement with Abel's expired, there was no way the business could afford her salary. She had continued to provide Michael with some support and advice over the subsequent three months without charging him, for which he was hugely grateful. He knew she didn't have the time. Her commitment to her father's business, her consulting work for Abel's, not to mention the demands of being a single parent, occupied her every waking hour. But she felt guilty for having left Michael in the lurch and so helped out when she could. More recently, though, she had become less and less available as her other commitments had grown. Michael hadn't spoken with her for at least four or five weeks. He ended his message with, 'I'm worried that the winds of change are about to blow my windmill down and I want to know what your father would do in such a crisis.'

Michael's young secretary appeared in his office to tell him that the poster had been booked for the next three months. She told him it would be a criminal offence to forcibly remove it, not that it would be possible to do so without the proper equipment given that it was thirty feet off the ground. She then handed in her resignation, having taken exception to the way that Michael had spoken to her.

Later that morning, Michael's mobile rang. Seeing that it was Jen, he answered it. 'What's up, Michael? I tried calling the office phone, but no one answered.'

'It's a fucking disaster, Jen.' He recounted what had happened and finished by saying 'I don't know what to do, Jen. Help me. What should I do?'

'About the secretary? Just get another temp in immediately.'

'No, not the secretary. Everything else. The business. Royston. This hatchet job on me. I can't believe they're allowed to do that, it's libellous. And Royston's cost-cutting; I can't afford to compete, it'll kill us. How can he possibly afford to offer cut-price funerals? I thought his business was on its knees. Then there's my house. My losses...'

'The first thing you need to do, Michael, is calm down. Go for a walk.'

'I can't just walk out. My funeral directors are all going crazy. They want to know what to say to their customers.

Many have already called to complain about being ripped off. The phones have been ringing all morning. Employees, suppliers, customers all want to know what's going on. The national media are also on to it. I got a call from a *Sun* journalist who was trying to link Dad's suicide to this; God knows what they'll write. That's why we've stopped answering the phones. Not that anyone else is here to pick them up anyway.'

'Michael, you need to calm down. Everyone can just wait. You need to think this through and work out how best to respond, rather than running around like a mad thing trying to put out every single fire.'

'I'm not even doing that. I'm doing nothing. Jen, is there no way you can come back to help me out? Even just for a few days?'

'Michael, I'm really sorry, but I can't.'

'I'll pay you. Whatever it takes. Everyone has their price.'

'Michael, no. You know it's not about money, and in any case both you and I know that you can't pay me. The money's gone; now you need to use your wits. In your message you asked me what my father would do. When everything was going wrong for him in China, he hunkered down until he found a way to flee to Hong Kong.'

'You think I should hunker down and put my head in the sand?'

'Until you get it in a better place, yes. Not for long, because you don't have much time. In a crisis, you need to act quickly and decisively. But you do need to think through how to act first. Maybe it'll only take thirty minutes, but you need to get your head in the right place, and then spring into action. So I would go out of the office right now for a short walk, get yourself a quiet coffee, probably not in that local coffee shop we used to frequent because they know you there, but somewhere where you can sit quietly and not be disturbed. Then you need to start taking small steps.'

'What do you mean by that?'

'Right now you're overwhelmed because your problems seem too big. They're not. You need to chunk it down into manageable steps. Here's a thought for you: the person who moves a mountain begins by carrying away small stones.'

Michael smiled for the first time that day. 'I miss your Chinese proverbs.'

'Off the top of my head, I would say that one of those steps should involve setting up a crisis-management team which should meet as soon as possible today. You need to share the load. You then need to work out how to handle the media and decide whether to stay silent and offer no response, or whether to take a more aggressive position. As an immediate first step, you might want to put the phones on answerphone with a message that apologises for not being able to take the call and asks for a number to call back on. Then you should try to return all those calls as quickly as possible once you've worked out what to say. You need to find out more about what Royston is doing and how he can afford it. Is this a one-off blast that you might be able to sit out? Or is it the first shot of a sustained campaign that might demand a different response?' Michael groaned at the thought. 'And obviously you need to reassure your team that you're in control. Now is the time to show those leadership qualities of yours.' What leadership qualities? thought Michael weakly.

He did as Jen had suggested, though. He considered who should be on the crisis-management team, a war cabinet as he thought of it. He decided it should be small and include Monica and his two best funeral directors. Monica gave him pause for thought, as it occurred to him that she would have split loyalties, but she was essential to the running of the business. He had no option but to include her.

Monica arrived early for the meeting and asked Michael if she could have a quiet word. They went into his office. She handed him an envelope and asked him to open it. Michael asked, 'What's this?' It was her letter of resignation.

CHAPTER THIRTY-FOUR

Vulture's nest

Hertfordshire. October 2000

The toughest day for Jack to stay undercover was when Royston's new campaign broke. He had managed to remain incognito for the best part of the year, only meeting with friends who could be trusted not to expose him, or contacts who were prepared to sign his non-disclosure agreements. The first six months had been relatively easy as Jack had been nursing his wounds and had no desire to interact with anyone other than Julia. But since breaking cover by meeting with the second Mrs Merriweather and then Royston and Wilfred, as he began to execute his plan he became more impatient. Whenever he felt he was losing his self-discipline, he reminded himself of his ultimate goal to destroy his brother. Jack would force himself to imagine Michael and Marianne in bed together to stoke his anger.

There was a bigger prize at stake, though. Jack knew he needed to bide his time, but found it almost unbearable to sit by himself in Julia's kitchen on the day everything kicked off. He would have loved to witness the moment Michael saw the poster on the side of his office. He couldn't even call Royston to find out what reaction it was all getting. They had agreed that they should have no contact whatsoever for the first few days of the campaign, anticipating that Royston might be followed. He had been tempted to get Julia or one of her colleagues to hang around near Michael's office, but had cautioned himself not to take any unnecessary risks. The time would come when he could reveal himself as the wizard behind the curtain; indeed he knew precisely when that would be – but for now, he needed to remain invisible as he pulled the strings that would lead to his brother's downfall.

Royston, meanwhile, was feeling the pressure of being the centre of attention. 'I don't see why I have to wear this fookin' jacket for a fookin' radio interview. It's not as if anyone can fookin' see me.' The coach Jack had hired to help navigate Royston through the turbulence of media attention patiently explained to her grumpy client that he needed to give an appropriate impression to the interviewer. 'And Royston, do watch your language. Don't forget your training.' When he emerged from the interview twenty minutes later, she hugged him with relief. 'That was perfect. Well done.' Royston brushed off her praise; he just wanted to get back to embalming bodies. He struggled to see what all this poncy media stuff had to do with the business of burying people.

He was relieved to get back to the sanctuary of his office, where he was greeted by his three harassed colleagues, run off their feet fielding a barrage of mostly positive messages and a significant uptick in calls wanting to know about the company's reduced prices. Just as Royston was starting to feel overwhelmed, and was wishing Jack were around, Monica walked through the door.

'I've done it. Just as we agreed: I've resigned.'

The moment was all too much for Royston. All the emotion of the day came rushing to the surface. Lost for words, he started sobbing.

'I thought you would be pleased to see me.'

'I am. I fookin' am,' said Royston through his tears. 'I'm sorry, but it's all been too much.'

'I just walked out. Michael didn't say a word; he was speechless. He didn't even try to stop me. God, it felt good.'

Jack and Royston had taken Monica into their confidence two weeks previously and made her an offer with a substantially larger salary than she received at Merriweather's. They also offered to pay her legal costs should Michael sue her for walking out to go and work for the competition. It helped that she had never actually signed a contract with Merriweather's. Jack calculated that his embattled brother probably wouldn't have the will or the resources to take her to court anyway.

'So where do you want me to start? What needs doing?'

To be reunited with Monica made everything Royston had gone through over the past year worthwhile. He no longer felt alone and out of his depth. With Jack directing and Monica doing, he would be free to get on with what he knew best: tarting up corpses at the end of their day. But he wasn't there yet, as he was about to find out. As much as Royston wanted to hide away in the back room with his embalming fluids, he was going to have to be patient. He had just become the very public face of the battle between two brothers, and, until Jack stepped forward, he was in the firing line.

It was the double-page spread in the *News of the World* the following weekend that spooked Royston. He called Jack in a panic. 'Have you fookin' seen it?' Jack said he hadn't. 'It's brought up that fookin' stuff about my arrest again. It as good as says I fookin' killed your dad. That fookin' fooker of a fookin' brother of yours.' Jack told Royston he needed to get a copy of the paper. He called back twenty minutes later with the article open in front of him. The headline read, 'Hero or Villain?' An old black and white picture of a glowering Royston, looking every inch the villain with his prominent tattoos and aggressive scowl, dominated the page. Jack was impressed. His brother had decided to fight back and fight dirty. There was little doubt that Michael was the anonymous source quoted extensively throughout the article. And Jack was surprised; he had expected a response from his brother, but hadn't expected him to resort to the national press quite so aggressively.

In an attempt to mollify Royston, he said, 'Have you heard the saying that all publicity is good publicity?'

'Fook off. What's fookin' good about being accused of manslaughter in the *News of the Fookin' World*?' He had a valid point, but Jack knew they stood to gain more than Michael by keeping the story in the public eye for as long as possible. They had more resources and were more media-savvy than their adversary. Ultimately, they had the bigger story: the little guy taking on the money-men who were stripping death of all dignity in their greedy pursuit of profit. The speculation about whether Royston did it or didn't do it might be more lurid and sensational, but that storyline had nowhere to go. Unless, of course, there was any new evidence to suggest Royston's guilt, but Jack was pretty confident that Michael had played all his cards in that respect. The article in front of him only rehashed everything they already knew. Jack just needed to shift the focus back to the nasty, money-grabbing accountants.

Later that afternoon, Julia called the *Daily Mirror* with an exclusive story about the new two-million-pound home of the accountant boss of Merriweather's Funeral Homes. 'They're even paying me £2,000 for it,' she told Jack, struggling to contain her excitement. When the story appeared two days later, Jack and Julia were delighted to see that the ego of her boss had got the better of him when the journalists had called him for a comment. He was plastered all over the article to such an extent that he appeared to be its source. 'It was brilliant,' said Julia to Jack that evening. 'Apparently, he only realised the magnitude of what he had done, in terms of breaching client confidentiality, when Mr Boyle Jnr himself called him in for a bollocking. Up to that point, he was showing everyone the article, bursting with pride at being in a national newspaper, the stupid, arrogant prick. Anyway, I think there may be a vacancy at the Baldock branch pretty soon. Perhaps I should apply for it.'

Jack felt a brief pang of sympathy for his brother when he saw the article. Its centrepiece was a picture of Michael's mansion, taken from the drive to make it look palatial. The headline – 'Vulture's Nest' – ran across the top. A mugshot of Michael was in the top corner, too. There was no other way of describing it other than a hatchet job. Jack reminded himself that there is no love lost in war and that this was going to be brutal to the bitter end.

Jack was brought up short when he turned the page. 'Julia,' he shouted, 'come and look at this.' His heart was beating faster as he waited for her to join him and he tried to make sense of the picture in the paper. 'Here look at this,' Jack pointed to a long-lens photo in the article of Michael helping his wife get their baby into the Jaguar. Jack watched as Julia as moved to get a closer look.

'Bloody hell, that's Cat.'

'Exactly, what the hell's going on?'

CHAPTER THIRTY-FIVE

Fatal flaw

Hertfordshire. January 2001

The one benefit, the only benefit, to Michael of the *Daily Mirror* article was that it led to an offer on the house. Substantially less than he had paid, but an offer nonetheless, and one his bank said he had no choice but to accept. It meant he had lost nearly half a million pounds on the purchase, and 400,000 of that he owed to the second Mrs Merriweather. Cat's parents paid the difference, for which Michael was hugely grateful, but not half as grateful as he felt guilty. Put bluntly, he had fucked up big time.

By any measure, Michael had clocked up several significant failures since leaving Abel's. Not that he saw it that way. He thought his only mistake had been to overextend himself with the house, for which he cursed his stupidity. By his reckoning, it had been a single act of financial indiscipline – although, admittedly a substantial one – that had led to catastrophe. He had made one big mistake and was being punished for it.

Michael, his wife and young daughter had been forced to swap their mansion for his childhood home, the apartment above the funeral home that he so despised. The one place in the world he had spent his whole life running away from, his father's old house, was now his home. From afar, Jack smiled at the poetic justice of such a comedown. Cat put on a brave face at such an extreme change in their circumstances. Michael, who had dreamed all his life of giving his children a better start in their life than he'd had in his own, found that he was bringing up Amelia in the self-same awful prison he had endured. He made sure the deep storage room, where the bodies were stored, was triple locked. The extra security might protect his daughter from an inadvertent encounter with a corpse, but returning to the scene opened the door to all his old nightmares.

Humiliated, impoverished and sleep-deprived, Michael resolved never again to put himself in such a position. Seduced by the adrenalin of power and dizzy in love, he hadn't been himself. The lesson he thought he had learned was not to take risks. But to admit just one mistake and only take one lesson, that of restraint, from the last year was still, arguably, delusional. He needed someone to help him see what he couldn't see himself; but the fact was that he now had no one else to tell him the truth.

Michael was well and truly on his own, having lost his whole leadership team. Such a loss pointed to numerous mistakes, but Michael didn't see it that way. He continued to have a blind spot about his brother, unable to see that Jack could have had a constructive role to play in the family business. He was pleased to have got rid of him and fatally incurious about what he might be doing with himself now. It never occurred to him that Jack could be an adversary, let alone that his own actions had turned him into one.

Michael had also underestimated how important Royston and Monica had been to Merriweather's. Not only had he allowed his prejudices to colour his judgment, but he had never taken the opportunity to get to know and understand the business properly. Had he done so, he might have appreciated that they were the glue that held the whole thing together. The old Mr Merriweather had known it, and Jack knew it. Together again, Royston and Monica now represented a significant competitive threat, but Michael failed to see it. Not only had their departure weakened morale within the firm, but having them agitating on the outside was doubly dangerous because they had the potential to unsettle the friends they had left behind. Even though Royston's Funeral Service continued to eat into Merriweather's business in its home territory, Michael convinced himself that the threat would pass. He still believed he would prevail in the long run.

Michael's only real regret was the loss of Jen, but he post-rationalised her departure to convince himself that it was never going to be sustainable for her to remain in the business for long. He told himself he had been lucky to have had her for fifteen months. He may have been right in this respect, but an alternative account of events might conclude that Jen would have stayed for more than those fifteen months if Michael hadn't messed everything else up.

It could have been different had he been prepared to work with his brother and had his actions not precipitated the loss of the inheritance money that was going to underpin all their bold plans. Then the business could have afforded Jen and she might have been more inclined to stay.

It would be fair to say that Michael was not demonstrating a great capacity for self-awareness in this time of need. He applied the same hairshirt resolve to the business as had been forced on his domestic life. He stripped the firm back to basics, letting go of the office lease and taking out all the central overheads, other than himself. Michael believed the fundamentals of the business were now in reasonably good shape and that the homes could more or less run themselves. His role was to oversee the financials through the system he had recently installed. Now, he told himself, was the time to hunker down. He thought he was taking different and more decisive action. Everyone else, meanwhile (and most notably his employees), saw him behaving just as he had since taking over the reins of the business: he was continuing to be the asset stripper that he had been pilloried as in the media. He was fatally flawed, but couldn't see it. And it was just about to get a whole lot worse for him.

Answering the phone, Michael was surprised to hear Wilfred's voice. The two men had had no contact since Wilfred had tied up all the loose ends surrounding Mr Merriweather's will. Michael had been grateful to the lawyer for engineering a stay of execution by arranging to convert the £400,000 he owed into a long-term debt to the second Mrs Merriweather. It was, though, extremely uncomfortable to be indebted to that woman. Michael didn't feel he could trust her – but he had no choice. Wilfred had assured him that she was delighted with her unexpected inheritance and so might be inclined to forget about the loan. Over time, Wilfred had speculated, it might be possible to appeal to her largesse and persuade her to write it off as a fair and just settlement of his father's will. Michael's memory of his uncaring and vindictive stepmother didn't square with Wilfred's account of a sweet, gentle old lady, so he thought this an unlikely outcome. He resolved to pay it back over time from the proceeds of the business. But Wilfred's call was about to kibosh that plan. 'I'm afraid we have a problem,' said Wilfred, 'or, to be more precise, I'm afraid *you* have a problem. A big problem.'

CHAPTER THIRTY-SIX

Hot Wheels

Swindon. January 2001

As his train passed the three large chimneys of Didcot Power Station, Michael remembered the first time he had made this journey to Swindon. Then, he had had no idea what was in store for him; now, he wished he *didn't* know. He recognised the ticket collector and wondered if every day since their last encounter had been Groundhog Day for him: checking tickets on the same train at the same time with an occasional angry passenger to break the monotony. Michael wanted to ask him what had happened in his life over the past two and a half years. He wore a wedding band. Had he sat down with his wife for dinner at home on every one of the 910 evenings that had passed since he last clipped Michael's ticket? Did he have children, and, if so, had they had left home? He was old enough for it. Perhaps a grandchild or two had arrived since he had last seen him. Maybe it was a complete coincidence that he was on the same train at the same time. Perhaps his job involved more

295

variety than it appeared and took him all over the country… Michael thought of everything that had happened to him since he had last met the ticket collector and felt some envy for the mundane life he assumed he must lead.

The train drew into Swindon on time. Unlike before, Michael was in no hurry to get to Wilfred's office. They can wait, he thought to himself as he stopped for a cup of coffee at the station. He thought about Jack. He had been shocked to hear from Wilfred that Jack, and not the second Mrs Merriweather, owned his debt. Wilfred sounded shocked as well. 'I have no idea how he pulled it off,' he had said over the phone. 'When we met, he gave every impression of wanting to make a clean break from it all. He certainly fooled me.' Michael realised at that moment that he had severely underestimated his little brother. He had been outmanoeuvred. Unlike two and a half years ago, Michael accepted Wilfred's invitation for the three of them to meet in Swindon. He had no choice. The fight was draining out of him. He was well and truly beaten and had no more cards to play.

Wilfred's office was unchanged other than that it was now immaculate. The front door was clean, the pictures on the walls were perfectly aligned, and the empty chairs were tucked under the table. Jack was already there, sitting, Michael couldn't help noticing, at the head of the table. He didn't get up when Michael entered the room; he hardly even looked at him. He simply offered a perfunctory, 'Hello, Michael.' And in those first five seconds, Michael knew this was not going to be a time for forgiveness and reconciliation.

Once they had all sat down, Wilfred started to open the meeting, but Jack cut across him. 'I think we can keep this short.' Michael noticed that Jack was still struggling to look him in the eye. He seemed uncharacteristically uncomfortable and appeared to be addressing the table. He was also tapping his foot. 'I asked Wilfred to call this meeting because I have a proposition for you which requires the presence of an independent, objective and legally qualified witness.' He paused. Michael and Wilfred exchanged a glance. For the first time in all of their interactions, Jack was clearly in control. 'As Wilfred will have told you, Mrs Cartwright and I—'

'I'm sorry, but who is Mrs Cartwright?'

Wilfred, pleased for the opportunity to be able to contribute, answered Michael's question. 'She's your father's second wife, the beneficiary of your father's will.'

Mrs Cartwright and I came to an agreement, which, among other things, has meant that your £400,000 debt has passed to me.' Jack paused again to be sure that this had sunk in. 'I don't know if you remember, but when we were young I once accidentally broke one of your Hot Wheels cars. You were insistent that I paid for it and wouldn't let me owe you the money, even though you knew at the time I couldn't afford it. Ironically, it was our stepmother who lent me the money, but not without a lecture about not playing with your toys. The lesson you taught me was that one must pay their debts. Whatever the cost.' Wilfred smiled inwardly at Jack's sangfroid and thanked his lucky stars that he was an only child.

'I'm sorry, but I haven't got £400,000. I promise to pay it back over time, but I can't now.'

'That's what I said about your Hot Wheels car.'

'It's not the same.' Michael began to feel the fight return. He had intended to accept his fate, but he wasn't going to be humiliated by his sanctimonious little prick of a brother.

'The principle is precisely the same.'

'I haven't got the money.'

'That's your problem. You shouldn't have bought that house. Lovely place, by the way. Julia and I had a look around after you vacated it.'

'Who's Julia?'

'Julia's my girlfriend. She works at Boyle, Boyle and Boyle.' Jack paused to let this little bombshell sink in. He didn't know if Michael would connect the dots and was pleased when Wilfred asked, 'Who are Boyle, Boyle and Boyle?'

'They're the estate agency that handled the sale of Michael's house. They did very well out of it. Two sets of chunky commission in a matter of months.'

'Your fucking girlfriend works at Boyle, Boyle and Boyle? She was the source of that leak?'

Jack was delighted that Michael had made the connection. 'No, of course not, she works at a different branch.'

Michael sat back heavily in his chair as something else struck him. 'You bastard. I always thought the timing of your renouncing the inheritance in the very same week that

I moved into the house was unfortunate, but you knew, didn't you? You fucking knew. It was no coincidence. You timed it to fuck me up completely.'

Now Jack looked Michael straight in the eye and smiled broadly. He had been nervous about the meeting, but was beginning to enjoy himself. He had spent most of the morning remembering all the little humiliations his brother had subjected him to over the years, to ensure he didn't go soft at the denouement. Deep down, he still wanted to impress his brother, and he didn't know whether he had it in himself to execute his revenge plan through to its conclusion. When Michael had first arrived in Wilfred's office, looking every inch the beaten man, Jack had become uncomfortable with the thought of turning the knife. He knew Michael was fundamentally decent and, although he couldn't show it, he felt a degree of compassion for his brother. But then Michael had reverted to his former bullying type, and Jack regained the resolve he needed to see it through.

Michael was beside himself with rage as he pieced together how his brother had artfully managed his downfall. But there was more to come. Jack hadn't yet given him the full picture.

'More coffee, anyone?' Wilfred broke the brooding silence. He feared it could turn physical. He didn't want blood on his recently vacuumed carpet. He might have chosen to serve the dead, but a corpse in his office would not be good for business.

The intervention helped Michael recompose himself.

'Look, I can't pay. I just don't have that kind of money.'

'Where there's a will there's a way. Isn't that what you once said to me, Wilfred?' The lawyer nodded meekly. 'I didn't have the money for your Hot Wheels car, but I found a way.'

'Shut up about that fucking Hot Wheels car.'

'Oh, and that reminds me, I nearly forgot. Silly me.' Jack reached inside his pocket and produced a small toy car, which he placed on the table with a theatrical flourish. 'You wouldn't believe how much this cost me. They don't make them like this anymore; I got this from a collector. It's in pristine condition and exactly the same as the one I broke all those years ago. I know I've replaced it once already, but out of the goodness of my heart, I've got you another one. A little reminder of your moral that a man should always pay his debts.'

Michael didn't know what to do with himself. He wanted to storm out of the room and slam the door behind him. He just wanted it to all be over but realised he had to suck it all up. Losing his temper would achieve nothing. Jack had engineered his entrapment so flawlessly that there was nothing he could do other than take his punishment. 'If I could pay, which I can't, when would you want it?'

'Immediately. I paid back my £400,000 months ago.'

'I honestly don't see where I could get the money. I don't think the banks will lend me anything after what's happened. Cat's parents have already helped us out, and there's no way they've got that kind of money.'

'I thought that might be the case,' said Jack, who

started fumbling in his briefcase. He brought out some documents, which he laid on the table in front of him.' I asked my lawyer to draw up papers to force involuntary bankruptcy.'

Wilfred gasped at Jack's audaciousness and cruelty. Michael just stared at his brother and said, 'But if I'm declared bankrupt, you won't get your money back.'

'I might get some of it, but, to be honest, it's not about the money. I've got more than enough.'

'What the fuck is it about, then?'

'You know perfectly well. It's about revenge. You fucked my girlfriend; you took every opportunity to demean me—'

'What?' Michael was bewildered. 'I never slept with Marianne.'

'Don't lie to me. I know you went to her in Paris.'

'I'm not lying. You have to believe me. I did see her in Paris, I'll admit that. I'll even admit that I wanted to seduce her, but she made it crystal clear that was not an option. She was already with Daniel by then.'

'Who's Daniel?'

'Her boyfriend, well fiancé now. So is this all about Marianne?'

'It's much more than Marianne.'

'I haven't slept with her, honestly. You have to believe me.' Michael grasped at a potential lifeline. 'You're mistaken. I haven't done what you think I've done. I'm sure we can work this all out.'

Jack had been momentarily thrown off course; it struck him that he had never given Marianne the chance to explain when he stormed out the café. But none of this made any difference. Michael admitted that he had tried to steal her and anyway this was about much more than that. He was not going to get derailed now. 'You abused our agreement to try to work together as Dad wanted. You forced me out. You gave me no choice.'

'Jack, I'm sorry.'

'I don't believe you. Anyway...' Jack found he didn't want to hear any apology from Michael, sincere or not. He wasn't after reconciliation; he wanted revenge. He wanted the opportunity to succeed where Michael had failed. In other words, he wanted the business. 'I've got an alternative proposition for you.'

CHAPTER THIRTY-SEVEN

The final nail

Hertfordshire. January 2001

Michael walked into their tiny lounge and slumped on to the sofa. 'It's all over,' he said.

'What's all over?' Cat, equally exhausted, having only just managed to get Amelia to sleep, was sitting like a zombie in the armchair. She could see in her husband the face of resignation and defeat.

'This. Everything. It's all over.' Michael explained to her how he had been comprehensively done over by his brother. Cat was flabbergasted by the determination, meticulousness and ruthlessness with which Jack had engineered his brother's downfall. She had a million questions.

'So he waited until we bought the house before renouncing the inheritance?'

'Yes.'

'But how did he know that he could trust your stepmother to pass the money on?'

'I don't know. I don't know what grubby little arrangement they made. He didn't say. All I know is that he pulled it off and has ended up with the bulk of the inheritance himself.'

'You've got to admit it's impressive. Awful for us, but a touch of genius nonetheless. God, I'm sorry, Michael. I'm sure it's not over between the two of you. Christ, you're not even halfway through your life. You've always been at war. Look at this as a setback.'

'Some setback.'

'You just need to work out how to respond. Take a leaf out of Jack's book and work out how to come back stronger.'

'It looks to me like game, set and match. I don't see how I can come back from this. Jack's got everything.'

'He hasn't got me.'

'That's true. Here am I thinking it's all over, but maybe he hasn't yet made his final move.'

'That's just paranoid.'

'Well, wouldn't you be? Given what's just happened to me? I've been humiliated, cheated out of two million pounds, slandered as a pariah in the national press, and now I've lost my business. What's almost worse is that I didn't see it coming. I *should* have been paranoid; I should never have allowed him to plot his revenge. I should have hired a private detective to watch his every move. The one thing I've learned from this is to trust no one and to take nothing for granted.'

'You can trust me.'

'Can I? Can I really?'

'Of course you can. "For better or worse, in sickness and health, for richer or poorer, as long as we both shall live" – do you remember that?'

'I do, but forty per cent of people who say that end up getting divorced. They're just words.'

'I meant it. I mean it. You're stuck with me.' Cat gave Michael a big hug. 'So how long has Jack been working with Royston?'

'I don't know – well over a year. At least, behind the scenes. Jack will have been the brains behind the relaunch and all that publicity. I could never work out at the time how Royston could have afforded it all, let alone have the wit to pull it off. But now it makes sense. Jack had the money and the experience. I have to give him credit for that. He always claimed that he had communication skills. That poster on the side of my old office was a masterstroke. The bastard.'

'What about those horrible stories in the national press about our house?'

'Yes, he was behind that, too. He wouldn't admit it as much, but clearly, he planted the stories. Fucking bad luck that we should end up using the one estate agency where his girlfriend works. He must have felt all his stars were aligned when that little gem dropped into his lap.'

'Was there no other option but to sell the business to him.'

'There wasn't. He had me over a barrel. And if I'm honest, it's a bit of a relief to be out of it. I still believe I could have made a success of it, but it would have been tough. Six hundred thousand is probably a fair price. He argued that it's worth much less and that was a generous offer.'

'How come?'

'He may be right. He had paid for a professional valuation, which, given that Monica, in particular, knows our business inside out, is probably based on sound assumptions. In the long term, it could be worth a lot of money, but right now it's not particularly profitable given all our recent investments. Yet again, either through luck or design, Jack has picked the perfect moment.'

'A bit of both, probably. Jack does seem to have a remarkable ability to always be in the right place at the right time.'

'The other thing that would depress the value of the business is the presence of an aggressive and well-funded competitor hell-bent on destroying it. Any potential buyer would think twice about entering that battle.'

'Didn't Jen advise caution about creating a competitor when you sold those homes to Royston?'

'She did, but had it not been for my bloody little brother, I believe we could have seen Royston off. He was struggling until Jack came along. My big mistake was to underestimate Jack. It'll be interesting to see what he makes of it now he's got what he wanted. He's going to find it a lot harder than he thinks.'

'Are you sure you're not underestimating him again?'

'Perhaps.'

'So what about you? What about us? What are we going to do?'

'First thing I'm going to do is crack open a bottle of wine. I need to drown my sorrows in alcohol. Will you join me?'

'I shouldn't.'

'Of course you should. Go on; I'll get two glasses.'

'Michael, there's something I have to tell you. I know it's terrible timing, but I'm pregnant.' Michael didn't know whether to laugh or cry. After a moment's stunned silence, he chose the former. 'That's wonderful. Perhaps there is a God after all.'

'Really?' She hadn't known how he would take the news, and after everything that had happened to him today she had feared it might be the final nail in the coffin. But he was genuinely delighted.

'Of course. It's what I've always wanted: A beautiful wife, two children and a Labrador. It's the first piece of good news I've had in months. It's brilliant, it really is. I'm sorry, but I'm going to have that glass of wine now. I'm sure you can have just one. Come on, we don't have much to celebrate; we must at least celebrate this.'

'Oh all right then, twist my arm.'

'I didn't realise you could get pregnant again so quickly.'

'Nor did I. It's quite a shock. You must be very potent.'

'Obviously. Crap at everything else, but an expert at procreation, that's me!'

'So, back to my question. What are we going to do? Presumably, we'll be homeless.'

'Well, yeah. Jack's given us a month's grace in this house. It was unbelievable how he had all the paperwork sorted for the sale of the business. That was why he had arranged for Wilfred to attend our meeting. He needed an independent lawyer who could witness everything. Normally a business sale takes months and involves endless toing and froing. This was done and dusted in thirty minutes. Admittedly, I was cornered and had nothing to negotiate. I had to accept everything he proposed. So, as of tomorrow morning, he owns the business, but he did say we could stay here for a month if we want. Quite frankly, though, I would like to be out as soon as possible. I wonder if we might be able to stay with your parents for a few weeks while we sort ourselves out?'

'Of course, they would be delighted. I can't wait to tell them there's a second grandchild on the way.'

'I didn't even ask, when's it due?'

'I don't know. I've booked an appointment with the doctor tomorrow. I guess it's six or seven months away.'

'I'd better get a job, then.'

'What do you think you'll do?'

'The obvious thing will be to go back to Abel's, if they'll have me. Richard's doing well there at the moment. Hopefully, he'll put a good word in for me.'

'Surely you don't need a good word.'

'Possibly...they did say I could come back, but a lot of water has passed under the bridge since then. I'm not sure that they would necessarily welcome back a business failure with open arms.'

'Michael, you're not a failure.'

'You can just imagine it: "Here's your new accountant. He ruined his own business, and so we think he's the perfect man to advise you on the finances of your business. He specialises in destroying family businesses."'

'Michael, stop it, you've not failed. All that's happened is that you've sold the business back to your brother for a tidy sum. You've nothing to be embarrassed about. They don't need to know the full story. And even if they did, the business hasn't failed. As you said yourself, you've taken some hard decisions that will, in the long term, make it stronger. You've got a lot to be proud of.'

'I can't see that they'll think much of me having been plastered over the national press as a money-grabbing asset-stripping accountant.'

'From what you've said about Abel's, I would imagine they would be *most* impressed by that. Isn't that what they're all about?'

'In a sense.'

'You should hire your brother to put a positive spin on your story. It seems he's an expert at that kind of thing.'

CHAPTER THIRTY-EIGHT

Micky and Jimmy

Hertfordshire. January 2001

Jack felt strangely deflated. He had won, but it didn't feel like a victory. On his journey home he reflected why he didn't feel elated. Today's *coup de grâce* had been the culmination of everything he had worked towards for the past eighteen months. It had occupied his every thought; he had forsaken his friends and any semblance of ordinary life; he had given everything to crush his brother. There was no doubt that he had succeeded, too. And yet he didn't feel triumphant. Maybe it was because he hadn't achieved what he set out to do in quite the way he had planned. His ultimate goal had been to beat Michael at his own game and prove that he was the better businessman. It didn't feel like he had done this. He had successfully outmanoeuvred his brother, but the end had come almost too quickly.

In his dreams, Jack had envisioned prevailing in a battle between two competing approaches: Michael's focus on cutting costs versus his more expansive model of investing in growth. This hadn't happened. Part of him wished he had been able to string it out longer, like a cat playing with a fatally wounded mouse, and conclusively prove to Michael that he was the more capable businessman. He consoled himself with the thought that, now he was in charge of the train set, he did at least have the opportunity to prove, to both his brother and his dead father, that he was up to the job. He was determined to make a success of it. The shame was that his opponent was already out of the ring.

Jack would soon find that Michael had done a good job of reshaping the business. He would always be able to point to any future success that Jack might enjoy, and rightfully claim that he had lain the foundations for that success. It was equally clear, though, that those foundations would not have been enough. Michael had been financially prudent and had introduced some sound systems, but he had failed as a manager of people and as a salesman. The business Jack bought suffered with a demoralised workforce and a lack of underlying growth. Jack did not doubt that Michael, left to his own devices, would have driven it into the ground. It would have become like one of those Roman architectural ruins, where a perfectly preserved under-floor heating system is all that is left behind. Jack regretted not allowing enough time for Michael's failures to reveal themselves, but he was at least grateful for the work he had done. It would make his task easier. It occurred to him that his father had been right in thinking that the two of them had complementary skills that could improve the business. His father would have been disappointed, though, had he

311

known that those skills were to be deployed sequentially rather than in concert as he had wanted.

Jack felt conflicted about what he had done to his brother. Throughout their life, it had been Michael that had borne the grudge, not him. It was Michael who hated him, not he who hated Michael. Before their father's death, Jack had accepted that he would never enjoy the close relationship with his brother that he desired, because Michael wanted it that way. It hadn't been his choice. This side of Jack, the one that yearned for love and acceptance from his elder brother, now felt guilty for having hung, drawn and quartered him.

Jack remembered the time when he had persuaded his father to buy him a pet. They had gone to the Baldock branch of Dogs and Other Exotic Animals and ended up with two gerbil brothers. Jack had been excited to get two brothers, and secretly named them Micky and Jimmy. The gerbil brothers gave every impression of being the closest of friends. Eight-year-old Jack would project himself into what he saw as the kind of relationship he was missing; and then one day, Micky and Jimmy had a ferocious argument that ended up with bits of Micky all over the cage. A horrified Jack witnessed this fight to the death but was helpless to intervene. Jimmy escaped with his life, but otherwise hadn't fared too well either. He had a shredded ear, and his tail was half the length it had been before his little fratricidal fracas. A week later, he also died. No one, other than Jack, was sure whether it was from his wounds or from loneliness. Jack knew that Jimmy had died of a broken heart. Life just wasn't worth living without the beloved brother he had inadvertently massacred a week earlier. It didn't escape Jack that he had now effectively done to Michael what Jimmy had done to Micky. Jack just hoped that, unlike his furry predecessor, he could recover from the shock of his brutality and its consequences.

Meanwhile, Jack's sympathy for his brother didn't extend as far as letting up in his battle for absolute supremacy. The public persona he had manufactured for Michael, as a money-grabbing villain, was too valuable to pass over. All is fair in love and war, as they say. Although Michael was now history as far as the business was concerned, he still had a useful role to play as a wicked counterpoint to the more humane and caring funeral service promised by Jack and Royston. The first thing Jack did the next day at the office was to send out a press release announcing the takeover of Merriweather's by Royston's Funeral Service. It read a bit like *Lord of the Rings* in its depiction of good triumphing over evil. It was unrelenting in pushing the comparison between Royston's humble origins and Michael's hubristic ambition. Jack decided, for now, and for the story, that Royston was still a good frontman. Unlikely though it seemed, Royston's non-conformist, edgy and somewhat intimidating character had become a perfect vehicle to give the business a human face. No other funeral business promoted itself in this way. Most were so hidebound by notions of discretion that they didn't advertise at all. The very few exceptions tended to do so with platitudinous statements and generic stock shots of elderly people looking wistfully at the sky. A foul-mouthed, heavily tattooed frontman would be an anathema to all his competitors, and hence was perfect for Jack. Not only was it different, and so stood out, but Royston was, with all his flaws, undeniably human.

Royston had been heavily coached to lose the *fookin' fooks* whenever on media duty. He more or less succeeded in this, other than a couple of slips. It wasn't a problem in the press; the *Royston Crow* simply referred to his colourful language without quoting him. Live radio was another matter. The North Herts local community radio station received a record number of complaints when Royston lapsed on their morning show. After that, the demand for Royston to appear on local live broadcasts began to dry up, but the incident had the benefit of reigniting the interest of the more salacious national media. Jack briefly entertained the notion of turning a negative into a positive and rebranding the business Royston's Fookin' Funeral Home. But even he could see that, in this instance, all publicity might not necessarily be good.

The issue of how they should rebrand the business became the topic of lively conversation one evening in the Bull. Jack, Royston and Monica had gone to the pub for a drink after work. Julia, Dale and Clayton turned up a little later. Jack took the opportunity to share some of his thoughts about naming the business. 'Julia and I got this great film out from Blockbuster last week, called *My Beautiful Laundrette*. It's about an interracial gay relationship. Pretty edgy. These guys transform a dingy laundromat full of old people into somewhere cool. They make it bright and sparkling, the sort of place you would want to hang out in even though it's only a laundrette. That's what we need to do with our funeral homes. They're all so dark and dingy. Who would want to spend five minutes there? Who wants to say goodbye to their loved ones in a Victorian parlour room with Crimplene curtains and piped music? Death is hard enough to deal with as it is; why do we have to make it so bloody depressing? We need to create a place where people can celebrate a life well lived and share joyous memories of whomever it is that has just snuffed it. We should rebrand our homes "My Beautiful Funeral Home". Seriously. Why are funeral homes always known by the name of the owner?'

'What's fookin' wrong with Royston's Funeral Home?'

'Okay, it was good for your business because it served a purpose to position it against Merriweather's, but now that we have a larger territory, and it's not just your business, I think we need something different.'

'Hmmph.' For all his complaints about his media duties and being dressed up 'like some ponce', Royston secretly liked having his name on the door. He could only imagine how proud his mam would have been. From humble origins to a name on the door via a C grade in metalwork: the boy done good.

Jack continued. 'This naming convention is a hangover from the past. It used to be that all businesses took the name of their founder, but that's so twentieth century. Actually, it's so nineteenth century. Why has the undertaking trade stuck with this tradition when other businesses have evolved? What does Merriweather's say? Nothing. It means nothing. It might have meant something when my father was involved; he was at least known in the community and commanded some local respect. Now, if anything, our name is probably more known as belonging to those two rich bastards who inherited millions when their dad topped himself in a crematorium. How's that going to help business? We need a name that means something, that stands out and that projects a positive image. Maybe "My Beautiful Funeral Home" is it.'

'And what about the interracial gay relationship?' Dale smirked. 'Are you and Royston going to engage in that?'

'Fook off.'

'How could we? We're the same race.' Jack put his arm around Royston in mock-affection, but was pushed off by the homophobic embalmer.

'Okay, then, just a straightforward gay relationship between you and Royston. That would make a good story for the papers.'

'Fook off, Dale. I've already had to put on a fookin' tweed jacket; I'm not going to fookin' fook him just to give the papers something else to write about.' The group burst into laughter at Royston, who appeared to be treating Dale's suggestion as a genuine proposition. Royston increasingly struggled to separate fact from fiction in this mystifying new world.

'What about "Heaven"?'

'What about Heaven, Monica?'

'We could call the business "Heaven".'

'What? After the gay nightclub in Soho?'

'No, not after a gay nightclub. What is it with you and gay stuff? Is there something you need to tell us? "Heaven" would be a great name for the business because it gives a positive spin on death. Our Christian customers would see it as a gateway to where they hope they're headed. The atheists could interpret it simply as a good place.'

'What about the Muslims?'

'Yeah, well that could be a problem. It might limit our market.'

'Thinking of names,' said Julia, 'I heard there's a wine bar in London called Planet of the Grapes. I just love that. It's so clever.'

'Exactly,' said Jack. That's just the sort of thing I want: a name that means something. I bet that name draws people in and they go there with high expectations.'

'You could call your business The Planet of Death,' Dale suggested. 'Royston would be a great frontman for The Planet of Death.'

'Fook off, Dale.'

'Maybe not.' Jack started drumming the table with his fingers. He was excited by the conversation. 'What is it that we're good at? Why do people choose us?'

Monica said,' We care, we're respectful, and we know what we're doing.'

'Is that any different from any other good funeral home? I'm trying to find the thing that sets us apart. If there's nothing, then we need to create it. Do you know where the word "undertaker" comes from?'

'Isn't it something to do with undertaking a task that no one else wanted to do?' said Monica.

'Yes, we shovel the shit that no one else wants to. It comes from the seventeenth century. Shit-shovellers for 300 years – it's high time we changed that and took more pride in our work.'

Clayton said, 'How about Happy Endings?'

'Name ourselves after a handjob. Great idea, Clayton.'

'Something you're familiar with, I suppose, Jack?' Dale then looked mischievously across the table, 'Julia?'

'Well, at least he's getting it, Dale.' It was common knowledge, mainly because Dale openly complained about it, that he had been banished from the marital bed. Dale raised a finger at her.

Monica returned to Jack's conversation. 'I've always liked a phrase your dad once told me about from an undertaker in the US. I've got it written down here.' Monica fumbled in her bag and pulled out a small notebook. 'Look, here it is. He described his mission as to "create a service so sublimely beautiful, in an atmosphere of such complete harmony, as to alleviate the sorrow of parting". He said that in 1915.'

'I like that. The difficulty is finding a name that conveys the right sentiment without sounding mawkish. There was an expression they used to use in the agency that I like: "It says what it does on the tin." I would love to find an equivalent. Something like My Beautiful Funeral Home does that, but I'm uncomfortable with the funeral home bit, which is the bit that says what it does.

'Wouldn't *Your* Beautiful Funeral Home be better?'

'Possibly. But what do you guys think about changing the name?'

'It doesn't feel fookin' right to me. We fookin' bury people; we're not a fookin' laundrette.'

Julia said, 'What about Seventh Heaven? Might that get around the denominational issues? And the gay nightclub issues?'

Jack jumped up. 'That's brilliant. That could be it. *Seventh* Heaven. Why didn't I think of that.'

'Maybe because you're not as creative as me.'

'How about The Departure Lounge?' Clayton added.

'I like that, too. This is great. We should have more business meetings like this here. You three,' said Jack, looking at Julia, Dale and Clayton, 'can be honorary members.' Jack felt the warmth of being with his closest friends and two trusted colleagues. All the angst he felt about his brother had begun to wash away. Three pints of Abbot had helped, but it was more than that; this inauspicious occasion, nothing more than a few drinks after work with friends and colleagues, carried some significance for him. It was as if his past had faded away into history and no longer needed to define his future. A week had passed since his meeting with Michael and Wilfred, but only now was he beginning let go of his feelings of guilt and finally look to a future that wasn't in his brother's shadow.

Looking over at Julia, he also realised that he had moved on from Marianne. He had been wrong about her and Michael, which was a relief. He should have trusted her more and not jumped to the wrong conclusions. But that was all in the past now, he could let go. And in the cold light of day (or at least in the alcoholic fuzz of the evening), he realised, perhaps for the first time, that Julia was a better partner for him. He had always put Marianne on a pedestal. Part of him had always felt as if he was hanging on to the relationship in quiet desperation. If he was honest, he always thought she was better than him and he didn't deserve her. Being with her had fuelled his sense of inadequacy. Julia, on the other hand, was more his equal. They didn't expect anything from each other, there were no hidden agendas, and over the past year together they had become very close. They made a formidable pair, as Michael had discovered. For although the revenge plan had been Jack's work, he couldn't have done it without Julia. It occurred to him that, given a choice, he would now choose Julia over Marianne without hesitation. He wouldn't have made that choice even six months ago.

It was over two years since his father died. For the first time in his life, Jack felt able to stand on his own two feet. He had been stung by Cat's comments at his father's memorial service that he never stood up for what he wanted. The truth was, he hadn't then known what he wanted. He had thought he wanted Marianne, but now he knew that had been little more than fantasy. Finally, he knew where he was headed and what he wanted. It had taken twenty-six years to get here, but he was where he wanted to be.

Nevertheless, there was still one unanswered question. As everyone else decided to call it a night and head home,

Jack asked Royston to stay on for a final drink. Once everyone else had left, and the two men were alone in the pub, Jack said to his colleague, 'I want to thank you for everything you've done over the past few years. In fact, also everything you've done before that. But particularly in the last year. I've put you through a lot, and I want you to know how much I appreciate your unwavering support.'

'You don't have to fookin' thank me for anything. If anything, I should be thanking you.'

'I guess we make a good team. I know I can trust you.'

'Yeah, I fookin' trust you, too. I wasn't sure at first, but now I know you're like your dad. I could trust him with my life.' Jack didn't say anything, but held eye contact, which prompted Royston to ask, 'Why are you looking at me like that?'

'I'd like to know what happened with my dad, Royston. You know you can trust me. I've never asked you about it, but now I need to know.'

Royston broke eye contact and looked down at the table. There was a long pause. A clattering of glasses from the kitchen signalled that the barman was clearing up and well out of earshot. Jack didn't take his eyes off Royston, who was clearly struggling to know what to say or whether to say anything at all. Eventually, Royston composed himself and looked up at him. 'Your dad made me swear never to tell anyone.'

'I need to know, Royston. You can trust me.' Royston let out a big sigh. Jack went on, 'How about I ask you questions, and you just nod or shake your head. That way, you're not telling anyone. Are you prepared to do that?' Royston gave a tentative nod.

'Okay. So. Did you have anything to do with Dad's suicide?'

Royston looked helpless. He tried nodding and shaking his head at the same time. His head looked as if it was on ball bearings. Jack burst out laughing, which broke the tension and helped Royston relax. 'Fook it. I may as well fookin' tell you. It's not simple. I can't tell the fookin' story by nodding my fookin' head. We'd be here all fookin' night.' He took a swig of his beer. 'Are you sure you want to fookin' know? And can I fookin' trust you?' Jack nodded.

'About three years ago your dad said he wanted me to test the fookin' cremator on the last day of every month at exactly the same time, 7.30 p.m. He told me not to ask why and never to tell anyone. His exact words were, "Whatever happens, don't fookin' tell anyone." Royston paused to correct himself, 'Well obviously he didn't say *fookin'*, but he said not to tell anyone. I thought it was a bit fookin' strange that he said *whatever happens*, but I didn't think that much of it at the time. I've been doing it on the last day of every month ever since. Still do it now. Probably no fookin' point, but he never told me to stop.'

'But Dad died on 2 June 1998. I remember getting the call at work.'

'That's when they realised he was fookin' missing. The last day of May was a Sunday. No one thought much about it when he didn't turn up to work on the Monday, but by Tuesday we began to worry that something might have fookin' happened to him. Someone found some unexplained ash in the cremator that Tuesday afternoon. He planned it fookin' well because he would have fookin' known that no was using the cremator that Monday.'

'But the letter he wrote to me was dated 1 June. How could he have written that then if he topped himself the day before?' Jack thought for a minute, then answered his own question. 'He must have deliberately misdated it. Wilfred only gave it to me a couple of days later. He must have given it to Wilfred sometime before.'

'As I said, he was a clever fooker. Good fookin' planner. Like you, in fact. Like father, like fookin' son.'

'But *why* – have you any idea why he did it?'

'For some fookers, it just all gets too fookin' much. Your dad was no fookin' different. I don't think he ever really got over the death of your mam. You'd be surprised at how many suicides of men in their fookin' fifties I have.'

'Like the shit-faced farmer,' Jack remembered.

As the two men left the Bull that evening, Jack patted Royston on the shoulder and said, 'Thanks, mate. It helps to know what happened.'

Royston had tears in his eyes. 'The silly fooker. I wish he'd fookin' talked to me instead.'

CHAPTER THIRTY-NINE

Life and death

Hampshire. July 2001

'We need to get to the hospital now.' Cat was in considerable discomfort. The baby wasn't due for two weeks, but Amelia had been early, so they were prepared. Since leaving Royston, Michael and Cat had moved in with her parents in Hampshire. Michael was grateful for their support. He had returned to Abel's on a freelance basis and was currently commuting into London three or four times a week. Freelancers didn't have status at Abel's, so Michael had dropped down a few rungs in the hierarchy. Richard's career, meanwhile, had accelerated in the opposite direction. It was humiliating for Michael to be on a different floor to his old colleagues and to take instruction from people who had qualified after him. But he felt so beaten up after his experience at Merriweather's that he was grateful for a job that didn't ask too much of him and helped him take his mind off his reduced circumstances.

Michael was worried about his wife, though; she was

in pain and complaining that she didn't remember it being this bad last time. His father-in-law, a doctor, reassured them that there was nothing to worry about, in that way that doctors always do. And it only increased Michael's anxiety. In his experience, when someone said there was nothing to worry about, it almost always means the opposite. His father-in-law did, though, advise that they should get to the maternity unit at the Princess Anne Hospital in Southampton as soon as possible.

Michael was impatient in traffic jams at the best of times. Being caught in rush-hour congestion and crawling into Southampton with his wife about to give birth and in pain, made his head want to explode. He contemplated flouting all the rules of the road and driving like a maniac, but couldn't bring himself to break the law. He chastised himself for being so pathetic. So he stayed put and followed the slow-moving flow. He kept a lid on his frustration for the benefit of his wife while Cat struggled with her torture.

Finally, they broke free. Cat was in such a state by the time they arrived at the hospital that Michael drove straight to Accident & Emergency, left the car at the entrance and ran in shouting for help. Cat was whisked away, leaving him to wait.

Six hours later, by which time his parents-in-law had joined him, a doctor sought them out and took them to a counselling room. 'I am very sorry to tell you,' he began, 'that although your new baby is safe and well, your wife has sadly passed.'

CHAPTER FORTY

Broken bridges

Hertfordshire. July 2002

12 July 2002

Dear Jack,

This is the first letter I've ever written to you. It's probably overdue. I've certainly been remiss in thanking you for covering all childcare costs for the girls. It's made a difference. I honestly don't know how I could have survived without the generosity, support and kindness of those around me.

Today is the anniversary of Cat's death. It's also Charlotte's first birthday. I'm afraid I've been unable to celebrate my daughter's birthday and so have left it to her nanny and their grandparents. I went for a long walk and have now taken refuge in my room. I don't know why, but I suddenly feel compelled to write to you. I have something to ask you, which I'll come on to, but otherwise I'm not sure why I particularly feel the need to write now. Perhaps *it's a form of therapy. Get it on paper to get it out of my head, as my therapist keeps advising me. So I'm just going to write and see where it takes me. I don't have to post it if I don't like what comes out.*

On that note, I'm going to get my sins out of the way first. I am genuinely sorry that I've been such a shit brother to you. As soon as I realised I couldn't possibly blame Cat's death on poor Charlotte, it dawned on me that I've been unreasonable in blaming you for our mother's death. I've always known this, of course, but I've hidden it behind my anger at losing Mum and my need to hold someone responsible. It suited me, or so I thought, to blame you. As you know only too well, that's the narrative I chose to adopt for our entire lives. I now see how wrong this is and how unfair on you it has been. When I see Amelia with Charlotte, I'm overwhelmed by a desire that they will support each other throughout their lives in this cruel world. I now, finally, understand why it meant so much to Dad to bring us together, and I am deeply sorry that I've been too wrapped up in my protective shell to let this happen. Perhaps the damage has been done. My behaviour over the past twenty-seven years may mean that any form of reconciliation is going to be impossible. Maybe too much water has passed under the bridge, but if nothing else I hope this letter might be a first small step towards repairing at least some of the damage.

The last three or four years have had an extraordinary impact on me. I feel as if I've been through the wringer. Everything I believed has turned upside down. My therapist has helped me see how I erected barriers in an attempt to control my environment to help make me feel safe. Dad's death and my career change took me out of my comfort zone. And now Cat's death, and my two beautiful girls, have forced me to confront the possibility that I had it all wrong.

I asked myself recently whether I would choose the same path again, given what has happened. If I knew beforehand precisely what kind of distress it would entail. Surprisingly – well, at least I was surprised, I decided I would. The pain of losing Cat has been unbearable. Had it not been for Amelia and Charlotte, I honestly think I might have followed Dad's example and killed myself. But as they say, it's better to have loved and lost than never to have loved at all. I wouldn't swap the time I had with her for anything. Certainly not for the dull, predictable path I was previously following.

Similarly, the experience of working in the family business, although it went badly wrong because of my pig-headedness, was life-changing. It's now eighteen months since I left; long enough for some perspective. I now see how ill equipped I was for the responsibility, and how toxic my dismissal of your contribution was. But the whole experience opened my eyes to the possibility that there could be more to working life than accountancy. The trouble was, I became seduced by the power of it all. I behaved in the only way I knew, which was to try to control everything to protect myself. But despite all my mistakes, given a chance to do it again, I would. This brings me to what I want to ask you.

My work with Abel's has been a godsend in that it has given me something to do. They've been very accommodating to my needs, letting me work when I want, and enabling me not to do so when I'm not up to it. I think I have Richard to thank for this, as it's uncharacteristic for Abel's to be compassionate. But I don't enjoy the work anymore. It seems so pointless and doesn't begin to compare with the experience of running a business. I know I fucked up a lot in my time at Merriweather's, but they were my fuck-ups. I still loved every single minute of it. I would take Merriweather's over Abel's any day. I thought now might be the time to do something about it.

Jack put down the letter as he poured himself more coffee. He was in Julia's kitchen. He still thought of it as her kitchen, even though he had been there for three years. Although they were now very much a couple, neither of them felt any need to formalise the relationship by buying somewhere else together. Jack didn't want to repeat his brother's error of buying something he would come to regret. He continued to live frugally and had ring-fenced as much of the inheritance as possible for the business. The only exception had been his decision to help Michael out by paying the childcare costs of his two nieces. It felt right that his father's inheritance should provide support for his grandchildren. Jack guessed what was coming next in the letter.

This might be a terrible idea. I would understand if you reject the suggestion outright, but I felt I should at least ask. I wonder if there's any chance we could still fulfil Dad's wishes and work together. Might what we've both been through be enough to wash away the poison in our relationship? It's true that I no longer feel the antagonism that I previously felt towards you. I would be prepared to try to rebuild our relationship. I suspect you may not feel the same. After all, you're now free from me. Why would you want to go back? You've so much more to lose. I've nothing left to lose.

So what I'm asking, I suppose, is the opportunity for a second chance. To try to put right some of my wrongs. To try to fulfil Dad's wishes for the two of us to come together. It embarrasses me to say that, previously, I had no intention of honouring this part of his will. I went along with it for several dishonourable reasons, but as you know, I never, at any point, entertained any serious consideration towards us working together. I see things differently now. Losing Cat in the same tragic way as we lost Mum, and having my own two beautiful and vulnerable girls, has led me to see family in a different light. Before, my only interest was in rejecting and denying my family. My life's purpose was to escape. Now I see family as the most important thing in my life. Living with Cat's parents has also changed my outlook. They are so close. They've given each other strength as they have come to terms with the loss of their only daughter.

Cat, too, played a big part. She was a mediator by

nature and used to say how moved she was at Dad's memorial service. She believed you and I had a duty to continue what he started. She thought we could make it work if only we could cut the crap and treat each other with decency and respect.

I'm not asking for a partnership or any sense of equality. I know that it's your business now and, from what I hear, you're doing a great job with it. I'm also not asking for any money or a stake in the inheritance. I accept the agreement we made and am more than grateful for your generosity in helping provide for Amelia and Charlotte. I'm simply asking whether you might consider employing me in a financial role. I appreciate that I might be too toxic, especially for Royston, and, as I've said already, I would understand if you want nothing to do with me after what we've been through. But it might be a good way to start rebuilding broken bridges. If it didn't work out, I would leave immediately. It might anyway only be a short-term move before I go and do something else. If I'm honest, I don't know if it's a good idea, but it's what Dad wanted.

I've probably said too much. I now need to consider whether to send this or not.

Your brother,

Michael

Jack sat back in his chair. The sun streamed through the open window. There was a sense of calm in the air. The coffee tasted good. Once his mug was empty, he rose and took his jacket off the coat rack. He carefully folded his brother's letter and put it in his top pocket. Then he walked out of the door.

Twenty minutes later, he was in the graveyard where his mother was buried. He stood by her grave for some time. His father's name had been added to the gravestone. Then he noticed a newly dug grave. He walked over to it. After a quick look to check that no one was watching, he lowered himself into the grave and lay on its floor, facing the brilliant blue sky above.

He wondered if this was what it would be like when his time came, and he was six feet under for the rest of his death. It's rather nice, he thought. Perhaps I could have a glass-topped coffin and ask them not to refill the grave. I could watch the passing clouds go by forever.

His thoughts turned to his father, commemorated less than thirty feet away. If only I'd known him better, thought Jack. I wish he had lived to see us – me – take over his business. It was all he ever wanted.

Jack took Michael's letter from his jacket pocket and re-read it slowly.

Why not? he thought. Why not indeed?

CHAPTER FORTY-ONE

Unfinished business

Hertfordshire. July 2002

Jack checked his watch. Michael was late. It crossed his mind that his brother might have been in an accident. Jack, conditioned by his brother's punctuality, had now been sitting in the Silver Ball transport café for a good half hour and was already on his third coffee. The caffeine was making him jittery. He cursed himself for his nerves. He had thought he was beyond this kind of thing, but despite now having the upper hand he realised that Michael was still his older brother and that twenty or so years of bullying couldn't be wiped away quite so easily.

It occurred to Jack that perhaps Michael might have changed his mind and decided not to come at all. Their phone conversation a couple of days earlier had been perfectly civil, if a little awkward. Michael had been grateful to Jack for taking his proposition seriously, but beyond agreeing a time and place to meet they hadn't said much to each other.

Royston, on the other hand, had had plenty to say about the latest turn of events. 'Fook off. I know he's your fookin' brother, but with all fookin' due respect, he's fookin' poison. We're doin' all right. Why fook' it up by having him fookin' back?'

'It's what my dad would have wanted.'

'Your fookin' dad didn't know the little fooker was going to try to fookin' stitch me up for fookin' killing him.'

'I think he's changed.'

'Like fook he has.' But Royston's bark had always been considerably worse than his bite, and Jack was eventually able to wear him down by persuading him that everyone deserved a second fookin' chance.

Royston was correct, though; they were doing all right. The business was thriving. Jack hadn't had to make too many changes. He had decided not to rush his revolutionary plans to transform the company, opting instead for evolution. Mainly, he had focused on restoring the morale of his team and improving service standards. He had deployed his substantial funds judiciously on pay increases and incremental upgrades, leaving the rest in reserve for when the time was right for more dramatic change. There was no rush: the business was reaping the rewards of the foundations that Michael had laid during his fractious time in charge. As much as Jack would have liked to take all the credit, he knew his brother had, in part, been the architect of the firm's current success.

Eventually, twenty minutes later than agreed, Michael walked through the door. It took Jack a few seconds to recognise him. His hair was short, almost a crew cut; he was wearing jeans, white trainers, a white polo shirt and sunglasses. He could have just walked off the set of *Top Gun*.

'Hi, Michael. Wow. You look different, I barely recognised you.'

'Hello, Jack. Yes, I've been made over. It's time for a new Michael.'

'It suits you. I've never seen you in jeans before, nor, come to think of it, trainers or sunglasses. And twenty minutes late – that's a first.'

'Yes, I'm now putting as much effort into *not* arriving on time as I used to put into being punctual.' Michael smiled.

Jack said, 'How are you?'

'I'm all right, thanks. It's been tough, but I'm surviving. Just.'

'Thanks for your letter. Look, I'm so sorry about Cat. I feel bad about not speaking to you at the funeral.'

'I wouldn't have noticed. I was in such shock. All I remember from the day is being driven back afterwards by Richard. There were four adults in the car, but we were all in such a state. None of us noticed that the kids' CD had come on automatically and "The Wheels on the Bus" was playing. Only when it finished did we realise we had driven out from the church car park with "and the wheels go round and round" blaring out at a not insubstantial volume.'

'That's all you remember from your wife's funeral; the wheels on the bus go round and round?'

'Pretty much. I suppose it's another way of saying life goes on.'

'Cat would have loved that.'

Michael continued, 'You know she still wanted us to find a way to forgive each other.'

'Is that why you reached out?'

'It's been in the back of my mind, but yes, in part it is because of Cat. The anniversary of her death prompted me to write that letter.'

'Is that why you're here?'

'Not only, but largely. And she was right. I owe it to you to try to make amends. Also, I owe it to Dad to give it a proper go. That is, if you'll have me back.'

'Don't you think you would be better off making a fresh start? Doing something completely different?'

'Like what?'

'I don't know. Starting a financial consultancy, perhaps?'

'To be honest, I'm not sure I could.'

There was an air of resignation about Michael. Although he looked as good as ever – heathy, trim, enhanced by the make-over – he was palpably less confident than he had been. Stripped of his armour, all the assumed superiority with which he used to lord it over his younger brother was gone.

'Coming back here is hardly an easy option. You didn't leave on a high. As you might imagine, Royston is not exactly cracking open the champagne at the prospect.'

'You might be right, it might be a huge mistake, but I feel I have unfinished business. Also, I know I can trust you.'

Jack was shocked. 'Really. After what I did to you?'

'We did it to each other. A bit like those gerbils of yours tearing each other to shreds.'

'It didn't turn out too well for them, though.'

'Unlike them, we've got the opportunity of a second chance.'

'What makes you think it'll be any different this time round?'

'I've changed.'

Jack raised an eyebrow.

Michael continued, 'I used to think that all I wanted was a normal life. Our family circumstances seemed so fucked up and so different to everyone else's. I thought we were abnormal. I wanted the opposite of that. From as early as I can remember, I was angry. It felt so unfair that I had lost my mum. I blamed everyone I could, especially you and Dad. I didn't feel I could trust anyone, so I wrapped myself in a protective shell and chose to make my own way in the world.'

'And you did well. A-levels, a good degree, professional qualifications. That's a lot better than me.'

'With all due respect, that's not a high bar.'

'Fuck off. Maybe not, though. But anyway, you did well. You set a high standard. Part of the reason I was such a fuckwit was I knew I could never compete. I had no choice but to play the class clown.'

'I did well to a point, but looking back I'm not sure how happy I was. I always felt enormous pressure.'

'Pressure to do what?'

'To keep up the façade. I'm not sure I ever knew what I wanted. I was striving for something I thought I wanted. I suppose I was after some kind of respectability. But looking back, I'm not sure why. And then Dad's death, and everything that came with it, went and punctured it all.'

'Well, it wasn't just Dad's death, was it? You took some persuading to change course and join the family firm. I never really understood why you changed your mind. One minute you were against it and then suddenly you were for it. What happened?'

'To be honest, Marianne happened. As soon as I met her, I knew I wanted to be with her. And I thought if I walked away from the family firm I might never see her again.'

'Wow.'

'I wasn't rational. Of course I could have found a way to see her again. But at the time she and the family firm all became entwined in my mind.' Michael paused. 'And then... well, you know what happened next.'

'Okay – but you haven't said why you've changed.'

'Look at me. I'm wearing jeans, for fuck's sake. And white trainers. When have you ever seen that? And I was late. What more proof do you need?'

Jack laughed and then said, 'I mean deep down. You may have changed your spots, but some things are more deep-rooted.'

'As I wrote in my letter, losing Cat has shaken me to my core. Other than the girls, nothing felt important anymore. Everything seemed so trivial and meaningless. It's only in the last few months that I've been able to pull myself together. The one thing Amelia and Charlotte have taught me is that family is important. And like it or not, you and I are family. That's a big shift for me.'

The two brothers sat in silence for a few moments, contemplating what Michael had just said. Eventually, Jack said, 'Well, in which case I'd like to offer you a job. Knowing how you like to do things by the book, I've got an offer letter here.' He pushed an envelope across the table. Michael opened it, scanned it, and looked back up at Jack.

'Is this for real?'

Jack nodded.

'An accounts clerk on minimum wage?'

Jack nodded.

The two brothers stared at each other. Neither knew whether the other was being serious. Michael didn't know whether this was a genuine offer or whether Jack was testing him with one of his provocative little jokes. Jack didn't know whether Michael thought it was a serious offer. He was, though, interested to see how he would react. Eventually, Michael said, 'Okay then, if that's what you've got, I'll take it.'

It had been a joke. Clearly, it had been a joke. But as with all jokes, it was rooted in truth. Jack had thought it would be funny to turn the tables on his brother by offering him a demeaning role that echoed the positions Michael had proposed for him in the past. But he was shocked that Michael accepted it. He might have been playing along with the joke, but it didn't seem like that. And nothing demonstrated to Jack that Michael had changed more than his meek acceptance of the demeaning offer.

'It's a joke.'

'Maybe not one of your best.'

'Would you really have taken it?'

'I would. I'm in no position to negotiate.'

Jack said, 'In terms of the family firm, you should know that I appreciate that the firm's current success is largely down to the work you did to get it in shape.'

'Thank you, that's kind of you to say so.'

'And so I do not doubt that you have plenty to bring to the table. We don't have a Financial Director, so that's an obvious role for you to take. But only on the understanding that it's my business and I'm in charge. Could you accept that?'

'Having just agreed to the position of accounts clerk on minimum wage, yes, I think I could accept a promotion to Financial Director. And yes, I understand that it's your business. I'll take orders from you, sir.'

Jack smiled, 'I like that. I like you calling me sir.'

'Yes, sir.'

'Maybe not; let's see how we go. One step at a time. Are you okay with that?

'I am. I don't mind what I do, or in what capacity. I just want to give it a go. After all that has been said and done, we are family.'

'As said Sister Sledge.'

Michael and Jack smiled at each other.

Acknowledgements

In my early twenties, I resolved to write a novel when I was in my fifties, and so it gives me particular pleasure that this, my first novel, has been published four months before my sixtieth birthday.

I want to thank Clare Christian of RedDoor Press for taking a punt on me. There are so many talented writers with great books out there that I feel fortunate to have landed a publisher, particularly one so supportive of first-time writers. I would also like to acknowledge Heather Boisseau and Lizzie Lewis of RedDoor Press for bringing this book to fruition.

I'm enormously grateful to Tim Lott. His brilliant masterclass – A Beginner's Guide to Becoming a Novelist – told me almost everything I needed to know in just three hours. I then engaged Tim to appraise my manuscript; his constructive feedback gave me confidence in what I had written as well as helping sharpen the story.

With their excellent resources and support, Jericho Writers helped me navigate the treacherous path towards finding a publisher and ultimately led me to RedDoor Press.

Finally, I would like to thank my long-suffering wife, Ros, and my two children, Jay and Natasha, for their enthusiastic support throughout.

Thank you for staying with me to the end of *The Better Brother*. I hope you enjoyed it.

Book Club Questions

1. Which brother do you think was most surprised by news of their father's death, and why?
2. Do you think Mr Merriweather (Snr)'s actions were justifiable?
3. What would have needed to happen in order for the two brothers to have worked happily together from the outset?
4. How different would the story and outcome have been if the protagonists had been sisters rather than brothers? Or brother and sister?
5. Would Michael have been better off sticking with accountancy? Is it better to live in the lethargy of boredom or in the convulsions of distress?
6. What do you think happens next? Will the brothers be able to work together?
7. Do you think the outcome is what Mr Merriweather (Snr) was hoping for?
8. Who is the better brother?

About the Author

Simon Gravatt is a first-time novelist who lives in South London. He's drawn from personal experience as a brother and business owner to write his tale of sibling rivalry and the combustibility of small business. Simon is married to Ros and has two adult children, Jay and Natasha.

simongravatt.net

Find out more about RedDoor
Press and sign up to our
newsletter to hear about our
latest releases, author events,
exciting **competitions**
and more at

reddoorpress.co.uk

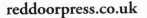

YOU CAN ALSO FOLLOW US:

 @RedDoorBooks

 Facebook.com/RedDoorPress

 @RedDoorBooks